The summer we all ran away

Cassandra Parkin

Legend Press

Independent Book Publisher

Legend Press Ltd, 2 London Wall Buildings, London EC2M 5UU
info@legend-paperbooks.co.uk www.legendpress.co.uk

Contents © Cassandra Parkin 2013

The right of the above author to be identified as the author of this work has
been asserted in accordance with the Copyright, Designs and Patent Act
1988. British Library Cataloguing in Publication Data available.

ISBN 978-1-9093953-1-2

Set in Times
Printed by CPI Group (UK) Ltd, Croydon, CR0 4YY

Cover design by Gudrun Jobst www.yotedesign.com

Cassandra Parkin grew up in Hull, and now lives in East Yorkshire. Her short story collection, *New World Fairy Tales* (Salt Publishing, 2011), won the 2011 Scott Prize for Short Stories. Her work has been published in numerous magazines and anthologies.

The Summer We All Ran Away is Cassandra's debut novel.

Visit Cassandra at
cassandraparkin.wordpress.com

or on Twitter
@cassandrajaneuk

acknowledgements

First, a huge thank you to my editor Lauren Parsons, as well as to everyone else in the team at Legend Press - for choosing my book, and for everything you do to support new writers.

Secondly, thank you to my family members past and present, who gave me the glorious summers and haunting stories that inspired so much of this book. Especially big thanks go to my grandfather Ken, who – against the odds – managed *not* to drive the car down Quay Hill, off Custom House Quay and into the harbour.

And finally, to my husband Tony and my children Becky and Ben - thank you, thank you, thank you, for believing in my writing, for being thrilled (but also completely unsurprised) when my novel found a home, and for always being on my side.

For Tony, Becky and Ben

chapter one (now)

This Thursday, in the middle of August, had been the most terrible, apocalyptic day of Davey's nineteen years on earth. Getting drunk seemed the only possible response.

Slouched hopelessly on the grey-white steps of Trafalgar Square, his rucksack between his knees, he forced the vodka down his throat. Was it supposed to taste like this? Or were his mother and stepfather storing oven-cleaner in the drinks cabinet for secret reasons of their own? He imagined it burning through his stomach and intestines, fizzing gently, creating thick yellow fumes. Stubbornly, he took another swill, and wondered if he might go blind.

Of course, if he did, then maybe he wouldn't have to -

"Alright there, mate?" said a companionable voice.

Davey squinted up through dust and sunshine to the policeman who stood, sweating amiably, by the steps.

"Bit early to be drinking, isn't it? Not even lunchtime yet."

Years of public school training smoothed over his terror.

"Er yes, sir. Sorry, sir." His words slightly blurred by alcohol.

The policeman nodded wisely.

"Good." His gaze took in the clean hands, the good jeans, the bottle of Stoli. The rucksack. The dark hair capping the young, weary face. The bloom of fresh bruises, one on the jawline, one high on the cheekbone. The crust of blood at the hairline. "You've been in the wars."

Davey flushed. The policeman sat down beside him.

"Need any help? Got trouble with them at home?"

Davey wondered what incarnation of *them* the policeman was picturing. An alcoholic mother. An unemployed father with a drug habit. A violent girlfriend.

"I'm f-fine," he said. His stammer peeking out from beneath its stone. Would the policeman read anything into it? "But, erm th-thanks."

The policeman looked thoughtfully at the rucksack.

"Running away's bloody hard, you know. You might think it solves everything, but it mostly makes it worse."

"I'm n-n-n-not erm - " Davey suddenly discovered he was a terrible liar, even to strangers. "How - "

The policeman gave him a penetrating stare.

"Look, you're not causing any aggro, so I'll leave you alone if you want. But you'd do better to sort it. If you're getting hit, we'll help, but you have to ask. Alright?"

Horrified, Davey stood up. The ground rocked treacherously beneath his feet.

"Where are you going?" The policeman had hold of his elbow, his grip firm and impersonal.

"Train station," said Davey, indistinctly.

"Yeah? Where you headed?"

Over the policeman's shoulder, a paper bag danced in the breeze. West Cornwall Pasty Company.

"Cornwall," said Davey, after a slight pause. "I'm g-g-going to visit my Aunt."

"Your Aunt in Cornwall? What's her name?"

"Dorothy," said Davey, desperate. "My Aunt Dorothy. I'm g-g-going to stay with her for a bit. G-g-get my head together. You know?"

"You've got money for the ticket?"

Just let me go.

"Yes, yes, plenty." Davey showed his wallet. "See?"

"You sure there isn't anything you want to tell me? 'Cos they'll do it again, you know. They always do."

"Not if I'm n-n-not there," said Davey, and grabbed his rucksack.

"Alright, son," said the policeman, resigned. "Off you go. Good luck."

A blink, and he was on the tube. How had he got here? He remembered a barrier, a platform, a ticket machine, a handful of change, but couldn't string them together into a coherent narrative. But he was going to Cornwall. Guided by a paper bag. Well, why not? He had to go somewhere. His contempt for himself had his stepfather's voice. *Only cowards run away, real men stick around and sort it out.* He drowned it with vodka, and felt a giant wave of collective disapproval break over his head.

Above his head, the adverts were moving. A girl on a poster winked at him. She was pretty and confident, and had saved up to one hundred and fifty pounds on her car insurance because she was a lady driver. Davey's stepfather had tried to force him into driving lessons, but so far he'd managed to resist. Two panels down, a man dressed as Nelson had also saved money on his car insurance. Was that because he was an Admiral? The parrot's gaze was knowing and sly.

The lines of the tube map made him feel sick. Lying on the floor was a newspaper, open to the showbiz pages. An iconic British actress had walked off a film set because her husband was sleeping with the actress playing her daughter; a battered California starlet had wrecked her car and checked into rehab. Their faces stared accusingly up at him, as if these events were his fault. Regurgitated vodka crept up his throat. Was he going to be sick? He picked up the newspaper in anticipation. The woman next to him edged away.

Another blink, and he stood at the foot of an escalator. The platform swayed beneath his feet. If he was on a ship, would the ground feel stable? Was this why sailors drank? The handrail's speed was treacherously slower than the escalator and he had to keep letting go and grabbing on again, convinced each time that he would fall backwards into the chaos below.

Staggering off the top step, he fell into a man in a suit.

"Jesus Christ, just *fuck off*, will you?" he snarled. Davey clung to the man's shoulder, trying to re-orient himself. "Let go of me or I'll fucking deck you." His expensive aftershave was like a scented cloud. "Are you drunk? Police, police, I've got a lunatic here, police!" A privileged voice, used to be being obeyed.

"No, I'm sorry, I'm *sorry* - " Davey let go and stumbled away. The crowd parted, then refused to re-form around him, leaving him for the policemen to find. He began to run, realised how stupid this was, forced himself to stop again. High-vis jackets over black uniforms appeared at the bottom of the escalator. The crowd rustled with excitement.

"I haven't got fucking time for this," said the man in the suit, and gave Davey a spiteful shove. "Piss off, you disgusting little shit." He straightened his jacket and marched away.

As if his departure proved that Davey was not, after all, a lunatic or a terrorist, everyone returned to their business. The police arrived, looked around, saw nothing, swore, began to ask questions. A woman with henna-red hair pointed them in the direction of the man who had called them.

Reprieved, Davey crept along the wall of the tunnel. His forehead was dewy with sweat. Was it against the law to throw up at a tube station? He began following a woman with a large suitcase, hoping she would lead him to the railway.

They crossed a huge white concourse, Davey's stomach clenching, the woman's sensible low heels clicking. Would more vodka settle his nausea? The phrase *hair of the dog* floated across his mind, but the thought of hairy dogs – stinking and drooling and wet – made him gag. The woman with the suitcase was climbing some steps now. Where was she going?

Clinging to the rail for support, he broke through the surface to open air.

Another blink, the smell of diesel, everyone with suitcases, whistles shrieking like birds. Was this the train station? A giant board filled with letters and numbers. Just when he'd got a fix on them, the display refreshed and he had to start all over again. Fast food smells coiled around his nostrils. Gulping desperately, he found the Gents, scrabbling in his pocket for change to get through the turnstile.

The steel toilet bowl looked dirtier than ceramic, even though it was probably more hygienic. The vodka tasted even worse coming back up than it had done going down.

By the basins, he took another deep swig from the bottle to cleanse his palate, aware of the basic stupidity of the action, but reluctant to disobey the stern signs over the taps: NOT DRINKING WATER.

"Where are you travelling to?"

A ticket-selling woman behind a glass screen, her voice coming to him via an intercom. There was a slight delay between the movements of her mouth and the arrival of the words.

Buy ticket. Get on train. Run.

"Cornwall," said Davey.

"Which station?"

"W-w-w - " His stammer loving the vodka. Was this why he'd never really liked to drink? "Which ones are there?"

"Information centre's over there," she said wearily. "Come back when you've chosen."

Davey found a touch-screen kiosk, but you could only operate it if you already knew where you wanted to go. Behind him, a woman sighed and said loudly, "You can't work it because you're *drunk* - " and Davey, ashamed, slunk away to a row of chairs. The carpet's pattern looked like germs swarming. He wondered if he was going to be sick again.

After a few minutes, the man next to him left. On his chair was a tourist leaflet.

A spreading ripple of movement and rearrangement, everyone

sitting up, paying attention. Davey opened his eyes. Strangers opposite him; stranger beside him. Wide glass windows. The sensation of speed. He was on a train. Which train? A huge ogre squeezing his way towards him.

"Tickets, please." The guard was enormously tall and fat, barely able to fit between the seats. Why had he chosen a job he was so obviously not designed for? Or had he been thin when he got it, then gradually grown into his present size?

"Ticket," repeated the ogre, holding out his hand. Davey groped desperately back through the blankness of sleep. Did he have a ticket? Could he have got on the train without one? He remembered the ticket office, he remembered queueing, he remembered not knowing where he wanted to go. He found his wallet; there was a lot less money in it than he remembered. The other passengers watched with interest.

Panicking now, Davey began to rummage through his rucksack. On the very top was a bottle of Glenfiddich whiskey, half-empty. Had he drunk that? He remembered vodka, not whiskey. Then something flickered in his brain, just a couple of neurons mindlessly firing up, and he reached into his jacket pocket and found a rectangle of cardboard.

Together, they inspected it dubiously.

"Railcard," said the guard at last.

Davey rummaged some more, found a holder with a laminated card. He held it out and waited miserably for the guard to pronounce his fate. The guard looked at it for a long time.

"So you're old enough to be drinking," he said. "I was going to confiscate that bottle, son. If you give me any trouble, I'll have you put off the train."

"Okay," Davey agreed meekly.

The guard was looking at the bruises.

"Change at Truro."

The carriage contained nothing but staring eyes. Davey slumped down into his jacket. Outside, the world unspooled like a roll of film.

"Where are you headed?"

The woman next to him was speaking. Davey, head reeling from the inch of Glenfiddich he'd gulped down in the toilet, tried to focus on his ticket. Where *was* he going? Was this still the train with the fat guard? Alcohol had turned his memory into a swamp; no clues on the surface, hideous monsters lurking below.

You've made a complete mess of your life.

It's for your own good.

I'm trying to help you.

He shivered, and stared downwards. The letters on his ticket flickered and danced and refused to turn into words.

"Can I see?" She took his ticket from him. "You need to change at the next station."

"Thank you."

"No problem."

He studied her in shy glimpses. She reminded him of Giles' mother. Small and soft, fair wispy hair. The train was slowing.

"Okay," she said briskly. "This is me. And you. Up you get." She chivvied him out of his seat, handed him his ticket, saw him off the train.

"Thanks," he mumbled again, not daring to meet her eyes. He was terrified of needing help or asking for anything. Since he was three years old, *getting in the way* had been the unforgiveable crime.

"I've got a son your age," she said vaguely, and he stared at her in astonishment.

"Are you Giles' mum?" he called out as she disappeared across the platform; but she was already gone.

A sudden jerking stop, a sign right outside the window. Another platform to negotiate. His rucksack caught in the closing doors. The stillness of the ground was too much, and he was painfully, shamefully sick in a bin. He could hear the sound of judgement being passed, and blood singing in his ears. As he straightened up, he heard seagulls.

He stood in a steep street, a finger of tarmac leading straight down to the quayside. There were no barriers. How good would it feel to ride a skateboard down, down, down and off into the oily water? Did he have a skateboard?

He rummaged hopefully in the rucksack, but was distracted by the Glenfiddich. His mouth tasted like a drained pond. As he unscrewed the cap, he suddenly remembered the terror of stealing it, less than twelve hours ago.

On the other side of the harbour, a rose-coloured house stood by itself. In a high window, a tiny light hung like a red star.

A worm of memory wriggled at the back of his sodden brain.

"Steady there," said a man, helping Davey aboard the boat. Dazed and mystified, whiskey swimming in his blood, Davey sat down on an iron park bench screwed tight to the wooden deck.

Where was he going now? On the quay was a shelter with walls of cool, cream-coloured concrete. He would have liked to rest his hot cheek against the wall and close his eyes, but instead he was on a rickety ferry that smelled of diesel fumes and sweaty humanity, going - somewhere. No-one else shared his bench. Did he now look so wild and unkempt that nobody dared sit next to him?

He realised he was starving, and looked in his rucksack again. Why on earth had he ignored the contents of the fridge and cupboards, but packed six pairs of black socks, a battered photograph album, a stolen newspaper and *Alice in Wonderland*? How could that have seemed like a good idea?

You're a total fuck-up from start to finish.

I don't know why I even bother any more.

The seagulls sounded like crying children. He was crying too, no tears, just a contortion of his face and a keening sound that escaped in gulps and bursts. The sea-spray had the approximate taste of tears but with more complex afternotes, like a good wine.

The boat sat alarmingly low in the water. Was it safe? Were there people who checked these things? The man in the wheelhouse smoked a cigarette and stared across the water. His expression reminded Davey of long-distance lorry-drivers at service stations; a professional surrounded by amateurs, inhabiting a different world.

The bump and scrape of wood against stone, ropes thrown and tied up. The same man who had helped him onto the boat now helped him off again. Davey marvelled at the un-self-conscious way he touched Davey's hand and elbow. At school, physical contact was governed by unbreakable rules. Shoulders and upper arms were alright, as long as you slapped hard. Legs were for kicking. Heads were for capturing in a headlock and thumping. Penises, bizarrely, were acceptable, in certain situations. Hands and forearms were too close to holding hands, therefore a shortcut to social death. He tried to remember the last time he'd been touched gently by someone who wasn't his mother, and remembered a nurse bandaging his arm one night in casualty. "How did this happen?" she'd asked him, and when he'd stammered out something about a broken glass, she'd smiled cynically and shaken her head. He still had a jagged, silvery line to remind him.

He was exhausted, but something in him was forcing him on. He climbed a steep, narrow street – barely wide enough for a single car – and opened the whiskey bottle, now nearly empty. A woman walking her dog glanced at him in disgust. He tried to apologise, but his mouth was too dry. The double yellow lines were like those on the floor of the hospital, guiding bewildered patients around the labyrinth.

I've got to get up high.

He was clammy with sweat and his head and his legs were agony. The sun had filled the harbour with molten gold. He could smell himself, a vile blend of vomit, sweat and alcohol;

but he could also smell the coconut of the gorse bushes.

Stumbling into the hedge, his hand slipped between the greenery and found granite. It was a dry stone wall, covered with plants. How long did that even take to happen? He'd seen dry stone walls in Yorkshire; the most they could manage was a bit of lichen, which the Geography master had told them grew by about one centimetre a century. The wall they'd crouched behind to smoke was six hundred years old. Dreamily, he dug his fingers into the wall and began to climb.

At the top was another gorse bush. He flung himself recklessly over, relying on his clothes to protect him, getting scratched as he tumbled down the other side. Then he was behind the wall, looking across a vast expanse of scrubby moorland towards a pink-walled house that stood alone on a ridge. His head cleared and he thought, *Yes! That's where I was going, that house, that light -*

He was desperately thirsty. He hadn't pissed for hours, he wasn't sure if he even could, every drop of water had been leached out of him. If he died right now, he wouldn't rot, he'd desiccate, just a sack of leather with clothes on. Stopping to rest, he put his hand down on a sheep's skull. It was oddly beautiful, clean and white, the huge ridged yellow teeth fallen from the sockets. He held it for a while, then put it carefully in his rucksack.

Instead of getting closer, the house merely got bigger, disclosing a whole private landscape surrounding it. He thought of the word *grounds*, and then the word *acres*. The sun was almost out of the picture now, and his body had achieved the clever but uncomfortable trick of being both sweaty and freezing. He wondered what else was out here with him in the twilight, and made his feet move faster.

Surrounding the rosy house was a rosy wall. It was high and smooth, and even if he wasn't starving, dehydrated and drunk, he'd never climb it. Still, it almost felt like enough, to have got this far, to have made this strange, difficult journey to another place, another world, another life. Keeping his hand against it, he began to skirt the perimeter of the grounds.

Why had it been built so high and so strong when the house was already so isolated? Periodically, the house hid behind trees, but the wall was his faithful companion, guiding him onwards and onwards. The dew began to settle, and he knelt and licked unashamedly at a clump of grass.

Then he was suddenly clinging to a tall pillar. Its identical twin was perhaps twenty feet away. Between them, a gravel driveway shot through with primroses led to a wide wooden door with a deep tiled porch before it.

Oh, thought Davey, blinking. *Oh. Yes. That's what, that's where I was going, that's exactly where I was thinking of - my God, I made it, I actually made it -*

He journeyed up the driveway on his hands and knees, barely conscious of the stones bruising his hands. His entire self was focused on the doorway, which he thought perhaps he had seen in a book, or a dream, or a photograph; it looked welcoming and familiar, planted long ago in a secret part of his heart, and waiting for all of the nineteen years of his life for him to arrive.

The porch floor was inlaid with black and white tiles in a diamond pattern. He lay down with his head on his rucksack and ran his fingers over them. He didn't want to knock on the door and present whoever lived here with his stinking, drink-sodden, disgusting self, but to his weary bewilderment the door was moving, light was spilling out, and someone with cool hands was kneeling beside him and touching his face gently.

"Good Lord," said a woman's voice from somewhere above him. He tried to focus, and saw a pale face with a generous mouth, large brown eyes and soft, mousy brown hair looking down at him. "Where did you come from? And what happened to you?" Davey tried to open his mouth to explain. "No, shush, it's okay. You're safe. Let's get you inside."

"Who is it?" asked a girl's voice from somewhere beyond the doorway.

"No idea. Can you stand up, sweetheart?" Davey tried, but the strength was gone from his legs. "Not to worry. Priss, can you get Tom, please? I need some help."

The shadow of someone else looming over him; a brief, interested pause, then footsteps passed by, crunched on the gravel, receded. Davey closed his eyes and abandoned himself to the bliss of that hand on his forehead, not stroking, not moving, just lightly resting there, like a kiss or a promise; like a balm or a blessing.

"What's going on?" A man's voice, anxious, ready for a fight.

"It's fine, Tom, no need to panic. We just, well, we seem to have this boy."

"What boy? Who is *that?*"

"Let's just get him in, shall we?"

"Well, if you're sure - "

The hand left his forehead, and then someone who smelled of fresh air and wood-shavings gathered him up in his arms, staggering a little as he stood up.

"Are you going to make Tom bring him in the *house?*" A girl's voice, Liverpudlian and incredulous.

"Why not?"

"He could be fuckin' anybody."

"Obviously he's *somebody*. But you can't just leave people out on doorsteps, it's not fair."

"Well, put him in the outhouse at least! He might be a psycho or a junkie or - "

"Shush, Priss." The voice sounded amused.

"You're too good to be true, you are."

"Be nice," the man's voice commanded.

"I don't need to be nice. You and Kate have got *nice* covered. I'm bein' fuckin' sensible."

"God always takes care of drunks and little children," said the woman. "Stop being horrible and bring up a jug of water. Can you hear me, I wonder, whoever you are? Don't worry. You're safe now."

chapter two (then)

On the surface, the evening was everything a housewarming party should be; cool, well-lubricated, surprising, stylish, scented with flowers and pot and trees growing tall in the warm West Country night, peopled by guests who were beautiful or talented or amusing or successful or sometimes a heady combination of the four. The cars scattered in the driveway were beat-up and bohemian; the clothes were dusty black or washed-out denim or else raggedy rainbow-coloured, cheap and tawdry and beautiful. Only by listening to the murmurs of conversations in corners could the sour undercurrent of envy be detected.

On the driveway, a girl in a green cheesecloth dress climbed out of a battered VW Beetle and pushed back her long, light, unfashionably tousled hair.

His manager finally found him wearing a pair of cut-off jeans and hanging large orange lanterns high in a Japanese Cedar. Red-barked branches grew horizontally out from the base for three or four feet before shooting towards the sky like a giant candelabra. A number of the maniacs he had on his books, Alan thought, would probably set fire to it, just to see how close a resemblance they could get. He brushed bits of vegetation from the sleeve of his new pistachio suit, watching his third most lucrative client hammering in nails as if it was the only job he'd ever have, and considering how to open the conversation.

He looked hard at Jack through narrowed eyes as he leaned out at a perilous forty-degree angle. The horrific skin-and-bone look of that last, disastrous tour was gone; he looked lean, brown and healthy. Time to get him back to what he does best. Jack continued to fool with the lantern, oblivious.

"Don't you have minions to do that?" Alan asked at last.

He couldn't see Jack's face, but he saw the deliberate way he stowed the hammer in his back pocket, the slow movements as he adjusted the lantern. He'd seen that carefulness a thousand times, before every interview, every gig.

"I don't know," Jack said at last, as casual as if they had seen each other that morning instead of fifteen months ago. "Do I?"

"If you haven't, you ought to have." Jack pulled himself further up the tree trunk. "Jesus, Jack, if you die falling out of a tree I'll - "

"Kill me?"

"Stop being such a wanker and get down here," said Alan.

On the ground, the two men surveyed each other.

"So, *are* you going to kill me?" Jack said.

"Whatever gave you that idea?"

"What, honestly? I think it was you saying, *Jack, I'm so pissed off with you right now that if I ever lay eyes on you again I'll wind your guts out on a stick and have them on toast.*"

"Did I say that? Okay, I probably did. Well, I'm still pissed off and I still might do it. But fifteen per cent off the top says I'll let you live till I've heard the new album."

"Who told you I'd written a new album?" asked Jack.

"Little bird. Is it true?"

"Yes, but… "

"Any good?"

Jack shrugged. "I like it."

"Of course you do, you wanker, you wrote it. Is it marketable?"

"How on earth would I know?"

"For God's sweet sake, why do I *do* this to myself - what's it called?"

"*Landmark.*"

Alan considered this. "Okay. Arrogant, but okay. Like, *this is it, world, Jack Laker's back.*"

"No, not really."

"Who else has heard it? Apart from your girlfriend, I mean."

"I haven't got a girlfriend," said Jack, bewildered.

"Yes, you have. That Evie bird who's stopping here at your expense, you met her in – you know – been here about three months now. Remember?"

"Oh! She's not my girlfriend."

"You absolute cold-hearted bastard," said Alan in amusement. "You can't sleep with a bird, play her all the songs from your new album, let her move into your house and throw a party on your behalf and then act all fucking baffled when she assumes you're an item." Jack opened his mouth to protest. "Forget it, I don't care, it's your life. Want me to try and round up the kids?"

"Are they still available?"

"Chance to work with a living legend? Trust me."

Jack grimaced.

"If you do that face in interviews I'll kill you. Send me a tape so I know what I'm letting myself in for. I'll start the jungle-drums rumbling. Will studio in six weeks do you?"

"You haven't even heard it yet."

"Does it look like I care? They'll buy it just out of curiosity. You can finish decorating this place. Maybe even put in a swimming pool."

"I don't want a - "

"Everyone wants a swimming pool. We'll tour the shit out of it, bank another dollop of money, go into the eighties with some cash behind us. And after that well, who knows? Maybe this'll be the last one, maybe not. But I've got faith. Deal?" There was a painful silence. Alan waited expectantly. "This is the moment when you say *Alan, you're a fucking wonder and I'm a lucky bastard, how often would you like your shoes polished and how many dates do you reckon you can sell?*"

"Sorry," said Jack. "No."

Evie showed people around and offered drinks, smile glued bravely on, chin held high, wearing her status as Jack Laker's girl like bright armour that deflected the mystified stares of the guests.

"Make yourselves at home," she said, elaborately casual. "Beer in the red fridge, white wine in the white fridge, red wine on the table. Food in the kitchen."

"And Evie the Nobody from Basingstoke in Jack Laker's bed," murmured a girl in a red jersey dress. She looked Evie up and down, taking in the long brown hair, the clear skin, the fresh, wholesome face. "What the hell does he see in her?"

Her companion laid his mouth against her ear. "I heard," he whispered, "they met professionally."

"She's in the industry?"

"Nope. The *other* kind of professional."

The girl's eyes widened. "You mean she's a prostitute?"

The boy snorted with laughter. "For God's sake! She's a *nurse*, you fool."

"A nurse?" She considered this for a minute. "Actually, that's almost worse."

"Musician's madness. Can't keep their hands off even when they're a few hours from death. I heard he did a groupie a night while he was out on the road." The boy glanced around. "Where is he, anyway?"

"No idea." She sighed. "And the house isn't even finished, half of it's still derelict. I only came here to get a look at him. He must know that's why we're all here."

The girl in green cheesecloth glared at the front door. She felt a deep distaste for this party, and for the man who'd sent her here (*a chance to make useful contacts,* he'd insisted, his eyes sliding sideways when she demanded, *Who? Why do I have to go to a party to meet them?* and the unsatisfactory answer *Just people, okay? Up-and-coming people. Like you*). The porch was like a room in itself. If she lived in this house, she would put a bench here so she could sit and stare down the driveway, and enjoy the sight of nobody coming to disturb her.

Try and meet Jack Laker, her agent had told her. *He's been off the scene for a while but he could still do you some good if he wanted to.* The memory made her grimace.

At last, she knocked on the half-open door. Nobody answered, but coils of cigarette smoke wrapped welcoming tendrils around her.

"Right then," she said, and stepped over the threshold.

"What did you just say to me?" Alan demanded. "Did you just tell me no?"

"I said *sorry* first."

"I think we both know what the important word was in that sentence."

"I'm not doing another tour, Alan. The album'll have to sell itself."

Alan looked at him in disbelief. "I can't be hearing this. I can't actually be hearing those words, in that order, coming out of your mouth. This just does not happen, Jack. Are you even listening to me?"

"Of *course* I'm bloody well - " He took a deep breath. " - Sorry. Yes, I'm listening. It just doesn't change the answer."

"You know this is what some people dream of, right?" Alan was trying hard to hold onto his temper. "You know right now there's kids years younger than you lying awake and praying for five minutes of my time? Just five minutes! And I'm here in your garden offering you the moon on a stick and you're bloody hesitating."

"But I'm not hesitating," said Jack, almost to himself.

"So," said Diane, sliding onto the sofa beside Evie.

"So," said Evie. They looked at each other and laughed softly.

"I can't believe it! You and Jack Laker."

"I know, I know! I have to keep reminding myself it's true!"

"And this house! I know it's not finished, but you can see the potential, it's beautiful."

"Bit of a step-up from the Cloisters." Evie's hand caressed the butter-soft white leather.

"It's not just about the house, though, is it?" said Diane. "I mean you do love him, don't you?" Evie's gaze was liquid and luminous. "Okay, sorry. It's just, you know."

"Not an easy life?" suggested Evie.

"The stories you hear, the stuff in the papers - "

"I've already seen him at his worst," said Evie, serene. "What's he going to do that's more terrible than that? Look, you don't need to worry," she went on, seeing Diane's expression. "It won't be easy, but so what? I love him and I'm happy. What else matters?"

"You look happy," Diane admitted. "God, you even look like you belong. I feel like a complete freak! Literally everyone else here is famous. Everyone! I can see them looking at me and trying to work out who I am. How did you know who to invite?"

"Oh, I asked his manager. He said it was a good idea. Well, actually first of all he said he didn't care if Jack was rotting away in a ditch. But I told him there was a new album, and *then* he said it was a good idea."

"That's hobnobbing," said Diane. "My best friend is hobnobbing with music industry moguls. Crazy." She picked up Evie's left hand and played idly with her ring finger. "Any chance of - "

Evie laughed. "It's still early days."

"I bet he's a handful to live with."

"No, actually he's great. Anyway, he's working a lot of the time."

Diane stroked the heavy brown silk of Evie's hair. "And is he as wild in bed as they say? Have you done it in every room in the house yet?"

"Not quite yet," she said briskly. "Fancy another drink?"

"Anyway," said Mike, spilling his beer as he put it down. "Oh, shit - " He blinked at the pool spreading across the terracotta.

"Isn't beer supposed to be good for terracotta?" Sheila snatched the roach from Sid, took a hit, passed it to Mike. "Go on, I want to hear this."

"Just a minute." Mike inhaled greedily. "God, that's so great. Whose is it?"

"Jane's," said Sid. "Tell us your story."

"It's not really a story," he said. "More like an observation."

"Alright then," said Sid patiently, "tell us your observation."

"Do you tell an observation? I think you make observations. Don't you make observations?"

"Speak!" Jane kicked Mike's ankle.

"Ow! Alright, I'm speaking." He passed the roach to Sheila. "So, it was at the gig in Camden, on that tour he did."

"Which tour?"

"*The* tour."

"You're saying it like he only toured once. He did loads before the *Violet Hour* tour, he wasn't just famous the way he was when he - "

"Do you not think the very fact you instantly know what I mean when I say *the* tour tells you it was, in fact, The Tour? Do you want to hear this story or not?"

"You said it was an observation," said Sheila.

"I might actually die of boredom before we get to the end of this," Sid announced.

"I thought I'd go backstage," said Mike, very loudly. "See if he'd got five minutes to speak to a mate. And my God, it was like - " he shook his head in disbelief.

"Like what?"

"Like nothing you ever saw," he said. "Not enough

security, too many fans, they obviously weren't prepared. All these girls – you never saw so many girls! – in these teeny little outfits, queueing up like they were trying to get into a nightclub, only it was Jack's dressing room and they were all obviously just after a screw."

"Awful," said Sid.

"Yes I *know*, but there's a limit. And then, there's all the other ones – the ones from before – kids with notebooks and pencils, looking like they'd just arrived from fucking Mars or something. Talk about worlds colliding."

"So basically what you're saying is, it was a room full of people who all worshipped Jack?" Jane tried to laugh.

"But that's the thing," said Mike. "I was just stood there, staring at this, this riot, and watching that toad of a manager, what's his name? Alan, that's it, going along the line of girls and really obviously picking one out for the honour of getting into the dressing room."

"For fuck's sake." Sheila threw the roach down onto the tiles. "What an utter cunt."

"Managers are always cunts."

"Not Alan, Jack! All that crap about *It's not going to change me,* and within a year he's turned from a slightly *recherché* musician into a mad superstar who won't speak to anyone and has girls sent to his dressing room."

"So I was watching all this happen," said Mike, "and then I felt someone push past me. And I looked round, and it was Jack. So I said *Hi, mate, how are you,* and he just looked at me – he looked like he'd died three weeks ago and no-one had bothered to bury him – and shook his head, and walked out. Next thing I know, he's on the front pages, being carried out of some hotel on a stretcher."

"And that's it, is it?" said Sid. "You got blanked by Jack Laker? That's your observation?"

"I just thought it was interesting that - "

"Fame turns everyone into a monster," said Sheila. "I just wish you'd known him before, he was just the sweetest guy."

"You weren't the only one who knew him before he was famous," said Jane.

"I never said I was."

"He should never have done it," said Sid. "The dozy sod."

"Done what?"

"Sold out. That tour was his downfall."

"He didn't sell out," said Mike. "He wrote an album that was a freak hit. Happens all the time."

"He didn't have to do the lifestyle as well. Nobody made him spend half his money on this place and shove the other half up his nose." Sid laughed. "Did you hear what he's got in the garden? A panther. An actual panther. What kind of pretentious tosser keeps a big cat?"

"Want some sour grapes to go with that beer of Jack's you're drinking?" asked Jane slyly.

"Sorry?"

"Genius is never recognised; nobody buys my paintings; therefore I must be a genius."

"You utter bitch, how dare you."

"Shut up and let me explain," Mike demanded. "I haven't finished my observation yet."

"Excuse me, but can you tell me where Jack Laker actually is?"

The group turned around and saw a tall girl in a green frock.

"Around," said Mike vaguely. "You could try upstairs. Why?"

"Doesn't he mind people wandering around his house?" The group looked at her blankly. "Never mind. Thank you."

"You're welcome," sang Mike sarcastically as she disappeared.

"For fuck's sake," said Alan. "Everybody tours. Everybody. You want to sell albums? You get your arse out on the fucking road and you work for it."

"I've done my time. I've got a fanbase. People buy my stuff."

27

"You know how fast they'll stop buying it if your profile drops? This is a business! New boys come on the scene all the time. They'll have your spot in the sun in a frigging heartbeat."

"And?"

Alan forced himself to take a deep, calming breath.

"Open up," said Jane, banging on the bedroom door.

"Who is it?" A man's voice, and a trickle of female laughter.

"The drugs squad." The door opened a crack. Jane dangled her bag of sugar cubes. "Come on, Jeff, let me in and I'll share."

The door opened wide, and Jeff, stripped to the waist, welcomed her inside. On the bed, Anna lay propped on her elbows, long black hair in plaits over her shoulders, smooth brown back gleaming with oil. A silver feather hung on a leather thong between her bare breasts.

"You're overdressed," she told Jane.

Jane peeled off her clinging nylon dress, revealing sunshine-yellow knickers. Jeff watched her with barely disguised lust. Anna patted the bedspread beside her. Jeff drizzled patchouli-scented oil onto his palms and began to caress Jane's shoulders. Jane offered Anna a sugar cube.

"Hardly need one in here," murmured Anna, gesturing to the hypnotic orange swirls on the walls. "This whole room is like tripping." She looked hungrily at the sugar cube. "I shouldn't, I really shouldn't."

"'Course you should. It's a party. Live a little."

"But I promised, oh, well - " she popped the cube into her mouth and sucked it luxuriously.

Jane wriggled with pleasure as Jeff's fingers probed the base of her spine.

"So what do we make of Mr Laker's place?" she murmured.

Anna shrugged. "The front's alright. The back's like a haunted house. Apparently he ran out of money."

"He's about to make a shitload more. I heard he finished

an album." She sighed, and blinked. "Maybe then he'll be able to buy a swimming pool. Is that wallpaper moving? It looks like it's moving."

"Where's everyone else?"

"Mike's in the library, holding court about I Knew Jack Before He Was Famous."

"Christ." Jeff shuddered. "Is it the story about the Irish builders?"

"Some observation about the last night of his last tour. I don't know, I got bored."

Anna was staring at the carpet. "Jeff, this is really good, you should try some."

"Happy as I am." Jeff watched in fascination as Anna's hand moved down Jane's spine.

"Are you Jack Laker, by any chance?"

The three of them glared at the girl in the green dress, embarrassed and annoyed.

"Why would you think I'm Jack?" demanded Jeff, pulling the sunburst bedspread over himself.

"You're having sex in his bed. Doesn't he mind?"

"Excuse me," said Jane, "but who are you, anyway?"

"Try the garden," said Jeff, guiltily.

"So, this is what you want, is it?" asked Alan. "Forget wild nights and adulation and a chance to share your gift with the world, you've got a near-derelict country manor with massive trees and a view of the North Atlantic. And no staff. And a panther."

"The front half's finished."

"*So?* It's fucking miles from anywhere!"

Jack patted the trunk of the tree. "This tree's been here for hundreds of years. Growing. Branching out, getting stronger. All that time."

"Imagine that. Do the tour."

"All the people who've come and gone, it's lasted them out." He picked up a pine cone. "Look at this. A whole forest, just waiting to grow." He grinned. "I might write a song about that. Maybe even a whole album."

"If you write an album about a Cedar tree, I really will kill you. Do the tour."

Jack threw away the cone in despair. "Why won't you listen?"

"I'm your manager. I'm not here to listen, I'm here to save you from yourself. For God's sweet sake, Jack, be kind to an old man. I've got your name etched on my stomach in peptic ulcers. Do the tour." Jack shook his head stubbornly. "Do you even know what you're saying? You get one chance in this business. One bite of the cherry. One moment to shine. And that's if you're lucky. Most people don't even get that. It's bad enough that you're buried down here, you need to be nearer London. And if you won't tour – *Jesus,* Jack, how the fuck am I supposed to – I thought you wanted to be a superstar!"

"I *never* said that," said Jack, suddenly fierce. "I said I wanted to be a *musician.*"

They stared at each other in the light of the lanterns.

She tried each of the bedrooms in turn, but they were all filled with guests taking drugs or having sex or both. Half the house throbbed with sound and blazed with light; the other half was enigmatically silent, as chilled and dusty as an unheeded warning.

"Like a carnival in Hell," she muttered in disgust. Was this what her agent meant by *up-and-coming people*? And where was her host, anyway? Escaping through a door at the end of a corridor, she found herself in the unfinished side of the house.

This was the bone beneath the skin, the unchanging skull beneath the pretty, fashionable façade. If this was her home, she'd keep this side exactly as it was, no matter how rich she became. Jack Laker, on the other hand, had simply run out of money. She wandered through lightless rooms with peeling wallpaper and abandoned, half-rotten furniture, wondering who had last collapsed gratefully in the pillowy beds, last rested their heads against the high chair-backs, last feasted at the long tables.

If she died in here, would she ever be found? Perhaps that had happened to her host. Face-down at an abandoned dining table, toasting a kindly convivial Death in the bottom of a bottle; or perhaps sprawled across a tattered chair, sightless and breathless, with a needle in his arm.

Down the half-rotten staircase, and then a sudden side-door led her outside. The garden was tangled and unruly, but the basic shape was still there, and she plunged gratefully into the silence beneath fat orange lanterns. Maybe Jack Laker wasn't even at the party. A man in a green suit and a lobster-pink shirt barged angrily past her and stormed off towards the house.

Then she heard a hoarse, snarling roar, a sound that said *I'm angry and hungry and you're on the menu.* She hadn't actually believed anyone would keep a panther in a garden. Was it loose? Was it near? Didn't they lie on tree branches and drop onto their prey from above?

In a clearing ahead was a red-skinned tree like a branching chandelier. Swarming up it would be like climbing a ladder.

"Hello."

Jack, propped in the tree and staring blankly out across the moorland to the open sea, was startled to find a girl climbing towards him. Automatically, he helped her up onto his branch. Her fingers felt cool and soft. Across the garden, the panther growled again, and he felt her flinch.

"Is it caged? Or is it roaming around?"

"What, the panther? It's in an enclosure."

She pushed her hair back from her forehead.

"No wonder it sounds so angry."

She had a long, elegant nose and wide cheekbones, and her eyes were a cool, pale grey. Her mouth was wide and rose-coloured. Her hair made him think of a lion's mane. He wondered if it would be rough to the touch.

"Er - " He was no good with women, he never had been. Even in those wild disastrous touring days, when girls in their hundreds had materialised backstage and unwrapped themselves like presents, he'd always been tongue-tied and mystified, by their beauty and by their interest. But for the first time in how long? Years? He wanted to make a good impression.

She was studying his face, her gaze very frank and undisguised. He envied her ability to look at a stranger without shyness.

"I thought it might be loose," she said at last. "I climbed up here to escape. Although now I think about it, it can probably climb much better than I can."

When she smiled, he had to restrain his hand from touching her cheek.

"So why are you in the tree?"

He considered the possible answers. "I suppose I don't really like parties," he said at last.

She had an unexpectedly dirty laugh. "No, me neither. This one's fairly disgusting. And I can't find Jack Laker anywhere." She sighed. "I'm supposed to try and meet him, but I can't think why. He sounds like an absolute maniac."

The knowledge that fairly soon he would have to tell her that he was, in fact, Jack Laker, sat in his stomach like a stone. "Is he really that bad?" he asked.

"He doesn't speak to any of his old friends, he had girls sent up to his dressing room, he slept with the nurses in rehab and he keeps a wild animal as a pet. What do you think?"

"My God," said Jack, in shock. "Where did you hear all that?"

"His friends." She considered this. "Well. I say *friends*."

"So what did you think of the house?" he said hastily.

"The finished bits'll date horribly," she said. "Right now it's probably the coolest pad in the Western world. Five years from now, people will look around it and say, *My God, this place is so nineteen seventy eight! Can you believe we thought a maroon bathroom was a good idea? And those curtains!* I think I prefer the empty half." She considered for a moment. "But thirty years from now it'll probably be the last word in cool again."

"And in a couple of centuries, the National Trust will preserve that gold-flocked orange wallpaper as a national treasure."

This time, they laughed together.

"Are you a guest?" she asked. "Or do you work here?"

"Does it matter?"

"You're the only person I've met who isn't vile. I thought that might be why."

He liked the crisp economy of her speech. He liked everything about her. Above her head, the orange lantern blazed like a torch. "I look after the garden," he offered. "Oh, and I feed the panther."

"You *feed* it? Is that what happened to your shirt?"

"Just doin' my job, ma'am. So why are you here?"

"In this tree?"

"At this horrible party."

"My agent sent me." He was amused by the venom in her voice. "I'm supposed to suck up to Jack Laker. Or maybe just, you know, suck Jack Laker. He didn't really specify."

He tried not to blush. "Are you a musician?"

"An actor. Maybe. I mean, in my head I already am one. But I don't make enough to live on yet."

The silence between them was warm and companionable. When she leaned against him, his blood leapt and galloped through his heart.

In the distance, the panther roared again. Unease tickled the back of Jack's neck.

Anna lay blissfully on her front, eyes half-closed, watching the wallpaper and listening to Jeff and Jane making love. A loose thread from the bedspread was becoming a line of light, enticing her through the doorway.

She took her time over the stairs, tucking the heel of each foot close against the back of each step. She was tripping; it was important to be careful.

"Hey, Anna." A group of people with purple hair and wide, stretched faces loomed out of the library towards her. "Um, do you know you're naked?"

She didn't like the way their faces looked, and hurried outside, where huge glowing oranges hung from the trees. The flowers made faces at her as she passed. Within moments she had lost her bearings, but it was cool and peaceful, the oranges were pretty and she liked the feeling of being alone. Time stretched out like a ribbon as she wandered beneath ancient trees, oblivious to the chill on her skin or the sharp leaves beneath her feet.

"Just take it easy," she whispered to the blooming night. "Don't do anything stupid. Remember you're, shit, what the - "

She had found an enclosure built into a deep hollow, with a smooth concrete wall and an iron gate, like a prison. Inside, a black-haired man watched her from behind grass-green eyes.

"What's the matter?" asked Mathilda.

"Sometimes he sees a rabbit or something." Jack was sliding clumsily down the tree. "And he makes that sound. That hunting sound. Just once, and then they run like hell and he shuts up again."

"He's still making it."

"That's why I'm worried."

"You're tripping," Anna told herself. "This isn't real. This *isn't* real." She rubbed her eyes fiercely, then put one hand against a tree trunk to steady herself. The bark sighed and softened beneath her fingers. The man in the cage looked at her pleadingly.

"The gate's locked," she told him. "I'm sorry."

Don't leave me. The words leapt from his head into hers. *If you come in here with me, they'll open the gate. Then we can get away.*

She looked uncertainly at the barred gate.

Go up the hill and slide down the inside wall. I'll catch you.

"I took something earlier," she confessed. "I'm not sure I'm thinking straight."

Help me. Please.

The ground felt spongy beneath her feet as she climbed. She sat cautiously on the concrete lip, her legs hanging over the edge.

"Shit! Fucking hell! Don't you dare jump, you stupid cow! Jack, where the hell are you?"

A man in a pale green suit danced in front of the gate, trying to get her attention.

"You can't keep him locked up," Anna told him. "It's not right."

"If you jump in there and that beast eats you and you fuck up Jack's career I swear to God I will - does anyone have a gun or something?"

Jack's blood ran cold. The panther paced the enclosure, lashing its tail. Above him, a girl with no clothes on was preparing to jump.

"You utter fucking idiot," Alan screamed at him. "See that? That's your entire career going down the toilet! She thinks she's rescuing it!"

"Stay there," said Jack to the girl. "I'm coming to get you."

"Too late." Her smile was brilliant. "Shall I count down? I think I'll count down. Ten. Nine. Eight."

"Give me the key." Mathilda held out an imperious hand to Jack.

"Who are you?" asked Alan.

"Why do you care? Give me the *key.*"

"You can't let him out," Jack said. "You can't."

"I'm not going to, you idiot. Key."

Jack took the key from around his neck and put it into her hand, then wondered wildly what he was thinking. As she ran towards the gate, Mathilda stripped off her dress.

"One," said Anna briskly, and slid over the edge.

Rooted to the spot, Jack felt his heart stuttering, slowing, failing. Two women were going to die in his garden, right in front of his eyes.

"Hey!" Mathilda's shout, the penetrating voice of a trained actress, echoed off the curved concrete wall. The panther, about to spring, jumped five feet straight in the air instead, and turned towards her.

Jack opened his eyes and saw Mathilda running at the panther, waving the green dress like a flag. The panther snarled, cowered, then crouched.

At the exact moment of its leap, Mathilda threw her dress. It fluttered out like a flag and covered the panther's head. While it clawed frantically at the thin fabric, Mathilda grabbed Anna's hand and dragged her to the gate. The panther tore its way free of the cheesecloth and leapt after them, but Jack was already slamming the door shut. They all felt the bars shudder as the panther's shoulder crashed into the enclosure. The padlock was back on and they could all breathe again. The night air was sweet and the orange lanterns blazed.

"Jesus Christ and all the little angels," said Alan, with great fervour. "I think I'm having a heart attack."

"Shit." Anna was crying. "Shit, I was supposed to rescue him, wasn't I? Why are you keeping a man locked in your garden anyway?"

"Sorry?" Jack wondered if he'd heard right.

"Of course it's not a man, you stupid mare," Alan sighed. "God Almighty, junkies."

A crowd of interested onlookers melted out of the trees to stare at their host, his manager, and two naked women. Jack stared back with undisguised horror.

"Who's with this stupid cunt?" Alan demanded, grudgingly putting his jacket around Jane's shoulders. "And who's got a coat they don't like?" A boy of about eighteen with a shock of black curly hair quietly removed an immaculately-cut zebra-striped jacket and offered it to Mathilda. "Good to see we've got a gentleman in our midst. Anyone owning up to this daft cow, what, you again? Proper Sir Galahad. Get her out of my sight, would you?"

As he led Anna away, the boy gazed helplessly at Mathilda, but she was looking at Jack, who was watching the gathering crowd as if they might eat him alive.

"Why don't the rest of you fuck off as well?" Alan demanded. "I think we can all agree the party's over."

Like scolded schoolchildren, the guests began to disperse.

"Right," said Alan. "I'll make sure they leave. Jack, if you don't do the tour after I sort this out, you're the most ungrateful bastard who ever walked this sorry earth, and don't you forget it."

Jack and Mathilda faced each other in the clearing.

"You're Jack Laker," she said.

"Well, sort of."

"Why on earth didn't you say? I'm sorry I was rude about your house. And your party."

"You were right. It was a terrible party."

"Then why give it?"

"Look," said Jack, desperate. "I didn't sleep with the nurses in rehab and I didn't have girls sent up to my dressing room, they just turned up there, and I stopped speaking to my friends because I couldn't even stand myself, never mind anyone else."

"But you do have a panther in your garden."

"Well, yes, but it's not how it - "

"It's wrong to keep wild things caged," she told him. Then, unexpectedly, she smiled. "Jack, it's kind of cold out here."

He put his arms around her and pulled her against his naked chest. The feeling of her skin against his sent a delightful shiver up his spine.

Delirious and drowning, he whispered, "I want to make you warm."

chapter three (now)

Davey was in a quiet, rosy darkness, desperately thirsty, and he was not alone. Someone held a tall glass of iced water while he gulped frantically. Within moments he knew it was coming back up again, and there was a hand on his back and someone holding a bowl while he retched.

"You don't do this very often, do you? Drink it more slowly. Here."

More water, sipped this time, and then the feeling of cool silk against his cheek.

He was awake again, alone this time, still thirsty, head throbbing, but there was a carafe of water with a glass over the narrow neck. He lay in a four-poster bed hung with heavy brocade. Cracks of light crept in around the edges of the curtains covering the tall window.

He drank deeply once again, and returned gratefully to sleep.

When he woke for the third time, the room was like a sauna and he was soaked with sweat. Sitting up, he discovered someone had undressed him. Undressed him and, it seemed, stolen his clothes, because the faded jeans and t-shirt on the captain's chair beside the bed were certainly not his.

He dragged at the curtains and sunshine swarmed joyfully in. The heavy sash window finally conceded two inches of fresh air. Gulping it down gratefully, he surveyed the room.

The wallpaper was alarmingly fashionable, a deep purple geometric pattern that clashed elegantly with the scarlet curtains and bedspread. There was a good high ceiling that went with the long windows, and panelled doors with glass door knobs that begged to be handled. Behind one he found a bathroom, austere and intimidating with a black suite and black and white tiles, and scrupulously clean. A single threadbare white towel hung on the rail.

To his mild surprise, the shower was merely a wall-mounted attachment over the bath. Coming out of the bathroom, he spotted his rucksack lurking furtively at the end of the bed like an imposter.

He held the strange jeans hesitantly against him. They felt good against his skin, possessing the worn-in comfort of long years of wear. If he was trying to buy them they'd be described as *vintage* and his stepfather would yell at him for wasting money on stuff that should have been thrown out years ago. The t-shirt was a faded decal of the *Jaws* poster.

Whose clothes were these?

The house around him was totally silent.

Reluctantly, feeling as if he was stealing from an exceptionally generous host, he put the clothes on.

Outside his bedroom was a long, wide corridor. The décor out here was also fiercely avant-garde; lime-green carpet and green-and-yellow wallpaper in a pattern of regimented flowers, like a collision between a maths book and a Van Gogh painting. Opening a door at random, he blundered into a space strewn with papers and notebooks and a girl's clothes. He backed out hastily and hurried away, too intimidated to open any more. At the end of the corridor, a staircase described a slow, stately descent.

Trying not to make any noise, Davey crept downwards.

As he reached the ground floor, he found the same odd conjunction of Georgian fittings and ferociously modern décor. The velvet pile on the wallpaper was soft beneath his palm; a long window was half-filled with a monstrous cheese plant. Now he could smell bacon and coffee and toasting bread, intoxicating smells that made his stomach growl. He heard the murmur of voices, and a woman's laugh.

The brass door knob felt cool and friendly. He turned it and found himself in a kitchen full of warmth and light and voices, and a sudden silence as he crept in.

"Hey, look." A girl a few years younger than him, her Liverpool accent thick enough to spread on toast. "The psycho junkie's woken up." She was almost intimidatingly lovely, with huge grey eyes and thick, lustrous fair hair tumbled carelessly about a classical, heart-shaped face; a show-stopping beauty that clashed defiantly with the thick silver nose ring, the variegated metal lacing the pinnae of her ears, the layers of black clothes, the stacks of cheap rings on her fingers, the chipped black nail polish. She was curled up on a long wooden bench, sheltering between a deep crimson wall and a battered pine table. A black notepad and a chewed biro lay on the table next to her, and a dark brown coffee cup nestled in her long, ink-stained fingers.

"I'm - " Davey felt his stammer begin to clamp down. "I'm D-D-D - "

"Dangerous? Dirty? Deaf? Dull? Dim-witted? Deluded? Damned for all eternity? Dead from the neck up?"

"Be nice, you horrible girl." A woman's voice from by the stove. She looked soft and motherly, her face crowned with soft brown hair cut into a neat, sleek shape. When she put a hand on his forehead, Davey recognised the cool comfort that had brought him back to life.

"I'm Kate," she told him. "Are you feeling better?"

His tongue leapt free of the stammer. "I'm Davey."

"Nice to meet you. This is Priss." Priss subjected him to a carefully blank stare. "And this is Tom."

Tom was wiry and tanned, grey hair just brushing his collar. Davey held out an awkward hand.

"How are you?" Tom asked.

"I'm *really* sorry about last night," Davey began.

"No," said Tom, "how are you? We were worried."

"*I* bloody wasn't," said Priss.

"And I'll leave today, of course I will, and - "

"Davey," said Tom patiently. "Stop it. Alright? How *are* you?"

"I - " Davey was speechless.

"Hungry, I should think," said Kate. She dipped into an orange saucepan and put a bowl of porridge in his hands. "There's cream and sugar on the table."

Davey sat down, feeling breathless. Priss closed her notebook and gave him a hard stare.

"You'd just better not be a psycho junkie," she said. "Alright?"

The porridge was marvellous. Davey spooned brown sugar into it, then added a generous slop of cream.

"I'm not."

"'Cos you were absolutely fuckin' out of it last night."

Davey had just discovered what was meant by *inhaling* food. It was hard to stop eating for long enough to answer her.

"I'm sorry."

"We had to carry you inside. And undress you. Your clothes were absolutely fuckin' disgusting." Davey blushed scarlet. "I wanted to put you in the outhouse."

In spite of how uncomfortable Priss made him, Davey found he was fascinated by the cadence of her voice, by the pace and the lilt and the soft Germanic consonants. He didn't like hearing girls swear – girls, he felt, were meant to be soft and pretty – but the word 'fucking', pronounced by Priss, became almost poetic.

"Priss," said Kate warningly. Priss rolled her eyes, licked the tip of her finger and began to eat sugar from the bowl. Davey reached the bottom of his porridge bowl, and stood up.

"Thank you," he said. "And I'm sorry. I mean, really, I simply can't, I don't, and I'll go today, of course I will - "

Kate looked at him in surprise. "Well, you can if you like, but you don't have to," she said. "You can stay as long as you want. There's plenty of room. We're not a hotel or anything, you don't have to pay," she added, seeing his expression. "But if you fancy it, you're welcome."

It was like being offered a million pounds by a stranger in the street.

"Oh, but, but I c-c-c-couldn't." Could he? "I mean you d-d-d-don't know anything about me, it's so nice of you to offer but really, I c-c-c-couldn't - "

"You're obviously running away," Kate said. "Hey, that's okay, most people do in the end. But why not stay here while you decide what you're going to do next? Priss, if you must draw on the table, draw us something pretty, hmm?" Priss rolled her eyes, and opened her notebook instead. "I liked your choice of book, by the way. But was there a reason you only brought socks?"

Completely off-balance, Davey was forced to resort to simple honesty. "I don't know. I wasn't really thinking when I packed."

"Not to worry. I'll find some stuff you can borrow. If you don't like your room, there are a couple more you could have instead."

"Um - "

"You don't have to explain anything if you don't want to." Kate was carefully not looking at him, stirring the ladle in the porridge. "We won't ask any questions, I promise. But you look like someone who needs a safe haven." She looked up from the porridge, and smiled. "That can be here, if you like."

"B-b-b-but - " he looked wildly around at the three people in the room. Kate radiant and motherly. Tom and Priss looking at Kate, who was clearly in charge. Tom's expression wary and questioning, Priss blank and enigmatic. "But, I mean, I can't, I don't want to intrude, it's not right, you don't want strangers in your home."

"Good Lord, this isn't our house," said Kate, laughing.

"Oh? Oh! So, you're just renting it for the s-s-s-summer?"

"You think we're a family?" Priss snorted. "Do I look anything like Kate and Tom? Do I sound anything like them?"

"We're squatting," said Kate, and winked. "Don't worry," she added, seeing the look on his face. "No-one comes here. You're absolutely safe."

Davey could hear the blood singing in his ears. "But don't you, um, don't you want to n-n-n - to n-n-n-know anything about - "

"We've all got secrets," said Kate, very gently. "We won't ask as long as you don't. Okay?"

Davey felt himself flush with guilt.

"Um, I mean, it's so nice of you, but I just don't know if - "

She had a nice, friendly smile, and a way of looking vaguely past him and onto more important things that made him feel curiously welcome. "You don't have to decide now." She glanced at the bright sky. "Maybe I'll put the washing out."

"I'll come with you," said Tom. "See about the garden." He glanced at Priss, who had disappeared behind her curtain of hair. "Priss - "

"Mmm?"

"Be nice to Davey."

"And feed him," Kate added, over her shoulder.

The kitchen when they left it became a more threatening, uncertain place. Priss glanced at Davey, then went to cut thick slices of bread from a crusty loaf and layer on thick rashers of bacon.

"So," she said, slapping the sandwich in front of Davey. "Anything you want to tell me?" She poured more coffee for them both, and sat down to watch him eat.

Davey had no idea where to begin.

"D'you know where the word *house* originally comes from?" Priss demanded, returning to the sugar bowl.

Davey looked at her warily, and shook his head.

"It comes," said Priss, looking smug, "from an old German

word. *Hud*. It means to hide. A house is somewhere to hide."

The bacon sandwich was obscenely good. Davey closed his eyes in bliss as salty grease oozed onto his tongue.

"It's actually quite rude to just sit there and eat and not reply to anything I say. Didn't your mam teach you that?"

"I'm sorry."

"Good. And you apologise too much."

"I'm s - " He stopped. Priss laughed, and licked sugar off her fingers.

Five mouthfuls of peace, and she began again. She was relentless, like a very beautiful woodpecker.

"So how much did you drink yesterday?"

"I don't know." Just the word *drink* made him feel sick. He washed it away with a swallow of coffee.

"Kate sat with you for hours. She thought you might die in your sleep. You know, like, choke on your own spew."

Davey put down his sandwich.

"Could you not talk about being sick when I'm eating? Please?"

"Just trying to stop you eating the pattern off that plate." She yawned, not bothering to cover her mouth. Davey glimpsed perfect white teeth and a clean, pink tongue. "What happened to your face?"

The sandwich suddenly lost its appeal. Davey put it down on the plate and reached blindly for his coffee.

"Are you going to talk to me about anything at all?" asked Priss, saccharine-sweet.

"I'm sorry. No, I'm not - " He had to stop himself from slapping himself on the forehead.

"Did you kill someone?"

Davey spluttered over his coffee.

"Why on earth would you think I'd killed someone?"

"You turned up here out of the blue, you were absolutely dead drunk, you were obviously running away in a hurry, your face is a fuckin' mess and all you've said since you got here is that you're *sorry*." She shrugged. "Murder's not the only answer, but it's a good one."

Davey stared at her in horror.

"So," she said, watching him with interest. "Did you?"

"No, I didn't!"

"Sure?"

"I think I'd remember!"

"Probably," she agreed. "You could be lying. But I bet you're a fuckin' useless liar. Which would you rather be, a bad liar or a successful murderer?"

"What kind of a question is that?" asked Davey crossly.

"Just pick one."

"But why? Oh, alright then, a bad liar."

"You'd rather be bad at something than good at something?" Priss seemed disappointed. "Do you want some more porridge?" Without waiting for him to answer, she took his bowl and filled it again.

"Thank you," he said, surprised. She shrugged.

"Kate told me to feed you. Thing is, the Holmesian method of deduction doesn't really allow for multiple possibilities. You *might* be a murderer on the run, but you might have come here 'cos you like the view, got drunk 'cos you think it's cool, smashed up your face 'cos you walked into a door, say sorry all the time 'cos you're an inadequate loser with no self-esteem, and only packed socks and *Alice in Wonderland* 'cos you left your luggage at the station. What?"

"How do you know what I brought?"

"I went through your bag, soft lad, to check you didn't have a gun."

"Why would I have a gun?"

"You might have brought one with you."

"Yes, but why a g-g-g - "

"You might have come to kill us."

Davey was beginning to find Priss irritating.

"Well, you went through my stuff while I was asleep. *You* might have been planning to kill *me*."

"It's not much of an MO, though, is it? Waiting in a house

in the middle of nowhere for people to turn up so you can do 'em over? That's the problem with haunted-house horrors, isn't it? You're relying on the victims to show up. If you were, like, deeply compelled to kill, you wouldn't just sit inside hoping someone's car'll break down nearby. You'd go out and find someone. Fuckin' Hollywood, sacrificing credibility for a great set." She seemed to have forgotten her original point, if she'd even had one. "Like, I love *Psycho*, but how realistic is it that you could just get rid of your mother and no-one would notice she'd gone, while still running a fully functioning motel?"

"Didn't he dress up as his mother?" Davey offered tentatively.

"Yeah, I suppose. But that wasn't my point, okay? My point is, logically speaking it's much more likely you're going to hurt us than we're going to hurt you." She sighed, and scribbled on the edge of the table.

"Kate told you not to do that," said Davey, seeing a chance to attack.

"No, she didn't. She told me to draw something *pretty*." Priss invested the word with a profound scorn.

"Are you going to?" asked Davey, fascinated by the notion of a household where drawing on the furniture was allowed.

"No I am fucking not. I don't believe in *pretty*. What a pointless goal to focus on. Pretty's the biggest fuckin' waste of time ever invented. Actually, no it's not, the biggest waste of time is love. But *pretty*'s a close second." Davey watched as she restlessly sketched a stick-man dangling from a noose. After a minute, she added a woman poking him with a stick. "See, most houses have knives and hammers and stuff. If you were in the mood to kill someone, I mean. But if you had a gun, chances are it'd be the only gun in the house. So if I had it and you didn't, I'd have the advantage."

"Look, I promise I'm not a murderer, okay?" said Davey desperately.

"If you say so." She smiled at him as if they'd been

exchanging small talk in a queue at a café, and picked up her notebook again. "That's quite disappointing, actually. I've never met a murderer." She considered this for a moment. "Well. I don't think I have. S'pose you never know."

"I'm sorry," he said again, unable to stop himself.

"Sorry 'cos you haven't done someone? Is there anything about your existence you're *not* sorry for?" She took the bowl of porridge out of his hands. "You're too much of a fuckin' drip to be a murderer. Right. I'll show you around. This is the maddest house you'll ever see."

He wanted to finish his breakfast and drink his coffee and rest his head against the wall and try and put together what was happening, but Priss was like a cat that wants something. Suddenly she was all over him, taking the cup from his hands, moving his bowl away, steering him towards the door, her hair in his face and her jewellery snagging on his t-shirt. It was easier to give in, so he did.

"Have you lived here long?" he asked, struggling up the stairs and down the long corridor of bedrooms.

"Kate's room," said Priss, tapping on one of the doors in the upstairs corridor. "Tom's room. This one's empty. This one's empty. This one's empty and it's got wallpaper that'll send you off your nut. This one's empty but it's got a massive black and red bath with gold taps, it's fabulous but knock first in case I'm in it. This one's mine, don't ever go in it without my permission or I'll have you. Empty. Your room. Empty."

Across a landing, a door loomed open to a dusty corridor with bare floorboards.

"What's through there?" asked Davey.

"The Dark Side. Only half the place has been renovated." She clattered ahead of him back down the stairs. "Don't go in on your own, the floorboards are dodgy."

"So how long have you all - "

"None of your fuckin' business." Back downstairs in the hall, she opened a door. "This is the office." The door disclosed a room of angles and functional steel, with black swivel chairs and a sharp grey desk that looked naked, or perhaps robbed. "What's wrong with this picture?"

"No computer," Davey said triumphantly.

"Forget that. Check out the ceiling."

Davey looked up. The ceiling was pierced with huge metal hooks.

"Game parlour," said Priss, waving an airy hand. "They'd hang the birds until the maggots dropped out. And then eat them. The birds, I mean, not the maggots. *What?*"

"Could we not talk about maggots?"

She was away and opening another door, as if this was beneath her consideration.

"Library."

A terracotta stove relaxed in a sunken pit scattered with cushions. Sleek leather sofas were surrounded by walls and walls of books. They began with names he knew only from being told he should read them: *Symposium, Lysistrata, Metamorphoses, The Odyssey, The Birds*. Then suddenly some familiar titles: *The Canterbury Tales, The Jew of Malta, The Revenger's Tragedy,* and an entire shelf of Shakespeare, collected works and single plays, including seventeen editions of *Hamlet*. He moved on through time, passing *The Life of Johnson, Evelina, Ivanhoe, Persuasion, Middlemarch,* old friends to remind him he had not tumbled entirely out of the world. Finally, two shelves of books he had only seen in charity shops. *Peyton Place. Valley of the Dolls. Tropic of Capricorn. Jaws. Princess Daisy. Firestarter.* The collection ended abruptly with half a case still empty.

"This is great," said Davey reverently. He took down a copy of *Kidnapped* and blew the dust off the top. Priss took it away and put it back.

"Later. Come *on*."

Davey wanted to linger, but Priss dragged him onward, into another hallway with an endless amount of doors. Davey began counting, then lost track when Priss tugged impatiently on his arm.

"Okay," she said, "now we're going to play a game."

"Do we have to?" begged Davey. His head was throbbing and his legs felt weak. He longed to go back to the library and collapse into a sleek leather sofa.

"What do you think?" said Priss over her shoulder. "It's called, *Guess what the fuck anyone ever needed all these rooms for anyway.* Ready?" She flung open the first door. "Big room with a lot of couches."

Davey trailed in behind her. On a wall of beige hessian, a stone chimneypiece poured in an unpleasant grey torrent from the ceiling and pooled into a hearth. Four sofas, square-backed but with extravagant round arms upholstered in vivid magenta velvet, filled the room. Purple curtains with contrasting green circles made his eyes ache.

"Drawing room?" suggested Davey wearily.

"You posh twat," said Priss.

"Sorry?" Her smile was so dazzling he almost failed to register the insult.

"Normal people call it a living room. Or maybe a lounge. And you get *nul points* and all, 'cos it's missing several key features."

"Like what? There's plenty of places to sit." Davey looked longingly at the nearest sofa. The colour boiled ominously in the pit of his stomach, but he could close his eyes.

"And then what?"

And then I'd go to sleep, he thought.

"I don't know, maybe, um, watch television."

"There isn't one."

"Alright, um, you could drink some coffee."

"No coffee tables."

"You could put the mug on the floor."

Priss looked at him scornfully. He glanced down and realised his feet were sunk deep in cream floor-covering so thick the word *carpet* seemed an insult.

"You could read."

"There's a library."

"You might want some privacy."

"And the light's shite an' all, you'd never pick this room to read in. So basically, this is a room where people do *nothing at all but sit*. Except those sofas are crap for sitting on."

"Really?" Davey sat experimentally, and found his knees were around his ears. He lay down instead, his head resting blissfully on the pillowy arm, and closed his eyes in ecstatic exhaustion.

Priss squeezed herself onto the edge and flicked his nose hard with her finger.

"Don't go to sleep when I'm talking to you. What do you reckon?"

"I don't know," murmured Davey, with his eyes shut. Priss flicked his nose again. Drifting, he imagined an unknown party of fellow sleepers, each marooned on their own magenta island. "A psychiatrist's office, maybe."

Priss laughed. "That's not bad, actually. I thought a drug-den. But I like yours better. D'you reckon the headshrinker sat in the middle on a big black leather chair and made them all talk about their sex-lives?"

"Maybe." Davey was nearly asleep. Priss flicked him on the nose again, then pulled his hair.

"Stay awake, or I'll make you tell me about *your* sex life," she threatened. "There's lots more to see yet."

The house unfolded around him like a half-finished puzzle-box. He was Theseus in the labyrinth, following an uncouth and dazzling Ariadne. A pair of huge double doors opened reluctantly onto a vast, echoing room with a battered grand piano, a double-height ceiling and no windows. Ornate stone coving surrounded blank alcoves containing a skim of bare plaster. At the far end of the room, the entire fourth wall was missing. A spindly nettle grew between the floorboards. "I reckon they had a fight about whether it was going to be a ballroom or a swimming pool," said Priss. "Can you imagine? I could get my whole *house* in here. Don't do that, soft lad, you'll go through the floor." She yanked Davey backwards, just as his foot pushed through dry, powdery wood into the cool damp below.

Wondering how she'd known, he followed her onto the next puzzle; a large room on the undecorated side of the house, containing a teak dining table with twenty-four chairs. This seemed reasonable, if unusually opulent – even his stepfather had drawn the line at twelve places – until Priss sighed and told him that they were as far as it was possible to be from the kitchen. "Are we?" he asked in bewilderment, and Priss snorted in disgust and dragged him onwards. In a room with an upright piano, a nice view of the grounds and faded wallpaper patterned with peacock feathers, she pulled aside a moth-eaten velvet curtain to uncover a space barely larger than a pantry containing an ancient record player, a lot of boxes filled with vinyl records, an old-fashioned school-desk, and a hard, uncomfortable chair. Lost from the beginning, Davey wondered if he would ever see his room, or the kitchen, or the library, or Tom and Kate, or anything he recognised, ever again.

"And this leads back to the hall," said Priss, opening another door.

To Davey's astonishment, they were indeed back where they'd started. There was the front door, and there were the stairs, looking different when approached from a different angle. He peered at them, suspecting them of having subtly transformed themselves during his absence. At the end of the kitchen, French windows opened out to a wide veranda. A surprisingly well-kept lawn led to a towering wall of shrubs where faint traces of long-buried paths summoned the brave into their green depths.

"Round two," said Priss. "Outside."

Davey's toes cringed at the feel of the cold wet grass beneath them, but he didn't dare ask Priss to let him go back and get his shoes. The trail – he couldn't call it a path – wound thinly between the massive, towering trees, making him think of forests in fairy tales. Several times he had to stop and pick holly leaves out of the soles of his feet. Priss strode ahead, talking at him over her shoulder.

"So what do you think to the library? Bet that was your favourite."

For as long as he could remember, Davey had fantasised about having his own library. His stepfather said books were untidy.

"It's great," he offered. Priss sniffed, and picked up the pace. Davey struggled to keep up with her. His head was throbbing and his eyes felt hot and sore. His forehead was drenched with a clammy sweat.

"Are you alright?" asked Priss unexpectedly.

"Fine," he gasped.

She stopped anyway, and he leaned gratefully against a tree and tried to catch his breath. Priss took her notebook out and scribbled in it. He had known plenty of people who carried notebooks as theatrical props, but Priss didn't seem to be doing it for his benefit. He found he liked watching her when she didn't know he was looking.

"Are you going to be an artist?" he asked at last, for something to say.

"Writer." She put the notebook away and set off through the shrubs again. They were climbing now, a small steep hill thrusting disconcertingly out of nowhere.

"What sort of thing do you want to write?"

"I don't *want* to write, I *do* write. That's what writers are. People who write."

"Sorry."

"You would be. I wrote a graphic novel with a friend last year. It's a superhero story for modern audiences."

"Really?" Davey had read *Watchmen* once, and found it bewildering. "What's it called?"

Her stare was as blank and innocent as an angel's.

"It's called *Crip-Boy and Enabler-Girl*."

Davey blinked, convinced he must have misheard.

"Sorry, it's called *what?*"

"*Crip-Boy and Enabler-Girl.* The hero's a guy in a wheelchair. Enabler-Girl's his carer, and also his girlfriend."

"Oh my God!" Davey was horrified. "You can't write that!"

"Why the fuck not?"

"Because - " His disgust was so huge he couldn't find the words to express it. "Because it's awful!"

She was walking backwards so she could hold him with her stare.

"How do you know it's awful?"

"You can't call someone in a wheelchair *Crip-Boy!*"

"'Course we can. It's a deliberately provocative title, it's meant to make you feel uncomfortable. It's playing with assumptions about disabled people, like, reclaiming the insult."

"But you're not disabled!"

"So?"

"But do you even know any disabled people?"

"Do you?"

As it happened, he didn't.

"And," she said triumphantly, "you haven't even read it! You're making all these assumptions without even *reading* it! You've got a problem with graphic novels, haven't you? You fuckin' intellectual snob."

"I am *not* an intellectual snob!"

"Then tell me what's wrong with that library." She jabbed a thumb in the direction of the house.

"How can there be anything wrong with a library?"

"It's lopsided. No Moore, no Miller, no Morrison, no Gaiman, and nothing after nineteen eighty." Her accent was becoming stronger. "I wasn't even *born* in nineteen eighty."

Her arrogance took his breath away.

"*So?* There's at least - " he did a quick calculation in his head " - at least three thousand years of literature in there! That should be enough for anybody. Even - " He stopped and bit his lip.

She laughed in triumph.

"Even a thick little Scally wid no fuckin' clue about anyt'in'?"

"I didn't *mean* that, I just - "

"I bet you went to an all-boys school, didn't you? And it cost thousands of pounds a term? And about, like, eighty-five per cent of youse go to Oxford or Cambridge? Am I, like, the first *poor* person you've ever met?"

"That's c-c-c-c-completely unfair, I d-d-d - "

"Despise people like me? Don't want to admit I've gorra point? Didn't know poor people could read? Did me mam round the back of the chip shop?" She laughed. "Do you always stammer when you feel guilty?"

His tongue finally unlocked and sprang free.

"Just fuck off, Priss!" he roared, then stopped, appalled at himself.

As if he'd given her a present, she beamed at him and took him by the hand.

"That's more like it. You're not so bad, you know. For a posh lad who's soft in the head." She dragged him up to the brow of the hill. "Now, look at *that*, and tell me it's not the most fucked-up thing you've ever seen in your entire life."

Together, they stared down into the hollowed-out concrete-lined lair. The iron gate had rusted half-open across the entrance.

Dear Mum,

~~How are you? I'm really well, I've found somewhere to live and~~

~~So, I thought it might be a good idea if I moved out on my own for a while~~

~~I couldn't stay any longer, I'm sorry, but I just couldn't~~
~~I just wanted to let you know I'm alright~~
Oh God. I can't do this. I'm sorry.

Love Davey.

chapter four (then)

From the edge of the lawn, Jack and Mathilda watched Alan
get rid of the party. His pink shirt blazed out like a beacon as
he snarled at the retreating waves of guests. Jack watched in
fascination. He'd had no idea that so many people had come
in the first place.

"Do you know all these people?" asked Mathilda.

"Some of them. What's so funny?"

"Don't you think it's strange to invite people you don't
know?"

"Hey, no business like show business. Actually, I think it's
ridiculous. I moved out here to get away from all that crap."

Jeff and Jane were pointing at the stars and laughing like
maniacs. Alan shoved Jeff crossly into the back of his car,
climbed into the driver's seat, and drove off into the night.

"He's one of the nastiest men I've ever met," said Mathilda
thoughtfully.

"Alan? He's not so bad."

"Yes, he is."

"He's good at fixing things."

"He's a bully." Mathilda said this as if there was no
possibility of argument. Jack felt he should defend Alan, but
couldn't think of anything to say. The panther was roaring
again. Mathilda looked over her shoulder. "Does he need
feeding or something?"

"I fed him earlier. He's just angry."

"I don't blame him. Can you imagine how frustrating it

must be, being locked up all the time?"

"I can hardly let him out."

"Don't you think the world would be more exciting with the odd panther wandering around in it? They say there are already big cats living wild around here. He could start a family."

"Why are you so keen on him? He could have killed you."

"But he didn't."

"But he could have."

"But he *didn't*. He was just doing what he's meant to do."

"Weren't you scared?"

She shrugged. "Of course I was."

"But you still did it."

"Don't you ever do things you're scared of?"

Jack felt his throat tighten up. "I used to. Not any more."

"Why not?"

A thin breeze was blowing through the trees. He saw her shiver.

"Let's go inside."

"Are you avoiding the subject?"

"Yes. No. Yes. Probably. Look, it's getting cold and my panther ripped your dress up. I think going inside is the reasonable thing to do."

She laughed. "That's because you didn't see what they were all doing in there."

He took her hand and led her to the bright kitchen.

"This place is a wreck," said Mathilda severely, picking her way over shards of glass. "Were they throwing these at the walls?"

"I knew there was a reason I never have parties." He pulled her towards him and laid his mouth over hers. The taste made him feel as if he was falling into deep water. Her hum of pleasure vibrated in his belly. Then she moved away.

"We ought to clean up."

"What, right now?"

"Do you want to come downstairs tomorrow and stand on it?"

He imagined the glass piercing her pale foot. "Okay, but don't you do it, I will."

"Let's do it together. Where's the brush?"

They rummaged through cupboards, Mathilda amused by his total bewilderment in his own kitchen. He found a dustpan and brush beneath the sink, exclaimed in triumph, and turned around to find Mathilda right behind him. He had to lean against the sink to stop himself from touching her.

"Here," he said, holding them up like weapons.

"Well done." She took them out of his hand.

"No, no - "

"Yes. I'm going to sweep up. You're going to tell me about yourself."

"I'd rather talk about you."

"Is that you trying to make me think you're a nice guy?"

He watched the flex of the long muscles in her legs as she knelt gingerly and picked up the larger pieces. The sink was cold against his back. Her features were strong and distinctive, far above the commonplace of *pretty*. She would dominate any stage all by herself, she filled the room.

"What part would you most like to play?"

"Hamlet."

"Really?" He swallowed the obvious objection. "Why?"

"Hamlet's the part every actor wants to play," she said, pushing her hair out of the way. "It's like, I don't know, playing Wembley for musicians. My God, if you asked Peter Sellers what part he'd most like to play if he could."

"But why?" he persisted. She looked at him severely. "I'm just curious."

"I used to know this bloke," she said, still sweeping glass into the dustpan. "He said you find in Hamlet whatever you bring to it. If you've just broken up with someone, you'll think it's about Hamlet's relationship with Ophelia. Girls think it was Hamlet's fault for being pushy, and boys think it was Ophelia's fault for not putting out. If you don't get on with your mum, you'll think it's all about Gertrude; if you don't get on with your dad, you'll pick Claudius. Public schoolboys with a classical education think it's about the inexorability of Fate. Angry young men think it's a rant against the class system and the expectations imposed on us by our parents - "

Boldly, he sat beside her and took the brush away so he could cradle her hand in his.

"What do you think?"

"I think it's about how it's easy to get trapped in a part you're playing. He starts off pretending to be mad, thinking that'll help him, but by the end - " she shrugged. "What do you think Hamlet's about? I'm presuming you know it."

He offered a silent prayer of thanks for the now-defunct privilege of a grammar school education. "I read it at school, when I was about fifteen. I thought he needed therapy. Who plans to kill people because a ghost tells you to?"

"But the ghost was right."

"So? He saw his dead father walk through the wall. That's no basis for a decision, is it?" Her eyes were fixed on his face. "So you think Hamlet's about someone who's mentally unstable?"

"I, did I - shit!" He laughed. "Did I just confess to being mentally unstable?"

"I told you we were going to talk about you."

"You did. I just thought I'd managed to divert you, shit. I was hoping to save my tortured-genius story for the second date."

"Would you call this a date?"

He flushed, but saw that she was smiling too. "What would you call it?" he asked, stroking her palm.

She gave this some serious consideration. Jack brushed his lips tentatively over her fingers.

"I don't know," she said at last. "Getting to know each other. Would that cover it?"

It was hard to know how to touch her. Dressed only in her knickers and Alan's green jacket, she was so close to naked that touching her anywhere seemed an invasion.

"So, um, do we need to do any more cleaning now, or do you think oh, Jesus - " She slipped a cool hand beneath the waistband of his jeans and squeezed; Jack staggered and clutched at the edge of the sink. "Oh - " She took one of his hands and pressed it hard between her thighs. "Jesus, Mathilda, that's absolutely beautiful - " He slid the jacket off her shoulders, kissing the exposed skin. The sink pressed coldly against his back. "This is crazy, I've got seventeen bedrooms, we don't have to do this in the kitchen - "

"There aren't any clean beds."

"How mmm, oh God, how do you know?"

"There were people in every single bedroom when I looked earlier - yes, just there - "

"There's one they won't have found - "

"Jack, are you ever coming to, oh!"

Evie stood in the doorway, her frock immaculate, her hair brushed and pretty, her brown eyes wide with surprise. He let go of Mathilda, guilty and annoyed with himself for feeling guilty. He'd forgotten Evie was even in the house.

"I thought you'd gone to bed," he said.

The look on Evie's face was hard to read. He could see he was missing something important, but couldn't work out what. Then, Evie suddenly smiled brilliantly at Mathilda.

"It's a good thing I'm not the jealous type, or I'd be scratching your eyes out. It's alright, don't feel bad, I'm used to it. No, really, it's okay you weren't to know. Why don't I find you a dress and I'll see you to your car?"

"But she's *staying* - " began Jack, furious.

"No, I'm not," said Mathilda, and shook off Jack's hand. "Sorry," she said to Evie, "I didn't realise."

"Didn't realise what?"

"That you really are Jack Laker," said Mathilda. "Seventeen bedrooms? Is that so you don't have to change the sheets in between?"

The scorn in her face was hard to look at.

"Oh, my God no, no, no look I wasn't, Evie isn't - "

Mathilda was already halfway out of the kitchen. Evie turned to watch her leave. Jack shoved her aside and ran after Mathilda.

"Please stay," he begged.

"I don't think so."

"Look, Evie's just staying with me for a bit - "

Mathilda shook his hand off her arm."Please don't touch me."

"She's no-one important - "

Her eyes blazed. "I said *please don't touch me!*" She stalked down the hallway and out onto the gravel.

"But she's not my girlfriend!" Jack yelled. "Why won't anyone believe me?"

But Mathilda was already gone.

Jack scrabbled madly through the bowl for the keys to his Jaguar. The roads were narrow, but if he was quick and not too careful on the corners -

"Don't you dare go after her!" Evie snatched the keys from his hand and threw them against the wall.

"What the hell are you doing?"

"Looking after you."

"I, what? I don't need looking after! And while we're at it, how dare you imply to Mathilda that - "

"How dare *you* speak to me like that!" Her face was white and furious. "How could you, with that girl?"

"What business is it of yours?"

"What business?" Evie's eyes were burning bright. "How can you ask?"

"Because we're not a couple!"

Evie slapped his face. Jack looked at her blankly.

"What was that for?"

"I'm sorry. I shouldn't have done that. But, what you - " her anger was dissolving into tears. "What you said, that was a horrible thing to say, why would you say that?"

"But I'm just telling the truth! I've never said I love you, I've never said we were an item - "

"So what the hell is this, then, if not a relationship? Me living in your house? Cooking your meals? Organising your parties? Phoning up your bloody manager, having him turn the air blue, then sweet-talking him into coming to see you? What does that make me, if not your bloody girlfriend?"

"But look, Evie I don't, you don't - " He had no idea where the sentence was going.

"Look, I don't expect you to be a saint," she said. "I know what it's like when you're out on the road. I know you're not going to be, you know faithful. I mean, all those girls, throwing themselves at you. What man wouldn't? And I'll live with that, I swear I will. I'll never even have to know for sure. Just be discreet, and come home to me afterwards." She tried to smile. "And just - not under our actual roof, you know?"

"This is insane."

"Why?"

"Because I don't love you!"

"But I love you. You know that. I always have. We're good together, we'll make it work, I know we will."

He thought about taking her hand, then decided against it. "Listen to what you're saying. This isn't how real people live!"

"Real people?" Evie snorted. "How's your life ever going to be *real*, Jack? You're not a person any more, you're a commodity. Do you think that girl wanted anything more than a notch on the bloody bedpost?" Her nose was running. She wiped it furiously with her hand. "All she wants is to brag about screwing Jack Laker, so she can get her name in the papers."

"She didn't even know who I was!"

"Of course she sodding well knew!" sobbed Evie. "She's an actress, you idiot."

Her words soaked through his skin, turning his bones to lead.

"It doesn't matter," he said at last.

"What doesn't matter?"

"I don't care if she did just want the notch on the bedpost," he said. "I don't care if she wanted publicity. It doesn't change how I feel. I saw her in the garden and - "

"And?"

"I think I fell in love with her. I'm sorry," he added weakly.

"You're *sorry*? And you *love* her? That's what you've got?"

"It's what I feel."

She stared at him. "Okay."

"Really?" He couldn't believe it was going to be this easy. Guilt prickled at his joints. "And you're sure you're okay about this?"

"I understand. You need to get her out of your system. Fine. I'll get out of the way for a while."

He rediscovered his anger. "Because I've got any fucking chance at all with her after what you just did."

"Oh, she'll come back," said Evie unexpectedly. "Don't look like that, it's not a good thing. She'll come back, and she'll use you to get what she wants, and then she'll walk out on you and you'll fall apart and all the work you've done will go down the pan."

He felt his hand coming up to, to what? To *hit* her? Jesus, no, he forced it back down to his side. "Don't say that. Please. Why would you say that?"

"You'll see. Is it alright if I borrow your car?"

The prickles of guilt were becoming needles. "You don't need to go tonight."

"No, it's alright." Her smile was worse than any accusation she could have thrown at him. "I'll go to my parents."

"That's six hundred miles away."

"Forget it. It's my job to cope, remember?" She wiped her cheeks. "I'll wait until she's broken your heart. And then I'll come back and pick up the pieces. I'll be waiting, I promise."

"Evie, seriously don't bother waiting for me, I don't want you to."

"And listen to Alan," she added over her shoulder.

Moments later he heard gears and gravel crunching, and the slow rumble of the Jaguar disappearing down the drive.

The silence was a deep base-note that made his head ring. From the mirror, a wild-eyed, bewildered madman glowered at him, a ghost from his nightmare past. What the hell just happened? What had he done? He winced, and began a slow tour of the premises.

It was just as Mathilda had said. Every bedroom had been used; every ashtray overflowed with cigarette butts and half-smoked joints; every table heaved with abandoned drinks; every bed was crumpled. The baths spilled flaccid bubbles and tepid water over their sides. On the mirror of the turquoise bathroom, the words 'Jack Laker gives the best parties ever!!!' were scrawled in orange lipstick. He wondered who'd written it, and whether he knew her. The basin was dusted with white powder.

Did he have a cleaner? Had Evie arranged one, along with everything else she'd done for him? A *relationship*. His *girlfriend*. How had he not seen this coming? He must be insane.

Abandoning the chaos, he crossed to the other side of the house. *I think I prefer the empty half.* Mathilda should have been here with him. Was that the ghost of her perfume in the air? How could he only have met her a few hours ago? And how could he have let her go again?

Behind the panelling of the deserted upper corridor was the entrance to the rooms Evie didn't even know existed. The rooms he'd paid the architect to hide, then painted and furnished himself, with things he'd chosen himself from ordinary shops in ordinary places, because they reminded him of his childhood. The catch was reluctant to yield, but he pressed persistently at the seam in the woodwork until the door swung open. In the bathroom, he opened the cabinet and stared in.

Looking back at him was his secret cache, the stash he'd been ordered to throw away, but hadn't. He had barbiturates to lull a thousand housewives to sleep, amphetamines to keep half of London awake, prescription painkillers to blot out a million years of pain. The capsules were big enough to hurt on the way down, but they'd make up for the brief discomfort by cleaning out his head. His hand was on the loose again, rogue rebellious entity with a mind of its own. This time, instead of hitting a girl, he was reaching into the cabinet.

There was a cautious knock on the bathroom door. He slammed the cabinet shut. His heart fluttered painfully against his ribs.

"Who is it?" he demanded.

"Mathilda."

"What? Really?"

"Yes, really. Why?"

He opened the bathroom door.

He wasn't dreaming.

"Evie passed me on the road," she said. "I thought I might come back after all."

"And find out if I really am Jack Laker?" He couldn't stop the ridiculous grin spreading across his face. The hideous scene with Evie hardly seemed real. He was so pleased to see her.

"Something like that," she said, and kissed him.

It had been so long since he had done this; so long since he'd felt the sweet shock of strange skin against his own. He was afraid of hurting her, then afraid of not pleasing her, and then simply afraid. When she put her hand on his cock and squeezed, her murmurs of pleasure set him on fire; he was sure he'd never be able to last long enough to satisfy her, and had to push her away. Then she put her arms around his neck and whispered, "It doesn't have to be perfect the first time, we've got all night," and he groaned in relief and hid his face in her hair.

A few hours later, he was woken by the bathroom light shining right into his eyes. Mathilda, wearing one of his shirts, was staring at the medicine cabinet in fascination.

"That's a lot of pills. Aren't you supposed to be clean?"

"I am clean," he protested. She looked at him disbelievingly. "No, really, I am."

"Why keep them then?"

"They're sort of like souvenirs."

She looked sceptical. "Most people steal ashtrays."

"It's a bit hard to explain."

"You're supposed to be a modern-day poet."

It was cold in the bathroom. He led her back to bed and wrapped the green eiderdown around them, smoothing her hair away from his face.

"When I was just starting out," he told her, "I met this record producer, Brian. He's dead now, but he owned an indie label called Gumshoe. They were going to sign me, but they went bankrupt. Anyway. He was ex-SAS, big Welsh lad he was, and he had a live landmine on his desk."

"Really?"

"Really."

"Why?"

"That was the thing, you see. No-one ever asked, because asking was cheating. You just acted cool and pretended it was totally normal to have a motion-sensitive bomb on the desk between you."

"And what did doing that get you?"

"Oh, you know, respect - " He loved making her smile. "So, we had a few meetings, and I was only a kid and I was a bit of a tosser, so I thought I'd break the rules and ask. And he laughed like a drain and slapped me on the back, and he said, *Jack, all men do this, I guarantee it. By the time he reaches forty, every man who's ever lived a life worth a damn has got something from his past that could blow up in his face and wreck his life. I just keep mine on display.*"

"And that's your explanation for a stash of pills you can never take? Okay, I'll think about that one. So what happened to Brian?"

"He had a meeting with this real angry young group. He was giving them advice about their live show, but they were white-hot and crazy arrogant. One of them thumped the table too hard." Jack shrugged. "Brian's past finally caught up with him."

"Proper rock'n'roll."

"I know. No-one knew whether to laugh or cry when they heard. His obituary was ridiculous. It was in *The Times*, but they got an NME journo to guest it. The headline was *An Industry Mourns*, but there were all these terrible phrases like *ground-breaking talent* and *Brian's death has left a huge void*, and no-one was quite sure if he'd done it on purpose." He felt the vibration of her laughter when she leaned against him. "Ask me what the band were called."

"Alright. What were they called?"

"You won't believe me, but I'll tell you. This is true, I swear, they were called, *Everything Explodes*."

"No! You made that up, I don't believe you!"

"I said you wouldn't. But honest to God, that really was their name."

Somewhere in the laughter, they began kissing again.

chapter five (now)

Davey was at a cocktail party, and someone was jabbering tirelessly away down his ear. He held a large martini glass festooned with umbrellas and cherries, and he was naked. He thought if he could start a funny conversation with the woman beside him, perhaps no-one would notice, but he couldn't make head nor tail of what she was saying.

"Sorry, could you say that again - "

" - said if you don't wake up soon, I'm eating it myself. I know you can hear me, mate, you might as well open your eyes."

Priss was sitting cross-legged on the end of his bed, draped in a silky red bedspread that made him think of lingerie. He looked hastily away.

"You're turning into a Morlock," she told him.

"Sorry."

"I'm going to put that on your gravestone. I brought you breakfast in bed."

"Thank you."

"It's a bribe," Priss continued. "I'm putting you in my debt so you'll be forced to come and talk to me instead of hiding in the library and pretending to write letters."

"I'm s - " Davey bit his tongue, and took the mug of coffee. Priss peeled off a long strip of fat and dropped it into her mouth before passing him the bacon sandwich.

"You shouldn't eat that," said Davey, before he could stop himself.

Priss shrugged. "I'm only sixteen, I can get away with it. Besides, that's the only bit I've eaten. You're about to eat the whole sandwich." She licked her fingers with her pink tongue. "Get a move on. I'm not very nice when I'm bored."

"Um, can you give me a minute?"

"To do what?"

"To get up."

"I'm not stopping you."

"I - haven't g-g-got any pyjamas on."

"You are *such* a fuckin' prude." Priss turned around. "Go on, then."

Davey scurried out from beneath the covers, grabbed an armful of clothes and locked himself hastily in the bathroom.

"I don't know why you're bothered," Priss shouted through the door. "I've already seen it."

"*What?* When?"

"When you was dead drunk and puking everywhere, soft lad, when d'you think? Are you stopping in there all day?"

"I'm sorry, I'm cleaning my teeth - " Davey chewed frantically on his toothbrush, struggled into his jeans, pulled his t-shirt over his head and unlocked the bathroom door. "But, but you're not even dressed!"

Priss looked at him challengingly and folded her arms. She was wearing a shapeless black jumper that exposed her left shoulder, thick woolly socks, and a pair of boxer shorts.

"Yes, I am."

"But you're only wearing - "

"If I wore this to the beach you'd think I was *over*dressed. You can't see my tits or my minge, can you?"

"It's j-j-j - "

"July," said Priss, leading the way down to the kitchen. "Justice. Juvenile delinquency. Jeeves." She switched to a bad approximation of an upper-crust accent. "Jolly good show. Just not on, what? No, that's fuckin' terrible, that, isn't it?" Davey wasn't sure what the polite answer would be, but fortunately she just kept talking. It was a bit like having the radio on. "Do posh people really use 'what' as a placeholder, or is that people like me are supposed to go round saying *Go 'ed* all the time? I've always wondered. Hey, Kate, look who I found snoring under his covers like a pisshead farm-hog."

"I don't snore," said Davey feebly.

Priss sniffed. "Like you'd know."

"Why are you always so horrible in the mornings?" asked Kate, ruffling Priss' hair.

"I'm horrible all the time."

"Yes, but you're worse in the mornings."

"The badness builds up overnight while I'm asleep."

"So you did sleep?"

"Don't fuss."

"Did you?"

"I was exploring the Dark Side. I found a dinner service in there. I think it's Meissen."

"What makes you think it's Meissen?" asked Davey.

Priss favoured him with a pale-eyed stare. "'Cos it's got a Meissen mark on the bottom."

Davey opened his mouth to ask how Priss knew what the Meissen maker's mark looked like, but then closed it again.

"It's not safe in there," said Kate. "And it worries me when you stay up all night."

"I'm a teenager," said Priss airily. "I'm supposed to have messed-up sleeping patterns and a shitty attitude."

"So you are." Kate put her fingers under Davey's chin and tipped his face up so the light caught his bruises, finally fading under the influence of time and rest and sunshine. "And how are you?"

"I'm fine," said Davey. Was this the start of an interrogation?

"Good."

"You look like George Best," said Priss. "All yellow."

"I'm sorry I slept so late," said Davey. He glanced at his watch and was appalled to find it was nearly eleven o'clock. He hadn't made it downstairs at a decent hour even once in the five days since he'd rocked up here. Priss was right. He was turning into a Morlock.

"Why?" asked Tom. "We're not exactly living on a schedule, you know. Have some coffee, it's fresh."

"But you keep f-f-f-feeding me and m-m-making me coffee and - "

"Oh, I expect we're just madly overcompensating for the hideous crimes of our past lives," said Kate.

Her tone was light, but for a moment, the whole room seemed to freeze in place.

Then, in unison, Kate and Tom began to move again. Tom said, "Right," and walked out through the patio doors. Kate murmured something in which the only distinguishable word was 'later', and disappeared into the house.

"We're going out for a walk," said Priss to Davey.

Davey wondered what would happen if he argued with Priss.

"Here's the thing," said Priss. "I really, *really* want to talk to you. And I'm tougher than you, and we both know it, so I'm always going to win any argument we have. Which means it's much quicker and less painful if you give in. Also, I brought you breakfast in bed, which, as I may have mentioned, was a bribe, and you took it, which means we've got a contract. Right?"

"We could talk in the library," Davey suggested.

"No we couldn't."

"Why not?"

"Never mind."

Davey noticed for the first time that Priss looked pale and tired, and she had dark shadows under her eyes.

"Are you alright?" he asked.

"'Course I'm fuckin' alright, why wouldn't I be?"

As they crossed the lawn, she slipped her hand into his. He was surprised by how small and soft her fingers felt.

"So," said Priss. "Is *Alice In Wonderland* your favourite book?"

They were sitting in the branches of a gigantic tree whose branches grew horizontally out from its red-skinned trunk and then shot up into the sky. The shape of the branches and the resiny scent made Davey think of a church.

"Yes. No. I don't know. I can't choose just one. I don't know why I brought it really."

She glanced slyly at him from underneath her hair.

"Is *self-knowledge* just a word beginning with 's' where you're from?"

"Okay then," he said. "If you're so clever, why do *you* think I brought it?"

"Ha! You ready? Answer one: 'cos it's about a fantastical journey from reality, and that's what you were hoping for when you ran. Answer two: 'cos it's a book in which altered states are a major feature, and you were absolutely off your face when you packed your bag. Answer three: 'cos it's a child's book, and you haven't been happy since you were a child. Answer four: 'cos you, like its author, are a shy, socially awkward misfit with a stammer." She laughed at the expression on his face. "I can keep going if you like."

"How, how, you don't know anything about me!"

"I know *loads* about you," said Priss loftily, without looking at him.

The wind rippled through the tree and blew Priss' hair away from her immaculate profile. When she wasn't speaking, he could see past the theatrical make-up and piercings to the classical serenity of her lovely face. He wished he could draw. Raphael, he thought vaguely, or maybe Caravaggio -

"It's really rude to stare," said Priss, still not looking at him.

Davey felt himself flush a deep and unbecoming scarlet. "I um, I wasn't - I wasn't st-st-st-st - "

"Stagnant. Strait-jacketed. Streaking. Stalking the girl from round the corner. Stuck up the chimney. Forget it. What do you make of the house?"

"It's great. The décor's really interesting."

"You know *interesting*'s what British people say when we mean *fucking awful*, right?"

"It's just, I don't know, it's fashionable."

"Fashionable?" Priss laughed. "Is that what you think?"

"My mother's really interested in interior design," said Davey, knowing he was going to win this one. "The retro look's been really big recently."

"Christ," said Priss. "I've met out-of-date cheese with more brains."

"Sorry?"

"It's not *fashionable*, you twat. It's so old it's come back in style."

Davey looked at her blankly.

"It's the original deal, thicko. Someone half-did that place up back in the late seventies and it's never been changed. That's why there's no books in the library past nineteen-eighty." She pulled the sleeves of her jumper down to cover her hands. "It's horrible. Like a tomb. Or a labyrinth. All those fucking rooms, looking out at us. Nothing matches up, I swear it moves around while we're asleep or something."

"But it's beautiful," said Davey, in surprise. "It's the best place I've ever lived in. I mean, I know I don't l-l-l-live there, n-n-n-not really, but - "

Priss laughed. "You need fuckin' analysing, you do."

"I've been - " Davey stopped suddenly.

"That figures," said Priss. "For all the good it bloody did you. Bet you had a crush on your therapist as well."

"I did *not*."

"Your problem is, you get distracted by appearances."

"I don't know what you're talking about."

"Hard to see through those rose-coloured spectacles, is it? You probably think this place is some sort of Paradise, right? Luckiest break of your life the day you turned up on the doorstep?"

"But it was! I don't know what I'd have done if - "

"Look, just 'cos I look like a fuckin' angel doesn't mean

you can trust me. And just 'cos Kate and Tom did one nice thing doesn't mean you can trust *them*."

"They saved my life!"

"So? Stop feeling grateful and start thinking!"

Reluctantly, Davey remembered the scene in the kitchen this morning.

"It's not their house, right? Although I reckon they only told you that 'cos they knew I'd say something, they didn't mention it to me for fuckin' ages. So what happened to the real owner?"

"I don't know and I d-d-d-don't care," said Davey resignedly.

"You mean you don't want to think about it. But you've got to, okay? *We've* got to. Just look at this place! Whoever owns it must have loved it once. Spent a fortune doing it up. Made it into a real home. And then, they just left. Walked away and never came back. Didn't turn the power off, didn't nick the light bulbs, didn't take the crockery, didn't take the pans, didn't take the books off the shelves, left all the clothes in the wardrobes." She looked meaningfully at Davey's t-shirt. Davey shivered. "And then one day, Kate and Tom walk in."

"So what?" said Davey.

With some difficulty, Priss tore off a cluster of long, needly leaves. "See, the thing is," she said, tugging hard at the tough stalks, "Tom and Kate, they don't bother you with questions. They just let you, you know, *be*. It's not like they don't care – Christ, *anyone* that'd mop up your spew, the state you were in – but they just, they don't pry." Her smile was brief, but bewitching. "They're, like, the opposite of parents. And I want to think they're everything they seem, I really do."

"Well, maybe they are."

"And maybe there's fairies living in the brook and a giant pink teapot orbiting the Earth and Our Lady really does make stone statues cry, but - really?" She wiped her nose on her sleeve, leaving a trail of wet silver. Even this disgusting action, when performed by Priss, seemed almost charming.

"Why can't you just let it go? I mean, why look a gift horse in the mouth? We're all happy here."

"Please," Priss begged. "Look me in the eye and say *Priss, you're a cynical cow and two adult strangers are being ludicrously nice to us 'cos they're a couple of living saints,* and I'll shut the fuck up forever, scout's honour. But tell me this. Why are they hiding in the middle of nowhere, in someone else's house? And how do they know they won't get caught?"

Davey shook his head stubbornly. Against all possible odds, he'd taken flight from an impossible situation and found a secret, magical haven. Now Priss was spoiling it all. Why couldn't she leave it alone? Why did she insist on making him see?

What was so great about the truth, anyway?

"Maybe they've done - something bad," said Davey at last, with deep reluctance.

"Oh, you reckon? Just man up and say the bloody word."

"Like m-m-maybe they m-m-m - "

"See, I don't *want* to think that," said Priss. "'Cos I love 'em. Both of 'em. I do. That's the trouble with love, though, isn't it? It stops you seeing the truth."

They sat in silence for a while, Priss tearing at her clump of leaves, Davey desperately trying to find the flaw in her logic. The scent of resin was enough to get drunk on.

"But," he said at last, "if you really think they've – you know, done *that* – shouldn't we go to the police?"

"We might be wrong! Do you want to go to the coppers just on the off chance you've caught a murderer? 'Cos I don't know about you, but I could do without stickin' my head over the parapet unless I really have to, you know?" Davey looked at her in appalled fascination, but she left no gap in the conversation for him to ask. "We've got to find out ourselves. I'm not dobbin' them in if they're just hiding from the taxman. I'll do it for a dead body, but not for anything else."

"But - "

"Look," said Priss, "These are the choices we've got. We

could walk away and say nothin'. But then what if they *have* killed someone? What would that make us? Or we could turn 'em in to the police. But what if it is just the taxman? Besides - "

"What?"

"I want to fuckin' *know*," said Priss. "I've got a million ideas and I can't stand not knowing which one's right. I mean, maybe Kate's husband was hitting her and Tom's her brother and he helped her get away, or maybe Tom's claustrophobic and Kate's agoraphobic and they met in therapy and decided to run off together, or maybe they're both on the run from some dodgy London gang. Or maybe they're cyber-criminals who've had half a billion off the Bank of England, or - "

"Or maybe they're star-crossed lovers," said Davey eagerly, "and they've waited decades for their children to grow up so they could be together, or - "

"Oh, shut up, you dozy twat. You think I'd hang around here for one fuckin' minute if I thought this was some soppy love story? One of the best things about getting old is you can stop bothering with all that hearts and flowers shite. Anyway, they don't share a room."

"And what if we do find out?"

"*When* we find out," said Priss, "we make a decision. Maybe we dob 'em in, maybe we just walk away." She tossed the tuft of needles away. "And if it's a good enough story, I'll change a few names and write a bestseller."

" - "

"Good. That's decided."

Was it? What had he just committed himself to?

And what if Tom, or Kate, or both of them, really had done something. Wouldn't that mean they could do the same to - ?

But would they do that after saving his life?

"Soft lad," said Priss. "You're fuckin' terrified, aren't you? We'll be alright."

"I'm not scared."

"You're always scared."

There didn't seem much to say to that, so Davey decided to

say nothing. Perhaps if he just sat in the sun for a while, this conversation would all have been a figment of his imagination.

"What's your favourite book, then?" he asked at last.

"The Bible."

"Really?"

"'Course not."

"I was only asking."

"I don't do personal information."

"You asked me."

"*So?* Life doesn't work the way it ought to. Where are you going?"

"To the bathroom," said Davey.

"That's a dainty way of putting it. You're not going right back to the house, are you?"

"Well, um - "

"Unless you're going for a shit, of course."

"Priss!"

"Oh, Celia, Celia, Celia shits," murmured Priss, closing her eyes against the sunshine. "Make sure the rabbits don't see. They'll complain to *The Times*."

Feeling prudish and paranoid, Davey scrambled down into the shelter of the woods. He glimpsed the half-open bars of the concrete enclosure, and turned away. He didn't like looking at it. He didn't want to see anything unpleasant. It looked like a prison. Who, or what, had been confined behind its bars?

As he re-zipped his jeans, a flicker of movement caught his eye. He opened his mouth to call out, then closed it again. The figure moving between the trees was taller than Priss, and the hair was the wrong colour for Kate, was it Tom? No, Tom was heavier and broader.

The man who emerged between two spindly rowan trees was a stranger.

His olive skin, black eyes and dark hair shot with silver made him look Italian, an impression enhanced by his crisp white linen shirt, stylishly half-buttoned over dirty blue jeans and tattered flip-flops. Davey, wondering if this was the owner come to reclaim his property, saw the stranger was carrying a bunch of flowers, seemingly picked from the woods. Davey recognised lilac buddleia cones, white rhododendrons with haloes of glossy leaves, handfuls of campion and forget-me-not, a splash of yellow dandelions. If Davey had picked those flowers, he would simply have a badly-assorted bundle of blooms, but in the hands of the stranger, they were graceful and lovely.

The man knelt beneath a beech tree, sweeping aside the litter of husks to touch the dry soil beneath. What was happening here? The man's head was bowed. Was he crying? Praying? Davey didn't dare move.

Then, whatever it was, it was over. The stranger laid the flowers down, stood up, dusted his hands, and saw Davey staring at him.

Davey's first reaction was profound embarrassment. A hot wave of shame washed over him from head to foot, dyeing him scarlet and stopping his tongue. When he could bear to look again, the man was watching him curiously. Then he put one finger to his lips and winked conspiratorially.

"Okay," whispered Davey. His throat was dry and the word was nearly silent, but the man must have seen his lips move, because he smiled, acknowledging their agreement, and disappeared into the trees.

Did that just happen? Should he tell Priss he just saw a man leave flowers beneath the beech tree? Should he mention that the man knelt and bowed his head first, tears on his cheeks as if in memory of someone who -

No, he thought. *It's probably nothing, nothing to do with Tom or Kate anyway. They probably don't even know him, we might never see him again. Maybe he used to work here and he buried his dog there, it doesn't have to be a person, that's ridiculous.*

Maybe I even dreamed it.

If I don't think about it, it never happened.

Trying to arrange his face into an expression of innocence,

Davey made his way back to the candelabra tree.

"So," said Priss as soon as he climbed laboriously back onto their chosen branch. "Who beat you up?"

"No-one," said Davey. "I f-f-fell over in the shower."

"Don't ever, ever go to Vegas. Was it someone at school?"

"I'm nineteen, I don't go to school any more, I'm g-g-g - "

"Gagging for it? Gangrenous? Gutted? Genghis Khan's distant relative? Sorry, I know I shouldn't interrupt but I can't sit and wait for you to finish, it's just not in me. My school was full of bastards as well. They never bothered me, but that's 'cos I'm horrible. They only pick on the nice ones."

"But they didn't, it wasn't - "

"If you don't tell me," Priss told him confidingly, "I'll just ask you and ask you and ask you until you go nuts. Did you go to boarding school?"

"How did you know?"

"'Cos you're fucked up and you talk posh."

"That doesn't m-m-m-mean anything. I mean I don't assume you go to some inner-city s-s-sinkhole just because you curse all the time and you've got an accent."

"Well, you should, 'cos I do." She paused. "Did. Were you buggered by the prefects?"

"No!"

"Just asking. Isn't it weird everyone's up in arms about Catholic priests, but when it's posh kids doing each other, no-one bats an eyelid? D'you reckon that's 'cos no-one really believes it? Or is it the inherent decadence of the upper classes?"

"Listen, I was *not* - no-one did *that* to me, okay?"

"They picked on you, though."

"You don't know that, how on earth would you know that?"

"You stammer when you get stressed. Bullies love predictable reactions."

"Well, you're wrong."

"Look me in the eye and tell me that. Come on, right in the eye and say, *I was not picked on at school* and I'll believe you."

"I was *not* p-p-p-p I wasn't p-p-p they didn't p-p-p - "

Priss looked satisfied. "Why didn't you just twat 'em back? You're six foot, easy."

"Six foot one."

"Mind you, posh boys are always bigger," she went on thoughtfully. "And triangle-shaped! Have you ever noticed that? It's, like, this special build you only get if you've got rich parents. D'you reckon it's genetic? Or do you lot do different sports to the rest of us?"

"Erm - " Memories of muddy fields and vicious kicks to the shins. Fortunately, Priss was still speaking.

"You could have had 'em if you'd tried. You only have to beat someone up really badly once, and they leave you alone for the rest of time. What?"

"You can't go round hitting people," said Davey.

"'Course you can, you daft twat. They get away with it. Why can't you?"

"Look, what's it got to do with you, anyway?"

"I'm just trying to work out why you're so scared all the time," said Priss. "And why you're so desperate not to think badly of anyone who's nice to you. It's funny, really. I'm way too horrible and you're way too sweet. I suppose if you average us out you get one normal person."

The silence hummed companionably in their ears. Priss was chewing ferociously on her thumbnail. Black nail polish freckled her teeth. The contrast was surprisingly pleasing, like a Dalmatian dog.

"Actually," said Priss suddenly, "if I had the choice of living in a deserted country house with a lad who doesn't take shit off anyone, or living in a deserted country house with a lad who's probably scared of wasps, I'd pick the one who's scared of wasps. At least you won't go bat-shit mental and kill us all 'cos you can't find a clean towel. Beta males are underrated. Do you want some lunch? I'm starving."

Why did Priss get to dictate everything, all the time? Davey wondered crossly as he slipped and slithered down the tree and followed her towards the house. And why did he go along with it? She was leading them past the caged enclosure. He didn't want to go that way.

"Can't we go back the way we came?" he asked.

He thought it sounded quite good, a decent approximation of innocence, but Priss was like a shark scenting blood.

"Why?" she demanded.

"Does there have to be a reason?"

"For you to suddenly assert yourself? What don't you want me to see?"

"I'm n-n - there's n-n-n - " Her stare was like being stuck with a giant pin. The beech tree with its bunch of flowers was right behind her.

"D'you know you're staring at something over my shoulder?" said Priss. "Who the fuck put those there?" She picked up the bunch of flowers and sniffed cautiously.

"I d-d-d - " This was the worst it had ever been; he had never felt so crippled, so trapped, so inarticulate. "I d-d-d - " He closed his eyes. "I d - "

"Why are you so stressed out?" asked Priss, baffled. "It's a bunch of flowers, mate, that's all."

Was he imagining it, or did the ground beneath the beech tree have a gentle swell to it, as if something bulked out the earth from below? He thought of Tom, who had been kind, of Kate, who had saved him. She deserved to be left in peace.

"I did it," he burst out. "I p-p-p-picked them, I was g-g-g-going to and then I felt stupid and I d-d-d-d - "

The stammer clamped down tight again, but it was enough. Priss was looking at him in astonishment, but at least she seemed to believe him.

"You're not right in the head, you're not," she told him. "I hope these were for Kate."

Why would she hope that? Was he such a ridiculous prospect?

"It's not bad, though," she said, inspecting the flowers critically. "Hidden depths, mate. You should give them to her."

Hours later, Priss and Davey sat in the warm, drowsy kitchen and watched Kate making spaghetti bolognese. Tom washed cutlery and stacked it with military tidiness into the draining board, then went to stand in the doorway. Davey, idly balancing a teaspoon on the salt cellar, watched Kate chopping courgettes, carrots, onions, mushrooms and garlic, and thought dreamily that Kate and Tom were the most restful people he had ever known. They asked no questions. They had no helpful suggestions about how to spend the day. They seemed to have no expectations of him whatsoever.

Was it possible, he wondered, that he might be able to stay here forever?

"Have you and Tom lived here long?" The question bubbled straight up from his gut, with his brain getting no say in it. Priss jumped, and glared at him.

"Mmm?" Kate looked at him absent-mindedly.

"I just wondered how long you'd lived here," he repeated.

"So long I can't even remember," said Kate, smiling to herself. "Why do you ask?"

"Oh, you know, I j-j-just w-w-w - oh, shit! I mean, sorry."

Standing in the door from the hallway, waiting patiently to be noticed was the man Davey had seen in the woods. Despite his resolve to forget what Priss had said to him, Davey found himself glancing sharply around at his companions, trying to catch them in the unguarded moment of an unexpected meeting.

Tom looked honestly surprised, and also apprehensive, looking at the stranger as if he might be wearing a bomb beneath his shirt. Priss looked as if she was doing long division in her head. Kate's face was filled with delighted surprise, and she held out her arms in greeting, laughed a name, *Isaac*, and offered herself for an embrace. But as she turned back for a minute to turn off the gas on the stove, Davey thought he glimpsed another expression, older and sadder, as if she had been expecting and hoping to see somebody else, and was disappointed.

chapter six (then)

Jack suspected he was losing the art of being with other people. Aboard the train to London, he tried not to flinch when a woman in her fifties took the seat next to him and began talking. She was visiting her daughter, who lived in Fulham and had just had a baby. By skilful questioning and a great feigned interest in the baby, he managed to deflect most of her questions; but his seat-companion still compelled him to admit that he'd recently met a girl, yes, a very nice girl, who, yes, he was hoping to marry one day, although no, he hadn't mentioned this to her yet. As they pulled into Paddington Station, he wondered what kind of Nice Girl the woman was picturing. Someone horsey perhaps, with a carrying voice and a long stride and a way with dogs.

The memory of Mathilda's tall, spare frame, her wide mouth and her light hair and her grey eyes, was like a talisman in his pocket. He remembered how she'd looked two nights ago, before leaving for London. She'd sat on the floor of the library while he, clutching his guitar and sweating with nerves, sang the tracks from *Landmark*.

"It's the Landmark hotel, isn't it," she'd said.

"Yes."

"I bet Alan thinks you meant *Milestone In My Career*, though, doesn't he?"

"Yes! How did you know?"

"Maybe I'm a genius too. It's very personal, you know, this album. Are you sure you want to show the world that much of yourself?"

"Doesn't it have to be personal to be good?"

"What are you doing in this industry?" she'd asked him then. "Oh, I don't mean that," she added, seeing his face. "It's brilliant, even better than *Violet Hour*. But you'll need to do interviews about it, and promote it, and answer questions about what it means and where it came from and that's not you at all, is it? It's all about the music. Being rich and famous is just the unintended consequence."

"How do you know me so well?" he had asked in amazement.

"Because I'm a witch," she told him. Then she had lain down in the spot where the firelight littered the tiled floor with flickers of light like leaves.

The rumble and whoosh of the approaching tube dragged him back into reality.

An hour later, Jack sat in a smoke-filled office on King's Road, watching Alan listening to the demo. Alan kept his face a smoothly professional blank, occasionally making opaque and miniscule notes on the blotter. Jack deciphered the words 'weepie', 'stad R???' and 'spine'. Was that good, or bad? Was it related to the album at all? Was Alan just planning his next session with his chiropractor?

"Mmmm," said Alan at last, and pressed the stop button.

Jack braced himself.

"You wouldn't think anyone'd still want poetry, would you?" he mused. "Didn't all that shit have its heyday back in the fifteenth century?"

"Pardon?"

"Poetry. Peaked with Shakespeare and Spenser, been declining ever since. I know I act like an ignorant tosser but even I've got my moments. Right?"

"So what do you - "

"Gather you and Evie split up."

"We were never together," said Jack in exasperation.

"Yeah, if you say so. Are you and that other bird knocking around together? That bird from the party?"

"Do you mean Mathilda?"

"Do I? Skinny, young, hair in a mess. Got her kit off."

"Saved someone's life."

"Yeah, that's the one."

"Yes."

Alan looked at him and grinned. "Got it bad at last, haven't you? You daft bugger. She here with you?"

"She came up two days ago for an audition. Why?"

"Just you be careful, alright? Not sure I like you being in love, to be honest."

"It's none of your fucking business."

"Simmer down. If it affects your work, it's my business." Alan rummaged in his desk drawer. "Want a coffin nail?"

"No thanks."

"Mind if I do?"

"Course not."

Jack watched Alan put a long cigarette between his lips, hold up a heavy gold lighter, summon the flame, inhale luxuriously, hold it for a second, breathe out.

"How about a coffee?"

"No."

Alan twinkled at him. "No what?"

"No! Just no! All I want is for you to tell me what you think of the album!"

Alan looked at him blankly. "But it's fucking brilliant, you wanker. We'll have *Landmark* and *2:43am* for the singles, maybe another couple if it goes well." Jack's spine turned elastic with relief. "You weren't actually worried, were you?"

Jack shrugged.

"You dozy sod. I told you, I'd take it whatever. But as it happens, it's the best thing you've done so far. Straight up vintage Laker, but with a twist." Jack winced. "Look, we're not all blessed with your magic way with words."

"I don't want to stand still."

"Nothing wrong with giving the fans what they want."

"It's not *for* the fans, it's for - "

"Give over," said Alan. "Let's talk about the tour."

Jack sat up straight in his chair. "No."

"We need the tour to sell it. You'll get rave reviews, I'm sure, but you can't count on airplay."

"*Violet Hour* got airplay."

"Shush. How many dates can you handle?"

'No' is a complete sentence, Mathilda whispered in his ear. She'd repeated this mantra to him over and over, in the deep warmth of their bed before she left to drive to London. That night, he'd lain against her pillow and breathed in the smell of her hair.

"No."

"We can cut them right down if you want. In fact, that might even be a good ploy. Make you rare."

"No."

"It'll sell out, I guarantee it. For a guy who's been invisible for over a year, you are fucking *ludicrously* in demand. People call all the time wanting to meet you. Not just ordinary people, either. *Real* people."

"What do you mean by a *real* person?" asked Jack, fascinated enough to deviate from his stonewalling.

"Oh, you know. Agents, actors, musicians, film producers, you know, *real*. Not just punters."

Jack nodded thoughtfully. "That's good to know."

"Take this seriously, you arsehole." From outside in her tiny cubbyhole, Alan's secretary buzzed him. "What?"

"He's here, boss."

"Count to twenty-five and send him in." Alan looked at Jack. "Actually, fifty."

"Okay."

"What are you up to?" Jack demanded.

"I'm not giving up on the tour, you know," said Alan.

"And I'm not doing it. I swear to God, if that guy out there is - "

"Yeah, we'll have that conversation another time. Sit down, you pillock, it's nothing to do with the tour, I've found this new artist who might do the cover. Found him at your party, actually."

"It wasn't my party."

"Alright, Evie's party." Alan grinned. "She was a good bet, you know. Better than that actress bird. Only room for one artist in the family."

Jack remembered Mathilda's intent face as she sat coiled in the window seat, murmuring lines under her breath, committing Ibsen's *Doll's House* to heart in less than three days. A process she described, to his astonishment, as mere preparation for the 'real work' of finding the character of Nora. He was awed by her commitment – all that work for a mere audition! – and moved by the happiness that came off her in waves; a self-sufficient, bone-deep contentment that was nothing to do with him, with his presence or his absence.

Alan was still talking.

"Anyway, I've asked around and apparently this kid's going to be a superstar."

"Do you know a lot of art critics, then?"

"I know a lot of rich people. That good enough for you? He's a nice kid. And a big fan."

"And?"

"And what?"

"And you're looking at me like I'm going to have a problem."

"No I'm not."

"Yes you are."

"Fuck me, Jack, but you sound like my missus sometimes."

"You're not married."

"That's 'cos I'm too busy nursemaiding idiots like you. Isaac's a decent kid. Just a little bit, you know, unique."

"You can't be a little bit unique. Unique is an absolute."

"Fuck off, you pedant. He's special. And bloody talented."

"He sounds utterly charming."

"Just meet him, okay? Try and be nice. Take him down to the studio, play him the new songs or something." Jack looked doubtful. "Come on, Jack, throw me a fucking bone here. Isaac's good publicity. That's got to be worth half an hour with a slightly strange foreign guy."

"Strange? Now he's *strange?*"

"Oh, God give me fucking strength - artistic, okay? Lot of ideas. *Strange*. Like you." He paused. "I must be insane putting you in the same room. You'll probably implode the whole bloody universe."

"In here," said Alan's secretary, opening the door. Alan changed his secretary every few months and Jack had long ago given up trying to learn their names, but they were always young, pretty and surprisingly competent. The latest girl had long blonde hair, thick black eyelashes and wore a black rollneck and alarming tartan trousers, which he'd been expecting. The young man, almost a boy, who followed her shyly into the room looked Italian and rather sweet, which he hadn't expected. Jack's mental image of an up-and-coming foreign artist was someone taller, thinner, grubbier, older and less healthy. He stood up to shake hands. Alan gestured half-heartedly from behind his desk.

"Isaac, Jack. Jack, Isaac." The phone rang. "Hang on."

Isaac caught Jack's eye and smiled. A number of half-formed thoughts: *My God he's younger than me / different generation almost / is this what people mean when they talk about 'in my day' / how long will my day last anyway / am I over the hill already* wandered across Jack's mind. Alan had his hand over the receiver and was looking at them both with a kind of calculating shiftiness. *This is like being set up on a blind date by your mother.*

"Sorry, lads," he said apologetically, "I need to take this. Take them down to the studio, will you, love?"

The secretary rolled her eyes at *love*, but led them away. Jack was interested to see that, as he passed the girl's desk, Isaac quietly stole a wad of paper and a pencil.

It was a pleasure just to stand in the studio again. Even the dank sweat leeching out from the booth recalled the select thrill of hearing his music captured, groomed, cleaned, perfected and finally sent out into the world. *It's brilliant, you wanker.* Would it be brilliant? Who cared? It would exist, that was what mattered.

The framed artwork from *Violet Hour* – a cityscape shot of him lounging moodily against a purple Mercedes-Benz, head bowed, chest bare – hung on the wall. Jack glanced at it, and looked away again. He'd approved it on the grounds that the photograph looked almost nothing like him. Isaac was studying it closely. Was he supposed to make small talk with this boy?

"Do you like it?" Jack asked, for something to say.

Isaac shrugged, that eloquent expressive gesture seen only on the Continent, sat down at the mixing desk and began drawing on his stolen paper.

One of the session guitars rested temptingly against the wall. It was a Gibson, well-used, without temperament, a reliable workhorse instrument you could depend on when your own was out of reach. Isaac wasn't looking at him at all, apparently absorbed in his drawing. Jack had the uncanny feeling Isaac was somehow willing him to become oblivious to his presence. He looked again at the Gibson.

The silence was companionable rather than awkward. Jack picked up the Gibson, put it down again, picked it up again, strummed a few chords, remembered he wasn't alone, forgot again. The opening notes of *2:43am* flowed out through his fingers. He'd have preferred a piano, but the guitar was alright. The train this morning had had the rhythm he wanted, that paradox of energy and stillness. There must be a way to weave it into the music -

When he opened his eyes, he found Isaac had moved closer and was quite openly staring at him, waiting patiently for Jack to come back from whatever world he was in.

"Jesus God," said Jack, swallowing his heart back down

into his chest. "Sorry mate, you startled me." Isaac shook his head affably, and continued to study Jack's face. "Um, look, could you please not do that?"

Isaac looked sad. Jack felt as if he'd unfairly told off a small child.

"You're not drawing me, are you?" he asked.

Isaac offered Jack his drawing. It was a deft caricature of Alan at his desk. Alan had eight tentacled arms and a malevolent expression. Jack couldn't help laughing. Isaac looked modest.

"I'd have liked something like that for *Violet Hour.*" Isaac glanced at the framed cover. "No need to be polite. It's hideous."

Isaac smiled shyly. Keeping his eyes fixed on Jack's face, he turned over the paper.

Even as a rough sketch, the image was arresting. An old-fashioned microphone – the beautiful old Deco style Jack had grown up loving and whose departure he still mourned – stood on an empty stage before a pair of heavy velvet curtains. The audience consisted of just one young woman, her face turned up towards the stage. Creeping unobtrusively up the right-hand edge of the paper in simple capitals were the words, *Violet Hour.*

"That's brilliant," said Jack. "Shit. That's absolutely brilliant." He looked again at the paper; the deserted stage, the audience of one, the seedy glamour of the curtains. "I swear to God, mate, if I could draw - " he paused. "Are you okay?"

Isaac was staring at a spot just behind Jack's shoulder. Jack turned around and, with a sense of foreboding, saw a girl with brown hair and an acid-green coat in the studio doorway. She looked familiar.

It was Evie.

Jack remembered the shifty look on Alan's face as he took the phone call, and vowed that as soon as he got back upstairs, he would pull the phone out from the wall and ram it down Alan's throat.

"Hey." Evie, trying to smile, trying to seem casual. He could read the cost of the effort in the lines around her mouth. "How are you?"

"Fine," said Jack grimly, trying to contain his utter fury. "I'm fine. How are you?"

"I'm great." Her smile was crooked. "Well, you know, I miss you, but, um, great." She turned her gaze to Isaac. "We've met before, haven't we?"

Isaac just looked at her.

"But I'm sure we - oh!" she stopped suddenly. "Oh, yes. Sorry. Um - how's she doing?"

Isaac sighed, and made a rocking gesture with his hand. *So-so.*

"I'm sorry," said Evie, sounding as if she meant it.

Isaac looked towards the door.

"Would you mind?" Evie looked grateful.

"There's really no need," said Jack. Isaac shrugged in gentle apology, and left. Jack took a deep breath and reminded himself to be fair.

"I asked Alan to call me," Evie said, before he could speak. "I rang him every day for a week and begged him to tell me when you were coming up. I told him he ought to be grateful to me, for looking after you so you could write it in the first place. And I've been waiting at a phone box round the corner since about six this morning and ringing every ten minutes to see if you'd arrived yet. I'm sorry, I know you don't want to see me but I had to make sure you were alright. I just had to."

Her frank confession disarmed him, replacing his righteous anger with a kind of guilty tenderness.

"I'm fine," he said. "There's no need to worry."

"I take it Alan liked the album."

"Yes, he did actually."

"I knew he would." There was no mistaking the pride on her face. "So when will it come out?"

"About three or four months, I think. Alan's trying to round up the band from *Violet Hour.*" He resisted the urge to look at his watch.

"And did that girl come back?"

"Mathilda? Yes."

"I told you she would."

"You did."

"Is she still there with you?"

"Yes." He wouldn't allow himself to say *sorry*. He'd never been gladder of anything in his life.

She moved closer, and took his hand between both of hers. He could smell the bitter aloe of gin on her breath. "Is she looking after you?"

He took his hand away. "I don't need looking after. She makes me happy."

"No, she doesn't! She doesn't, she can't, she - "

"Yes, she does! Remember that feeling when you find someone who completes your world? Waking up and your heart skips a beat because they're next to you in the bed? And you can't sleep because you'd rather lie there and watch them?"

Her eyes were bright. "Are you saying this to try and hurt me? Be honest."

"No, of course I don't want to – well, I want you to understand, so maybe a bit – look, we're not in fucking therapy any more, I don't have to tell you everything."

"You just did."

"Evie - "

"That feeling you described. That's not happiness, it's obsession. If you're going to do your best work you need rest and quiet and - "

"What makes you think you know what I need?"

Despite all she could do, the tears were spilling.

"I knew enough to keep you alive. I helped you get clean and sober, I ran our home all those weeks, we talked every day, we laughed about things, *that* was happiness, *we* were happy, you were working, it was great - "

"Evie, I want a lover, not a housekeeper! And definitely not a nurse! Oh look, please don't cry, but you have to understand, I just don't love you, okay? And I don't understand why you ever thought I did." His guilt had the taste of bitter chemicals. "If there was a nice way to say it, I would, but there isn't."

"Then why did you ask me to come and live with you?"

"*Stay* with me!" The craving gnawed at him, that fierce compulsive demand for something to numb the pain. They'd warned him in rehab – *when you get stressed, when you're upset, an automatic response, you'll have it for life* – why was he having this conversation? Was this his punishment for trying to be happy? The chemical taste was growing stronger. He was being haunted by the Ghost of Addictions Past. "I asked you to stay with me. Remember? Because you - "

"Because I got fired," she said. "And whose fault was that?"

The answer – *yours, for sleeping with one of your bloody patients* – was so obvious, he was paradoxically convinced he must be missing something.

"This isn't getting us anywhere," he said instead. His mouth was dry and tasted of burning.

"There's no point pretending it didn't happen," she said.

"I'm not trying to pretend anything, I - " he stopped. "My God, look at that." A slender trickle of smoke had begun to coil delicately around the edges of the doorframe.

"Stop trying to change the subject, that's just childish."

"No, you don't understand, there's a fire."

"What?"

"There's a bloody fire! Come on, we're getting out of here."

"No, I don't believe you, you're making it up, stop trying to get out of this, we're going to talk about it whether you like it or - "

He was surprised by how strong Evie was. As he dragged her across the room, trying to be gentle, he could feel her heart pounding against his arm. He wrenched the door open and a wave of choking smoke boiled towards them. Alan was pounding down the stairs, looking furious. When he saw Jack, he glared.

"Is this anything to do with you?"

"Of course not!"

"You sure? It's the sort of thing you might do."

"When have I *ever* set fire to your offices? We need to get out! Has someone called the fire brigade?"

They scurried out of the door onto the street. Outside, a crowd was collecting. Alan's secretary stood on the pavement with her arms folded crossly, as if the whole thing had been staged solely to disrupt her day. The dirty plate-glass windows of the conference room shattered. There was no sign of Isaac.

"What are you doing?" Evie grabbed onto him.

"I can't see Isaac."

"Shit." Alan went white. "Didn't he come out with you?"

"He was in the toilet," Alan's secretary said.

"So he's still in the building?" Another window shattered. Jack winced.

"Don't you dare go back inside," said Evie.

"Of course I'm not going back inside," said Jack. "Let go of me, I'm just going to check he's not round the back."

Behind Alan's offices, a narrow alleyway stank and festered, but was overlooked by the frosted windows of the bathroom. Orange light glowed from the windows. Jack clambered onto a dustbin, put his hands on the ledge, felt the heat of the blistering paint and recoiled from a tongue of flame that tried to lick his cheek and realised how insane this was but decided to do it anyway. He pushed up and got his head and chest through the window and into an appalling furnace of heat, swallowed a sour lungful of smoke. Someone was pulling him back down. Evie again, trying to save him? He kicked out, but couldn't shake her off. Another breath, and he had to stop fighting because he was coughing so hard. He slithered back out of the window, and found the person he was fighting was Isaac.

"How did you get out?" he demanded, still coughing. "I

was about to go in after you." Isaac looked horrified. "Look at those flames, that must be the soundproofing going up. What the hell happened? Did you see it start?"

Isaac looked at Jack for a moment. Then he sighed, put his hand in his pocket, and took out a box of matches.

"No," said Jack. "I don't believe you."

Isaac looked affronted.

"Seriously? But God, why the hell would you, you could have killed someone!"

Isaac rummaged in his pocket again, found a pencil and paper, and drew hastily. He showed Jack a tiny sketch of a man on horseback, dressed in armour and carrying a long lance.

"You set fire to the studio to rescue me from Evie?"

Isaac's smile was radiant and his face was smudged with smoke. He looked, Jack thought, like a rather grubby angel. The fire engine arrived. Hordes of firefighters poured into the street. Jack glimpsed Evie's bright coat, and felt a treacherous spasm of relief.

"You're insane," Jack told him. "Do you know that? You're absolutely insane. But, oh, Christ, am I actually going to say this? Thank you." He shook his head. "Look, I'm supposed to be meeting someone. If you swear you won't burn the café down I'll buy you a coffee."

They met Mathilda in the Rainbird Café at three o'clock. As soon as he saw her, he knew the audition had been good; her skin glowed and her eyes were dazzled. For the moment his mouth brushed hers, there was no-one else in the café.

"It went well," she told him, economical as always.

"They said yes?"

"They want me back when they've cast Torvald. How did it go with Alan?" She put her nose against his shirt. "Have you been in a fire?"

"Kind of."

"You're not hurt, are you?"

"I'm fine. Can I introduce someone?"

Isaac was guarding a large battered rucksack by the door. Jack was slightly unnerved to see Isaac's gaze fixed on Mathilda, not staring exactly, but studying the planes and contours of her face and body as a visitor might study a sculpture in a gallery. "This is Isaac. Alan wants him to do the *Landmark* cover."

"Do you know Jack's work?" Mathilda asked Isaac, as they drank strong, sweet coffee from heavy Portmeirion mugs.

Isaac nodded.

"What do you think of it?"

Jack shifted, uncomfortably.

"Jack hates people talking about him," Mathilda told Isaac.

"I don't mind when I'm not there to hear," said Jack. "I'm a reasonable man. Just, you know, don't tell me about it. Let me live with the delusion I'm not public property."

"How did you ever end up a star?" asked Mathilda, laughing.

"Freak accident? Mistaken identity? Alien intervention?" He drained the last of the coffee in his mug. "I'll get more coffee."

It wasn't until he saw him from across the café that it fully dawned on Jack how good looking Isaac was. His skin was smooth and brown and flawless, his hair thick and curly, his eyes black and liquid; a Hollywood fantasy of a young Italian peasant. Mathilda's long legs were folded beneath her on the wooden chair. He could see her hands move as she talked. It occurred to him that Isaac and Mathilda were probably around the same age.

Stop it, he told himself, and sat down, conscious that as he arrived, Mathilda fell silent and they both turned their faces towards him.

"Is it okay if Isaac stays with us?" asked Mathilda. "While he works on the *Landmark* cover, I mean."

"You want to do it?" Despite his misgivings, he was pleased.

"He needs somewhere to stay. Do you mind?"

"Of course not, do *you* mind?"

Mathilda laughed. "It's your house."

"So it is. Maybe I'll fill it with bass-players and bunny-girls."

"You'd get sick of them before I did."

"How did you get to know me so well?"

Mathilda's laugh of pleasure was low and sweet. She ruffled his hair and returned to her coffee. Jack took Mathilda's hand and held it for a second beneath the table, then brought it to his lips and kissed it.

It wasn't until he emptied his pockets in the hotel room that night that he remembered the sketch Isaac had given him. He unfolded the paper and studied it by the dim light of the bedside lamp. It was amazing what Isaac had accomplished so quickly with a stolen pencil and a sheet of cheap typing paper.

As he looked closer, admiring the deft little strokes that subtly suggested the heavy pile of the curtains, he realised that the face of the girl was familiar to him. Standing in the empty theatre in front of the drawn curtains, her face raised hopefully and a tear on the curve of her cheek, Isaac had drawn Evie.

chapter seven (now)

Davey awoke a few days later to find a bone-deep chill and a thin West Country rain falling like mist. When he dressed, his clothes were clammy and he could see his breath in the air. Beguiled outside by the rain's gentle appearance ("It's like walking in a cloud," he declared poetically, trying not to mind Priss' snort of derision), he found himself drenched within twenty minutes and wandered disconsolately back to the warmth of the kitchen, where Priss, shivering and trying to hide it, sat on the floor by the Aga with her arms wrapped around her knees.

After a few minutes, Isaac joined Davey at the scrubbed pine table. He had been mysteriously absent for the whole of the previous day, returning at some unknown time after midnight. He looked tired but content. He carried a chewed-up pencil stub and a stack of paper held together with a giant bulldog clip, and he wore an ancient oiled-wool sweater that glistened with flecks of rain. Davey, trying to concentrate on *The Cruel Sea*, found himself distracted by Isaac's insistent gaze. When Davey caught his eye, Isaac looked at him questioningly and made a miniscule gesture towards Davey's rapidly-fading black eye.

"It's nothing," said Davey defensively, wishing he had long hair like Priss that he could hide behind. Isaac looked disbelieving. "I don't want to talk about it, okay? Sorry."

Isaac leaned over the table and turned back the hair Davey had combed over the crusty scab along his hairline. He looked at Davey sternly.

"It's *nothing*," Davey repeated. "Really. It's nearly gone now."

Isaac put one finger to his lips, and then glanced out of the veranda windows. Tom was just visible through the rain-kissed glass.

"Oh my God," said Davey, horrified. Isaac shook his head and repeated his *shhh* gesture. Davey lowered his voice. "Of course it wasn't, you don't think I'd stay here if he'd, you know, b-b-b-beaten me up, do you?"

Isaac's gaze was unflinching. Davey had never realised how disconcertingly intimate the act of looking into someone's eyes could be.

"Look, it wasn't Tom, okay? Why does it matter, anyway? It's not going to happen again. What? *What?* It's *not*, okay? I w-w-w-wouldn't let anyone d-d-d-do that to me ever again, it was a w-w-w - " he stopped in exasperation. "A one time thing. Alright?"

Isaac continued to look at him.

"Why are you asking, anyway?" Davey whispered. "Kate and Tom never ask, never. Even Priss doesn't ask." Isaac was studying the stain of bruises that spread down Davey's neck. Could he tell how much further they spread, underneath the thin blue cotton? Isaac looked again at Tom. In his eyes was an unmistakeable warning.

"What is it? Why do I need to be careful? Do you know him or something? Why do you think he b-b-b- why do you think he might have d-d-d-d-d – shit – why would you think he hit me?"

Isaac shook his head in surrender, and returned to his pencil and paper. He was drawing Priss as she sat by the Aga. Isaac, Davey thought jealously, seemed to draw Priss a lot. Was he interested in her? Surely he was far too old to think he had a chance. He wondered if Isaac made a living from his art. Probably not. If he had money, why would he sleep in an ancient tent pitched on someone else's lawn?

Kate, looking uncharacteristically harassed, came through the French windows carrying two hemp bags of shopping.

"Priss," she said.

"Mmm?" Priss was flushed and drowsy with the warmth of the Aga. Davey thought she must look like that first thing in the morning, before she hid behind her make up.

"And Davey as well, come to think of it," said Kate. She put the bags down on the table. A bunch of overripe bananas slid furtively out and made a bid for freedom. Isaac put out a hand and caught them without looking.

"Yes?"

"I want you to do something for me," she said. "I want you to promise you'll stay out of the other half of the house."

Davey blinked. Priss held her face carefully blank and smooth. Isaac watched with intense interest.

"Why?" asked Priss.

"I think you know," said Kate, so sharply that Davey flinched and Priss blinked in surprise. "I'm sorry, I didn't mean to, but I think you know."

"Because it's dangerous?" Davey asked.

"We're not stupid," said Priss. "We can look after ourselves."

Kate sat down, reached across the table and took his hand, a warm and intimate gesture that caught him off-guard. Then she beckoned Priss to come and sit with them. She reached out to stroke Priss' hair. She flinched, then let her.

"This house," she said. "It's beautiful, of course it is. And you're welcome for as long as you want. But you have to be careful too. It's - " she hesitated. "It's very old. It has ghosts." Priss shook her head in disbelief. "I don't mean *ghosts* like people walking around dressed in white sheets, I mean bad memories. Old secrets. Things that are best left undisturbed. Do you know what I mean?"

To Davey's horror, Kate seemed close to tears. Davey didn't dare move. Priss' eyes were huge and her face was a milky white. Isaac was watching them intently.

"Sometimes it's best to let the past lie undisturbed," she

continued. "If you wake it up, it can be dangerous. So I want you to promise me you'll stay away. Not stir things up. Be safe. Okay?"

"Okay," said Davey instantly. Kate squeezed his hand and smiled.

"Thank you. Priss?"

Priss had got the colour back in her cheeks. "Alright," she said.

Kate looked unconvinced. "You really mean it?"

Priss met Kate's gaze head-on. "I promise."

"Thank you." Kate tucked a strand of hair behind Priss' ear, and stood up. "Then that's settled. I'm going to make some bread."

Priss looked guilty. "I'll help," she said.

"No, I don't mind."

"Then give me something else to do. It's not on, you running round like a slave." Priss poked Davey hard in the chest. "And you can do something useful an' all."

Davey put down his book obediently and waited for orders.

"Are your rooms tidy?" asked Kate, laughing.

"Yes," said Davey.

"No," said Priss. "But I'm the only one who sees it so it doesn't matter."

Kate shook her head mockingly. "Didn't your mother ever tell you to tidy your room?"

To Davey's astonishment, this question seemed to impale Priss like a bayonet. She stared at Kate speechlessly, her mouth quivering. Kate put her hand up to her mouth. Davey felt he should rescue the situation, but had no idea how. Then Tom, his arms loaded with logs, banged impatiently on the veranda door, and Kate went to let him in. Priss sat back down by the Aga and pulled her hair over her face.

"This'll keep us going for a bit," said Tom. "The bedrooms'll be cold, but we can get warm before we go up. Which room do you want a fire in?"

"We've got a fire," said Priss, yawning and stretching.

"You can't sit there," said Kate. "I'm making bread. You're in the way."

"We can have cornflakes."

"With dinner?"

"Why not?"

"Because Kate said so," said Tom. "Pick a room, this is heavy."

"Or Weetabix," said Priss.

"Or I could make bread," said Kate. "Just be told, Priss. You're not spending the day in front of the Aga. In fact, that goes for all of you. I want everyone out of the kitchen. Leave me to commune with the dough." She was trying to keep her tone light, but she looked strained and tired.

"Let's go in the library," said Davey.

"Library it is." Tom strode off. Priss trailed after him. Davey stood up to follow him, then felt Isaac's fingers close around his wrist. He tried to snatch it away, but Isaac's grip was surprisingly firm. Something slipped into the palm of his hand. When Davey tried to look, Isaac pressed his fingers tightly closed. *Not here.*

In the hall, he found Isaac had given him a folded sheet of paper. Of course. What else would it be? His skin itchy and uncomfortable from the unwanted contact, Davey stuffed it into his pocket without looking at it and went into the library.

"There," Tom said, crouched on the hearth. "Keep it topped up, but not too much or you'll likely crack the oven." He picked splinters off his jacket and dropped them into the flames. They danced and leapt like fireflies. "See you later."

"Are you going out?" asked Priss. "It's raining."

"I don't think I'll melt."

"But it's fuckin' freezing," Priss said. Tom looked at her reproachfully. "Sorry, but it *is*. It looks alright, but it kind of soaks you all the way through and gets into your fuckin' bones - look, I can't help it, it's how I was raised."

Tom smiled. "I like being outside. Behave yourselves, okay?"

As soon as he was gone, Priss snatched Davey's book out of his hands. "What the hell was all that about?" she demanded.

"All what? I was reading that."

"Read it later, daft lad, this is important. About the other half of the house."

"She doesn't want us to go in there."

"But why?"

Davey remembered his brief glance into the chilled ruin that lay behind the connecting door, and shivered. "Because it's dangerous. I think she's right. It's horrible in there."

"Or maybe because there's something she doesn't want us to find." Priss bit her thumbnail. "She was warning us off, wasn't she? And I've looked in there, I've looked everywhere, I couldn't find a thing! I was really starting to think - shit. *Shit!* I wanted to be wrong, Davey, I really did." There were tears on her lashes, which she blinked furiously away. "Is every good thing in this whole fuckin' world a fake?"

"I think you're wrong. Kate and Tom are lovely, Priss. They're *lovely*. Where do you think we'd be if they hadn't taken us in?"

Priss wiped her nose on her sleeve. "You'd be lyin' dead in the outhouse, mate," she said. "No way I'd have dragged you in over the doorstep and then mopped up your spew all night."

"And how about you?" he asked daringly.

For a moment, he thought she was going to answer. Then she laughed, and kissed him lightly on the nose.

"Nice try, posh boy. But you don't need to know *nothing* about me. What was Isaac talking to you about?"

"Nothing. He never says a word to me." A spasm of jealousy stabbed the backs of his knees. "Does he talk to you?"

Priss looked amused. "There's no need to be jealous. I'm not interested in him."

"I d-d-d-didn't mean that! That's disgusting, he's far too old for you."

"He's not bad looking, mind you," said Priss. "He'd be alright for breeding purposes."

Was she trying to make him jealous? "I doubt he wants a baby at his age."

"Well, he wouldn't *have* a baby, would he, I would. We'd get a council flat and live off benefits."

"Would you?"

"Of course I wouldn't, you dozy twat."

Her face was radiant in the firelight. He thought of Botticelli's Flora, of the swell of her belly beneath her gown, female and disturbing and mysterious. "Do you want to get married and have children one day, though?"

Priss laughed. "You know what love and marriage really are, posh boy? Stockholm Syndrome. All those centuries of oppression, it was the only way women could survive."

"But that's not how it is these days. Women aren't property or anything."

"And that's why the institution of marriage is collapsing. We don't need you any more. These days, we can fuckin' bin you off as soon as you've knocked us up. Fifty years from now, men and women won't even bother trying to live together. We'll just maintain separate residences and meet up for a shag occasionally. Romance is over, mate. Here. Have your dodgy war-porn book back. And don't talk to me for a bit, alright? I need to think."

The flames shone on Priss' hair, and the wood crackled. This whole setup, Davey thought gloomily, was wrong. He should be making a move, maybe sliding his arm around Priss' waist and moving her closer, or putting one hand under her chin and tilting her face to his. Instead he was trying to justify his existence as a man, and to explain why he didn't – yet – believe that the kind, gentle woman making bread in the kitchen was some kind of murderer.

Davey found Tom in the garden, inspecting the vegetable beds. The existence of an actual working kitchen garden, like the library, was another astounding miracle Davey couldn't get used to. The beds were well-tended, their borders cleanly defined, the weeds kept in check. Tom was hardly ever in the house, and when he was, he was constantly looking towards the doorway. Was this where he spent his days?

"Want to help?" Tom asked, offering Davey a wooden basket half-filled with bean-pods. Drips of water rolled off the sleek grey strands of his hair and down his collar. Davey hunched himself deeper into his jacket in sympathy.

"Is it these ones here?"

Tom plucked a ripe pod from the long green coils of a stand of beans, broke it open, and breathed the scent deep into his lungs.

"Just the big ones," he told Davey. "Careful," he warned as Davey reached clumsily into the centre of the tripod. "Don't knock them over."

"Sorry." Davey laid the beans carefully in the basket, took a step backwards and knocked into another tripod. "Oh, shit I mean, sorry - "

"It's okay." Tom took his elbow to steady him.

"I d-d-d-didn't mean to wreck all your work - "

"You haven't. It's fine. See?"

"But you must have worked really hard on these, um, planting them all out and everything."

"No harm done," said Tom. "We'll need more wood for tonight. Want to come and help?"

Davey followed Tom down the path, pondering his response. "No harm done." Was it simply a kind attempt to reassure him? Or was he elegantly sidestepping Davey's attempt to discover how long Tom had lived here? The paper Isaac had given him was like a shrieking mandrake in his pocket. The contents of this letter had united in his mind with a theory of his own to produce a brilliant but as-yet-un-established whole. If he could find a way to prove it, dazzle Priss with his solution -

In a dilapidated stone building that could have been a barn or a stable or an unusually opulent garage, the walls were stacked several feet deep with logs. In the centre, a chopping block waited. A stack of newspapers had sprawled out across the floor, *The Mirror, The Guardian, The Times, The Express, The London Evening Standard,* recent editions as far as he could see, although no visitors had come to the house since he had been here. Was this what Tom did every day? What was he looking for? The phrase *something nasty in the woodshed* slunk through his brain.

"Does it get cold here in the winter?" Davey asked Tom.

Tom was gathering the newspapers back into a pile, his movements slow and careful, almost as if he were acting the appearance of casual ease. "We'll be alright. We'll keep a few rooms warm."

Again that evasive switch of focus from the past to the future. Was it deliberate? Or was he simply sensitised to it?

"I've never lived anywhere without central heating," said Davey, then had to stop himself from wincing. He was glad Priss wasn't here to laugh.

"No," said Tom. "No, that makes sense. Davey, since you're here - "

Davey felt a spasm of alarm.

"Look, I'm not going to pry," Tom continued. "Everyone's entitled to their past. But, the thing is - " he hesitated. "Is there someone who'll be worrying about you? Someone you ought to get in touch with? Just to let them know you're alright?"

His cheeks burned as if Tom had slapped him. "I wrote to - "

"Yes, but did you send it?" asked Tom, very gently.

Davey couldn't answer.

"I can post it for you. It's alright," he added, "I'll take the ferry. They won't trace you from the postmark."

"Do you know where there's a p-p-p-post box?"

Tom swept a few splinters of wood from the top of the block. "Davey, all towns have post boxes. Pass me some of those logs, will you?"

"I ought to go myself," said Davey. "You don't have to."

"It's okay, I don't mind."

Tom swung the axe. The log fell apart in two halves with a satisfying *thunk*. Keen to look useful, Davey heaved another log over. *Thunk*. The slicing of the wood was clean and quick. Was Tom willing to go because he had nothing to hide? Or was it because he was hiding in plain sight?

"Want a go?" Tom was holding out the axe towards him. Davey took it warily. "You'll be fine as long as you're careful. Hold it there, and there. No, further up the handle. Swing with your whole upper body, not just your arms. Now try."

Davey swung the axe. It went in, but stuck halfway down the log. He pushed down hard on the handle to force the log to split.

"Careful, you'll wreck the blade." Tom levered it carefully out. "Let me show you again." *Thunk*. The log split effortlessly in two halves that showed their creamy insides as they fell. Davey watched in frank admiration. "So, do you want to try again? Or do you want to tell me what you came down here to ask?"

Davey looked at him miserably. "I just - " he began. "I just - "

"Yes?"

"I just wanted to, I wanted to, I just thought I ought to - " The guilt compressed his tongue like a scold's bridle. How could he accuse Tom of committing a crime? "Oh, God - "

"Can I give you some advice?" said Tom. "Confession is overrated. It really is. There's no point going over the mistakes of the past. We do the things we do, and we live with the consequences, and then we move on. That's it. That's all there is. Looking back, trying to find answers, it'll drive you mad." He placed a log on the block. The axe swung. The log fell in two perfectly bisected halves. "Do you know what I mean?"

"Is this your house?" Davey blurted out.

Tom looked at him for a long time. Davey noticed how silent the garden was, how sharp the blade of the axe as it whistled through the air. How Tom was between him and the door.

"For what it's worth," said Tom at last, "that's a consequence I'm living with. I gave up all my rights to ownership a long, long time ago. I don't think I'll ever really own anything ever again."

Outside, the drizzling rain continued to drench the gardens.

"That was amazing," said Davey, sighing. "And we've eaten all the bread, sorry - "

"Cooks like people to eat what they make," said Kate. "Don't apologise."

"But it's not fair on you," said Davey. "You cook for us all the time."

"I like to cook."

"No-one likes to wash up," Tom pointed out. "But half the time you won't even let us do that."

"I like looking after people." Her smile, Davey thought, was the warmest he had ever seen. Kate, when happy, could light up an entire room.

"You should make me and Davey do it," said Priss. She had been quiet this evening, and half her bread was rolled into meticulous little grey-white pills arranged around the border of her plate.

"I don't mind," said Kate, and began to clear the plates. Isaac, looking guilty, tried to help her, but she slapped his hands away and pushed him back into his chair. Isaac glanced at Tom and shrugged. *I tried.* Priss was fumbling with something underneath the table.

"Look what I found," she announced, dropping a long, flat cardboard box on the table. "Cluedo. Who wants to play?"

No-one other than Priss seemed desperately keen, but she was already unpacking the box, dropping weapons into rooms and sorting through the character cards. "Who d'you all want to be?"

"The yellow one," said Tom. Priss flicked over the Colonel Mustard pawn.

"Have I got to?" asked Davey.

"Yes you have. Pick one or I'll make you be Miss Scarlett."

Davey muttered something inaudible, but obediently took the pawn for Reverend Green. Isaac, who had shed his fisherman's jumper, revealing a faded lilac t-shirt with a ragged hem, took Professor Plum.

"I'll be Mrs Peacock if you like," said Kate.

"No-one's picked Miss Scarlett yet."

"Mrs Peacock's fine."

"Okay. So I'll be Mrs White."

"Why?" asked Kate.

"'Cos she's got a nasty, mean face and she looks like a horrible person," said Priss. Davey saw she had bitten the nail of her left thumb down far beyond the quick, and the skin was ragged with dried blood. Glancing round the table, he saw Isaac noticing the same thing. Davey picked up the dice hastily.

"Who goes first?"

The game got under way. To his surprise, Davey found himself enjoying it. The kitchen was warm and the pawns made a pleasing *click* against the board. Tom was going out of his way to be friendly towards him. Their conversation that afternoon might never have happened.

"It's strange," Davey said as he counted out squares, "to be playing a game about a murder in a country house, while I'm actually in a country house. *Ow!*" He looked at Priss reproachfully. "What was that for?"

"Nothing," said Priss. "Foot slipped. Make a suggestion."

"Oh. Sorry." Davey stared blankly at the board. "Okay, I think it was Reverend Green, in the conservatory, with the candlestick."

"Why?" asked Priss.

"What?"

"Why pick that person in that room?"

"Because it's a game of deduction," said Davey. "You've got to start somewhere."

"You know you just accused yourself of murder?"

"Well, it might have been me just as much as anyone else."

Priss sniffed. "He looks alright on the card."

"It's a game of chance, it's got nothing to do with how anyone - look, have you got anything to disprove it or not?"

"You go clockwise round the board," said Priss, looking smug. Kate shook her head. Isaac held the candlestick card out to Davey. Kate threw a two and inched towards the conservatory. Isaac threw a six and made it into the study.

"Suggestion," said Priss.

Isaac was scribbling on his notepad. Everyone tried not to stare. After a few moments, he laid the paper down on the table. In the library, Miss Scarlett loomed over the prone body of a man, clutching a piece of lead piping in her hand. Her face was savage and beautiful. Priss laughed in delight.

"That's brilliant," said Davey reluctantly.

"He is brilliant," said Kate, and reached behind Davey to ruffle Isaac's hair. Isaac looked modest. Everyone sorted through their cards. Kate showed him something from her hand. Isaac nodded. Tom threw a five. Colonel Mustard made it into the lounge.

"Reverend Green," said Tom, yawning. "In the ballroom. With the dagger."

Priss held out a card under the table. "Why have you all got it in for the vicar?"

"It's a game of deduction," repeated Davey. "It could just as well be Reverend Green as - ow, will you stop kicking me!"

"I'm just interested," said Priss. Her ravishing face was a picture of innocence as she gazed at Tom. "Why are you all picking on the man of the cloth?"

"Why are you defending him?" asked Tom. "Are those Catholic roots showing?"

"How'd you know I was raised Catholic?"

"Lucky guess."

"Well, I don't believe," said Priss, frowning.

"In lucky guesses?"

"In God. In the church. Anything. It's all bullshit."

Kate looked scandalised. "Sorry, I don't mean to be, like, disrespectful or anything, but that's what I think."

"I agree," said Tom. "We're responsible for our own actions. All there is, is what there is now. We shouldn't waste a second of it."

"So can we stop playing this game then?" asked Davey. No-one took any notice.

"Doesn't that make you sad?" asked Kate. "Thinking there's nothing after we die?"

"Death isn't frightening," said Tom. "It's programmed in. When the time comes, our bodies know what to do. But truly, what an obscene waste, worrying that some magical eye-in-the-sky's judging us and everything we do - "

Davey realised he was staring.

"Okay," said Tom. "Sorry, Davey. Rant over. Priss, your throw."

Mrs White took the secret passage.

"Why is there a secret passage from the kitchen to the study?" Priss asked. "Professor Plum, in the study, with the lead piping."

"Because they're at opposite corners of the board," said Davey. "Here."

Priss glanced at the card he held out, and crossed *study* off her list. "But why connect those two rooms?"

"Maybe Dr Black liked to snack in the middle of his experiments," said Kate.

"What experiments?"

"Well, he's called Dr Black and he lives in the middle of nowhere. I'm thinking Bond Villain. Something pointless, insane and spectacular." Isaac passed a sketch to Kate, who laughed and held it up. "Something like that."

A man in a black suit wrestled a triffid-like plant with the face of a beautiful woman.

"So if Dr Black was evil," said Priss, "should we even be trying to find out who killed him? Maybe the murder was, like, for the good of society."

"It's never okay to kill someone," said Kate.

"Not even if it was, like, Hitler or someone? *What?*"

"I was just invoking Godwin's Law," said Davey smugly.

"Alright, then, Slobodan Milosevic. Would it be okay to kill Slobodan Milosevic?"

"Is this before or after the massacres?" asked Tom.

"Does it make a difference?"

"Well, it's a different proposition. If you kill someone before they do something terrible, you're assuming you're infallibly right and they were definitely going to. And if you kill them after they did it, you're just punishing them."

"So is it ever alright to do it?" Priss persisted.

Tom shrugged. "What do you think?"

"I want to know what you think."

"You're young. You're supposed to have all the answers."

"That's a really shitty thing to say," said Priss. "I know I'm only sixteen but I'm not so fuckin' dumb I think I know everything yet. Don't treat me like an idiot, okay?"

Tom was very carefully not making eye contact with anyone. "Alright," he said slowly. "For what it's worth, I think sometimes you have to make a choice and live with it. And if your best judgement is you absolutely need to kill someone, you accept you'll live with it hanging over you for the rest of your life, and if you get caught, you'll probably go to jail for it. Good enough?"

Davey's spine felt like a rod of ice. He didn't dare move or look at anyone. Priss nodded thoughtfully, and turned to Kate.

"What do you think?"

Kate moved Mrs Peacock into the dining room. "I think," she said, "I'm ready to make an accusation."

"You can't be," Davey protested. "We've only played three rounds, there are hundreds of combinations - "

"I'm ready," Kate insisted. "I think it was Miss Scarlett, in the hall, with the dagger. Right, I'm having a look." She opened up the envelope, and smiled. "Told you." She spread the three cards out so the rest of the players could see them.

"How did you know that?" asked Davey in disbelief.

"Because it's *always* Miss Scarlett," said Kate, shrugging. *"Cherchez la femme."*

Dear Joshua,

The beans are ripe now, and the tomatoes are finally starting to ripen. If I'm still here next year, I think I'll put in some raspberry canes. The soil's good for it, nice and light and sandy. Good for everything, really. I'll put in some potatoes for next year too. West Country potatoes are famous, apparently. Kate tells me people sell them by the sackful at the roadside, and tourists take them home with them along with their dirty washing.

I'm writing nonsense about the garden because I'm still nervous. In fact, I'm still frightened. Weeks and weeks and weeks since I ran for it, and I'm still looking over my shoulder the whole time. I get nervous when I'm inside. I don't like the door being shut just in case I can't get it open again. If I saw a doctor, it's possible he'd have a name for it. Claustrophobia, maybe? Post-traumatic stress disorder? Those decades in a cell have taken their toll.

I ought to say I'm sorry, I suppose. When I started writing this letter, that's what I meant to do. It was a terrible thing I did. But I had a chance, and I had to take it.

I don't deserve any of what I've got now. And believe me, I've got a lot. I don't have any money, or even a real name, but that's okay. I've got a roof over my head and food in my belly, people I can more or less call friends, and a garden I can call my own.

I don't deserve any of it, but I'm grateful. I didn't deserve the chance to escape either, but I got it.

You know, I've written so many letters to you, but this is the one I might actually post. It's been a whole summer, and the world hasn't ended because one man escaped prison. I'll travel a bit so the postmark won't match and you won't have the dilemma of coming to look for me, and then I'll post it.

I hope all's well with you.

Tom

chapter eight (then)

"Why does he sleep in a tent when we've got so many bedrooms?" asked Jack.

Mathilda was lying on the rug by the open window in the library, basking in the late afternoon sunshine, her eyes tightly shut, a dog-eared copy of *Hamlet* beside her. Jack, tired with the thankless effort of composing, thought she had never looked so beautiful as in this moment of uncharacteristic laziness. But then he had this thought at least twenty times a day. Her face, far too arresting for the commonplace nothingness of "pretty", fascinated him from every angle. He'd seen Isaac watching her too, on golden afternoons where the two men lay around the lawns or the veranda, juggling pencils and beer and guitars and paper as Mathilda, as unselfconscious as if she were utterly alone, experimented with incarnations of Nora.

"He said permanent structures made him uneasy." A breeze ruffled Mathilda's hair and blew a strand across her mouth. She blew it back impatiently.

"How could he possibly tell you that?"

"Oh, you know Isaac. He's good at getting his point across."

"I suppose."

He glanced at his notepad. He didn't like any of the words or any of the music. Was it always this difficult to start? *Landmark* had been a picnic compared to this new project, but then, *Violet Hour* had seemed that way compared to *Landmark*.

He looked at Mathilda again. He longed to lie beside her and peel off her rainbow-patterned t-shirt and faded bell-bottoms, to kiss her stomach and her long thighs and make slow, clumsy love to her in the sunshine. Today, and unusually for the last few weeks, they were alone. Isaac was the most perfect house guest imaginable. Although he spent hours every day with them, watching and listening as Jack desultorily experimented with words and melodies and Mathilda transformed herself into other people, Jack rarely felt his presence as intrusive. But today he'd disappeared entirely, leaving a note on the kitchen table consisting of a child's sketch of a boat with a triangular sail and a clock with a moon drawn next to it.

Mathilda's cool white skin had borrowed the gold of the sunlight. Jack considered the word *Baltic*, crossed it out and replaced it with *frozen*, reconsidered, put *Baltic* back in again. Neither word said what he really wanted. He looked again at Mathilda, felt his heart squeeze tight.

Did Isaac lie awake on these warm scented nights and dream of her? Did he strain his ears for the sound of Jack making love to her, stroking himself to a silent climax, fantasising it was him instead?

"He gave me a present yesterday," he said out loud.

"What was it?"

"A painting."

"That's nice. What of?"

"He said it was a whale's pancreas. Apparently I'll understand what he means one day." Mathilda snorted with laughter. "It's sort of great, in a weird way. I was going to hang it in the bedroom. If that's alright with you."

"Why wouldn't it be?"

"Apparently some people find it hard to sleep in rooms containing the internal organs of large aquatic mammals."

"Really?"

"They did a study. It was in the paper the other day. I should have saved it."

She turned over onto her stomach and rested her chin on her hands. "I want to ask you something."

"If you want my whale's pancreas, it'll cost you."

"Isaac wants to paint me."

Jack felt as if every muscle in his body had winced. He forced a casual shrug. "Okay."

He was insane to be worried. Neither Isaac nor Mathilda had done anything to give him reason to be jealous.

"You're sure?"

"Would it matter if I wasn't?"

"Well, of course it matters. I love you," she continued, as if this was obvious, "so obviously what you think counts. I mean, if it was a role where I had to be naked, well, that's different, that's my job, but this is just for a friend. Are you alright?"

"Could you possibly say that again, please?"

"It's just for a friend."

"No, the first bit - "

"Oh!" She smiled. "Why? Do you need reassurance?"

"*Please.*"

"I love you," she said, with a shrug. "Do the words make such a difference? You knew anyway."

"No, I didn't know, of course I didn't, how could I possibly know? I had no idea - "

"How could you not know?"

"Because you never *said!*"

"I'm living here with you, aren't I? I get into your bed every night, don't I? I gave my agent your phone number, that's about as committed as actors get."

"How can you be so calm about this?"

"It's just three words."

"Describing the most important emotion on earth!"

"Why are you so angry?"

"I'm not angry, I'm - "

"Yes?"

Frantic, he thought. *Lost. Ecstatic. Bewildered. Besotted.*

Adoring. Crazy for you.

He put his arms around her. Words weren't enough, words were tricky and confusing, he was tangled and lost in words. He could only show her with his body, with his fingers and his tongue and his cock, with the slow rhythm and melody of two bodies perfectly in tune. The sofa seemed too impossibly far away to even contemplate. He loved her on the sun-warmed floor instead, oblivious to the hard surface beneath them, the words beating in his blood. *I love you. I love you. I love you, so -*

When they lay speechless in each other's arms, Mathilda drowsing and drifting towards sleep, he forced himself to focus on the memory of her face as she said it. The other word, *naked*, gnawed at him, but he refused to dwell on it.

I love you, so -

As if it was so obvious no-one could miss it.

As if no-one could ever doubt it.

He woke to an agonising cramp in his left leg and the sound of the telephone. Mathilda was still deeply asleep, her head on his shoulder, her arm flung across his chest. Trying not to yelp with pain, he eased himself out from beneath her. She sighed and stirred, but did not wake. He had noticed before that when she slept, she would stay locked in her own private realm whatever happened around her, impossible to rouse until she was ready. He grabbed his jeans, limped into the hall and picked up the receiver.

"I'm still not doing the tour," he said, pulling on his jeans.

"Yes, you are, you just don't know it yet. The kids are all set, studio at the end of next month. We'll be in Soho, since you burned my place to the ground."

"I *didn't* burn your office down - really, all of them? Even Joey?"

"Even Joey."

"I thought he signed on with Badwater."

"I signed him off again. Guess how I did it."

Jack pulled the zip cautiously upwards. "You clubbed him over the head and dragged him away by his hair?"

"Promised him the tour of the century."

"You what?"

"You heard."

"You - you utter unbelievable arsehole!"

"You utter ungrateful tosser! I have pulled off a fucking *miracle* here. I got your kids back from some of the hottest fucking acts on the planet, just so you can have the right back-up to do this album how you want. The least you can do is - "

"Give you my soul?"

"What the fuck am I going to do with your soul? Just give me thirty dates. Three months, that's all I'm asking!"

"No!"

"Too late. Done deal. See you in Soho. Details in the post. Bye."

As Jack slammed the receiver down, Isaac wandered in through the doorway.

"Oh," said Jack, without thinking. "I thought you were out for the day." Isaac looked towards the door. "Sorry, I didn't mean it like that." But of course he had, and he suspected Isaac knew it.

Isaac picked up an envelope from the doormat and held it out.

"Is that for me? Thanks." He knew without looking it was from Evie. She'd written every few days since he saw her in London.

Isaac looked at him reproachfully.

"I'll open it later," he told Isaac.

Isaac looked sceptical. In spite of himself, Jack remembered the pile of unopened envelopes stacked up in his bedroom in the hidden annexe. It was an act of cowardice to ignore them, he knew.

"How was the boat?" he asked. Isaac mimed choppy water, then seasickness. In spite of himself, Jack laughed. Isaac was almost maddeningly likeable. Despite the rat's gnaw of unease over Mathilda, it was impossible to stay angry with him.

Determined not to play the jealous lover, Jack deliberately stayed out of Isaac and Mathilda's way for the next few days. He found things to do in the garden, in other parts of the house, in the outhouses he was slowly reclaiming from the ivy. One was now stacked to the brim with load after load of logs, purchased from the imperturbable farmer, fifteen miles away, who also supplied him with meat for the panther. Jack had grown up with open fires, but had never split his own logs and kindling before. After an hour or so of dangerously hit-and-miss efforts with the wood axe, he finally began to find the rhythm, and chopped wood like a maniac until he was soaked with sweat and his palms were covered in blisters.

"Soft Southern wanker," he said out loud, inspecting his palms. "Never done a proper day's work in your life." Were you supposed to prick blisters, or leave them? He leaned the axe tidily against the wall of the shed, and wandered down through tangly rectangles crossed with thin paths that the estate agent had assured him were the kitchen garden. One day, he supposed, he would have to get around to doing something with them. Should he hire a gardener? Did gardeners even exist any more? He thought of the imperturbable farmer, whose expression had never varied from the moment they'd first met, when he had personally witnessed the arrival and installation of the panther. ("Sorry," the vet had said, as the men unloaded a snarling, rocking crate from the truck while the farmer stood and waited for the drive to be clear so he could get his tractor back out. "I knew that dose was light but you never like to overdo it when they're underweight."

"Afternoon," the farmer had said, nodding in Jack's direction. "Logs in the shed like you ordered."

"Sorry about the racket," Jack replied. "It's, well, to be perfectly honest with you, mate, it's a panther. Sorry."

"Ah? Right you are then. You still needing that side of pork for tomorrow?"

Jack took his boots off and padded through the house, enjoying the small sounds of wood settling and pipes creaking. The thrill of owning such a vast, impractical space – to say nothing of the incredulous shock of having enough money to run it – still gave him a childish pleasure. And now there was the delight of knowing that somewhere in these grounds, these rooms, was Mathilda, reading or learning lines or trying out speeches or simply lounging, waiting to be discovered and unwrapped like a present. He could hear her voice in the library, a low sleepy murmur like bees. The door was open a crack. He glanced through.

Mathilda stood in the middle of the floor, looking back over her shoulder at Isaac, who sat nearly at her feet, close enough to touch her. Mathilda was naked.

"I suppose you're right," said Mathilda, laughing. "But, you know - "

Isaac shrugged. He was concentrating on the surprisingly large and clean sheet of paper on his lap. Jack noticed that he'd taken the full-size reproduction of *Birds of America* to rest on.

"The thing is," said Mathilda, "most of the time, it's lovely."

It was a terrible idea to listen. He listened anyway.

There was a pause, and a gesture from Isaac.

"I think he's just got this urge to help people," she said, as if Isaac has spoken. "You know that girl, that crazy girl who keeps writing to him, what's her name? Evie, that's it. She got fired from her job, so he said she could stay with him. She thought he was asking her to move in."

Another pause, and a low, dirty chuckle from Mathilda.

"Yes, but that's just Jack, isn't it? For someone so fuckable he's really quite lacking in self-awareness."

Was that a compliment? He took a savage chunk out of his thumbnail.

"I know, I should be more grateful. A huge country house, a man who worships me. The classic fairy tale. All we need now are some enormous hairy dogs and a couple of over-privileged children."

He knew what Isaac was asking her. He himself had never dared.

"Oh, I don't know maybe one day." She sounded impatient. "There's so much I want to do first."

Isaac put his hands on her thighs and gently turned her towards him. Jack, still standing silently behind the door, glimpsed her thick thatch of pubic hair as she moved. Was that why Isaac had turned her around? So that he could stare at her? There? He was close enough to kiss -

Stop it, Jack thought. *Go outside and chop things.* But the command had no power.

"Oh, the usual." Mathilda laughed. "Travel the world. Play every great part. Be famous. But I'll settle for making a living."

Isaac glanced around the library.

"I don't want it all on a plate," Mathilda said. "Life's no good served up in bite-sized portions. You have to go out into the wild and hunt it down - savage it with your teeth." She pushed her hair back from her forehead. "But I do love him, Isaac. I really do. I'm just afraid of what's going to happen. I want his time and his energy and his support, and his ideas, and his inspiration, and for him to read every part I play and talk to me about it, and to admire my work, but from a position of knowledge. And there's all the other things I want that have nothing to do with him like success, and the chance to pick the parts I want to play, and space to grow, and time to myself. I want so much – so *much* – and I don't know if he's strong enough. He'd be better off with Evie. All she wants is to look after him." Abandoning her pose, she sat beside him on the floor and rested her chin on her knees.

Isaac laid the book and paper carefully down, then put an arm around her. Jack closed his eyes and leaned his forehead against the door jamb.

"Having someone love you," Mathilda continued. "That's

a huge gift. The biggest gift anyone can give you. But that's the problem. It's so huge, it takes all your time and strength to carry it. He's given me this massive present, and I don't know if I can afford the baggage."

Isaac patted her shoulder reassuringly.

Later that evening, as they sat in the kitchen drinking coffee and laughing, he realised with a chill he would never have guessed any of what she felt. Mathilda leaned happily against his shoulder and laughed at his jokes, dropping grapes into her mouth and then his. Isaac was the same as he always was, shy and charming and odd. Talking to Isaac, Jack thought, was like telling the bees; they listened, but never told, and afterwards they carried on about their own complex and absorbing business as if nothing had changed. The breeze blew the distant roar across the lawn and in through the open veranda doors. Jack glanced at his watch.

"Cat needs feeding," he announced. Mathilda frowned. "Don't look like that. What do you want me to do?"

"It's not right to keep him locked up."

"I didn't *put* him in a cage, you know," said Jack. "He was already in one when I got him."

"Why on earth did you buy him, anyway?"

"I won him in a poker game."

"You *won* him?" Mathilda laughed. "Actually, that's even worse. You ought to atone by letting him out."

"Ha ha ha. He'd starve."

Isaac drew a sly little sketch of a sheep on his notepad. The sheep wore an expression of beatific stupidity. In the grass behind it, two rounded ears were just visible.

"Okay, then he'd eat the sheep and get shot. Is that any better?" Isaac and Mathilda were both looking at him with a conspiratorial naughtiness that made him feel old, humourless and excluded. "Or he'd rip Isaac's tent to shreds and eat him instead." Isaac laughed silently. "Don't joke about this, mate. You do know he could do it, right?"

Isaac held up his hands in a gesture of surrender, and wandered out onto the lawn.

"Shit," said Jack, feeling guilty. "Have I upset him?"

Mathilda reached across the table and took his hand. "He's fine, he just prefers it outside. You do know we're not serious, right?"

He tried not to focus on the word *we*. "And you do know I'm always far *too* serious, right? I'm famous for getting hung up on the little stuff. I'm completely missing the not-taking-things-too-seriously gene."

"That's okay. It's quite endearing really."

"How can it possibly be endearing? Even I can't stand me sometimes. Is that the phone?"

"I'll go." She smiled at him, a dirty come-hither smile that made his hands tremble. "You need to go and feed the beast."

The leg of pork was already collecting flies. He filled the water bucket, and snapped on the lid. Then he wrapped the meat in a plastic sheet and slung it awkwardly over his shoulder.

The panther was pacing hungrily by the gate, staring intently down the path. Jack raised a hand in greeting. The panther snarled.

"Miserable bugger," said Jack. The panther had come to him without a name. The old man had simply called him 'the cat', and until they reached the cramped concrete cage with the pile of shit in the corner, Jack had thought they were going to see an ordinary moggy. The panther glared and continued pacing.

"Clean-out day," Jack told him, climbing the hill. He opened the chute and dropped in the meat. The panther padded inside. Jack lowered the inner gate. The panther roared.

"I know, pal. If it's any consolation, cleaning your shit's no fun for me either." He'd often wondered if the closing of the inner door reminded the panther of its previous prison, the stinking cage at the end of the neglected garden, the amiable old drunkard poking a half-frozen chicken through the bars, accidentally tipping over the dirty water bowl as he did so. Did animals other than man look back on the past and shudder? The panther shouldered the bars half-heartedly, then settled down to eat. Jack slithered back down the hill, took the key from around his neck and opened the cage door.

Sitting cautiously on the floor of the enclosure was the closest he could get. The panther smelled wild and gamey and its teeth crunched against the bones. Would it smell that strong in the wild? Surely any prey would scent it long before it made its leap.

The panther's tail was a thick black rope of silk. If he reached through the bars, he could hold its warm weight in his hand; but if the panther took exception to this, it could whip around and take Jack's hand off with one swipe of a huge front paw. Jack sat on his hands to stop himself being tempted and watched the glossy highlights on its flank as it gulped down its meat.

He had touched the panther only once, after the vet shot it with a tranquilliser dart so he could be transported to his new home. The panther had flinched and growled, then paced around the cage before finally succumbing to the ketamine. "Want to stroke him?" the vet had asked. "Once in a lifetime chance." So Jack had gone into the cage, knelt beside the sleeping animal and run his hands all over its rough, unkempt coat, feeling the ribs beneath the pelt, the skull beneath the velvet muzzle.

"He's about twenty pounds underweight," the vet observed. "He needs to put on muscle, though, not fat, don't overfeed him or he'll turn into a tub of lard. Stick to the feeding plan and it should happen naturally." He slapped the animal on its thin flank. "He's had a shitty few years, poor wee lad. But he'll get over it."

You and me both, mate, Jack had thought, and felt the tears come to his eyes.

Threading his way between the trees, he was frozen in his

tracks by the sight of Isaac and Mathilda embracing on the lawn. Mathilda's head rested on Isaac's shoulder, and Isaac stroked her back. They looked good together; the right age, the right height, a good mix of colouring, Isaac so dark and Mathilda so fair. The sight was both erotic and painful.

Isaac looked up and saw Jack watching them. Without taking his arm from around Mathilda's waist, he beckoned Jack impatiently over. As soon as Jack arrived, Isaac disappeared.

Mathilda smiled, but there were tears on her eyelashes. He guessed what had happened before she spoke.

"Who got it?" he asked gently.

"No-one. A backer pulled out. The production's cancelled. They're going to do *Oh! Calcutta* instead." She shrugged. "So it goes."

"I'm sorry."

"There'll be something else."

"Of course there will." He could feel her trembling in his arms, and he kissed her forehead.

"I'm being ridiculous," she said. "Actors get turned down every day. At least it wasn't my performance." She wiped her face. "It's because it was the only thing on the horizon. I should have had other things in the works. My own fault for being lazy. I'll go up to London tomorrow and see Irving."

"Give yourself a few days first."

"What for? This is what acting's like. Ninety per cent of the job is rejection. We're not all geniuses. Some of us have to hustle a bit."

"Hey, I did my apprenticeship."

"How old when you signed your first album?"

"Nineteen, but it barely sold - "

"And how old when you got the NME review?"

"Which NME review?"

"Okay, people, I'm calling it. Jack Laker won't sell in the millions (mainly because he doesn't feel like writing crowd-pleasing pap) but he's going to be the *musicians' musician for the next thirty years. You heard it here first. Now worship me*

as the God of Prophecy that I am. And worship Jack Laker while you're at it. That NME review."

"You learned it by heart?"

"You've got a framed copy over the toilet, you poser."

"Only so I don't take myself too seriously. Anyway, we're talking about you."

"I've forgotten what we were saying."

"I was telling you to take some time."

"Acting doesn't work like that. There's no room in the theatre for delicate flowers."

"I thought you were modelling for Isaac."

"I am."

"And the weather won't last. We should make the most of it."

"You just want me to stay here so you can carry on fucking my brains out five times a day."

"That's not true." She looked at him disbelievingly. "Hey, it's really not. I'll settle for four. I'm a reasonable man."

"I'm not sure I've got the energy for four. I'm getting nothing done as it is, neither of us are."

"Then I'll settle for two," he said. "Or one. Or none. I'll settle for just having you here. That's enough for me. Okay?"

"I'm not earning a thing."

"I've got plenty for both of us."

"You're a soft touch, Jack. I might be a gold-digger."

"I don't care if you are. I love you anyway."

"Then you're an idiot."

"You're supposed to say, *I love you too.*"

"That's the predictable answer." She hesitated. "Till after the weekend then, okay? Then I really have to go up and see Irving. Let's go to bed."

He chased her joyously up the stairs and down the corridor, catching up with her by the concealed doorway.

He woke again at nightfall. Truth, that unlikeable hag, sat heavily across his chest.

He wanted to pretend it was for her and for Isaac, these four days he'd wrung out of her. He wanted to pretend she needed time to get over losing the part which had meant so much to her. He wanted to pretend she needed his protection. But he knew in his heart she was as tough as old boots, far stronger than he was.

He wished he had a cigarette, but he'd forced himself to quit that drug too. So instead, he tore the cover of a spiral bound notebook into meticulous shreds, and forced himself to be honest.

He was relieved the production had fallen through. He would do whatever he could, whatever he could get away with, to keep her here with him. He couldn't bear to part with her. He wanted her here with him, now, tomorrow, always.

chapter nine (now)

He stood in the doorway and stared into the room like a criminal.

The house had the special silence that falls when only one person remains in it. Tom had, as he'd promised, taken the ferry to the mainland. Kate had gone with him. Priss was, as she put it, 'not at home to visitors', a state which apparently required her to have exclusive use of the library with no interruptions. He had not seen Isaac since breakfast, but he had never seen Isaac venture upstairs.

He was alone, he reminded himself. The house was old, its joints creaked. He would hear anyone coming in plenty of time. All he had to do was cross the threshold.

He couldn't make his knees bend. He told his feet to shuffle forward, but they weren't listening.

Late last night, he'd lain beneath his billowy crimson bed canopy, wandering through the border-country that led to sleep, when he heard Kate and Tom talking on the landing.

"She's so ridiculously beautiful," Kate said. "When she's asleep she looks about nine."

"She'd kill you if she heard you said that," Tom replied. "She told me beauty's a waste of time."

"No, she didn't."

"Yes, she did."

"No, she didn't. She said, *Beauty's the biggest fuckin' con on this entire fuckin' planet apart from fuckin' falling in love.*"

"Actually, that's exactly what she said. How did you know?"

"She said it to me too. How does anyone get to be so cynical before they're twenty? Or is that just modern youth?"

"Davey's not cynical. He's as sweet as they come."

Lying in the dark, Davey blushed.

"It's lovely having them both here, isn't it?" Kate said then. "Like having a family of your own, only not."

"I suppose it must be."

"Do you? Have a family, I mean?"

"No."

"Not anyone? Not even nieces or nephews?"

"No. Do you?"

"Just me."

"Did you ever want, you know, children?"

There was a pause while Kate considered this. Davey wished he could see her face.

"Maybe," she said at last. "But somehow - and then, of course, I was too old." He heard the door of her room open. "Goodnight, Tom."

Priss had insisted from the start that Kate and Tom were strangers to each other, but until now he hadn't really believed it. How had she known?

And if she was right about that -

Go on, he willed his feet. *Go into her room. Just do it.*

Once he was over the threshold, it became easier. There was a terrible secret pleasure in being in Kate's room when she wasn't. He had no idea how women lived behind the closed doors of their private spaces. His mother's room had been off-limits since he was five. Because he could, he opened a drawer, and discovered a mound of cloud-soft garments in soft neutral colours that conjured the mysterious word *twin-set*. The drawer below contained more practical things; cotton t-shirts, heavy sweaters. Had she brought all these clothes with her, or were they borrowed? They certainly seemed to fit her, but then the clothes in 'his' room fitted him too. He opened the smallest drawer at the top, glanced in, glimpsed a sensual nest of silk and lace and closed it hastily.

Uncorked, the flask of perfume whispered Kate's presence. The sensation made him feel guilty, and he replaced the top and moved on. On the bedside table, the only reading matter was the newspaper he remembered picking up from the floor of the tube. The sight made him swallow reflexively and look away. A pair of reading glasses rested on the top. He'd never seen her wear them, but of course almost everyone her age needed glasses for something, didn't they? Beneath the mirror by the window, Kate's cosmetics seemed oddly simple; a gold-cased lipstick, a bottle of cleansing milk, a box of loose powder with an ancient-looking powder puff. Maybe she kept the rest of them in the bathroom.

The avocado bath suite looked almost pretty against the clean white tiles. He could see why, many years ago before everyone knew better, it could have seemed like a good idea. The soap reposing in the dish was Imperial Leather, its black and red label still clean and new-looking. In the cabinet, a bottle of paracetamol sat disapprovingly on the shelf next to a box of brown hair dye.

The hair dye, like the glasses, seemed almost unbearably intimate, a reminder of the small vanities of humanity. He turned away, opened the drawer in the pine table in the corner. On top of the long box of disposable contact lenses (so that was how she managed during the day!) was a small plastic case. He opened the case and found himself staring at a strange plastic contraption, like a miniscule skullcap made from pliable beige plastic.

"Don't you dare touch that, you mucky bastard," said Priss in his ear, and Davey nearly swallowed his tongue.

"Jesus!" he hissed furiously, as soon as he could speak again.

Priss took the case out of his hand and snapped it shut. "Trust me, when you realise what it is you'll thank me. What are you looking for? No, I can guess." She laughed, far too loudly. "And I thought you didn't believe me! Didn't think you had it in you."

"I don't want to believe you, I just thought while everyone was out I'd - "

"Did you find anything?"

"No, not a thing. We must be wrong."

"Absence of proof isn't proof of absence. Did you look in Tom's room?"

"Not - no. Look, I don't think we should be - "

Priss was already out of the door.

"Well, at least it's clean," she said dubiously, peering into Tom's room. "Come on, what are you waiting for?"

Looking through Tom's meagre belongings felt even more dreadful. Kate's possessions had a certain softness, a whisper of luxury and feminine grace, that lent the search a dreamlike, sensual quality. But there was nothing glamorous about Tom's four ancient sweatshirts, over-washed and immaculately clean, or the single pair of jeans with the bottoms carefully taken up and the crotch neatly patched, or the six pairs of thinning cotton underpants with only the ghost of the name Marks & Spencer still visible on the label. In the bathroom, a cheap plastic razor was lined neatly up beside a bar of soap.

"I feel awful," said Priss at last. "What the fuck are we doing this for, Davey? Let's go outside."

As he walked out through the veranda windows, Davey found he was haunted by the thought of Tom walking through another, more forbidding door. Could he have been let go? Surely someone would have been assigned to supervise him. But then, people disappeared from the system all the time.

"I tell you what," said Priss. "I'm glad they've gone out for the day. I feel weird being around them."

"Really?" said Davey crossly. "Why could that be, then? Do you think that might be because you've got it into your head that one of them's a m-m-m-m - "

"Maverick. Manticore. Mermaid. Man-eating tiger. Market gardener. Manufacturer of lemon-scented - "

"Stop it!"

"Hey, you've got your fuckin' irritating verbal tic, and I've got mine. Come on."

"Where are we going?"

"Birmingham."

"Sorry?"

"Come on, soft lad. Use your fuckin' loaf. Where do you think we're going?"

Davey glanced at Isaac's tent, which he was inexplicably sleeping in despite the abundance of spare bedrooms.

"Not as thick as you look, are you? Might as well do the lot while we're at it." She looked thoughtfully at the tent. "Maybe we'd be safer sleeping out here too."

"You'd freeze."

"I wouldn't."

"Have you ever slept in a tent?"

"No. Have you ever slept in a house with no central heating and no meter money and no chimney so you can't even burn stuff to keep warm?"

Davey looked at her in horror. "Have you?"

"I might have," said Priss, staring at the house and frowning. "Or I might just be messing with you, using the power of class prejudice and stereotypes about poor people. Your choice. Which is my room?"

"Sorry?"

"That row of windows. Which is mine? I know it's one of them 'cos I can see the garden from it."

"How would I know?"

"It's a funny thing. I can never quite work out the layout of this place. There's always bits that don't quite match up."

"Are there? I hadn't noticed."

"That's 'cos you only ever see what you want to see. Christ, this tent is ancient, it doesn't even have a groundsheet. Have a look."

Against his better judgement, Davey peered in. A bedroll rested on a stand made from four forked sticks wedged in the ground, with two branches balanced in the forks. A folding tray-table with a scratched reproduction of Van Gogh's

Sunflowers held a stack of paper, and a giant Smartie tube filled with pens. The only extravagance was a downy quilt made of exquisite embroidered silk patches.

"I knew he'd been nicking my pens," said Priss. "Right, I'm having that one back. And that one. And that one."

"How do you n-n-n-know they're yours?"

Priss ignored him. She was flicking through the pile of sketches. "He's really good, isn't he?"

"I don't think you should be looking at them."

"Well, I don't think you should wear those jeans with that t-shirt, but you don't hear me complaining." She held out a sheet of paper. "Look at this one."

Davey looked. It was a pen-and-ink drawing of him asleep on the sofa in the library.

"I d-d-didn't know he'd done that," he said in surprise.

"He gets everywhere," said Priss. She replaced the drawing in the pile. "D'you know where he's gone?"

"Why would I know where he's gone?"

"I don't actually think you know, daft lad, I'm just setting you up so I can tell you what I know. He's gone to post a letter."

"So what?"

"So it's got no address and it's just a blank sheet of paper. I had a look at it while he was in the kitchen. What d'you think he's really doing?"

"Is this another question I'm not supposed to know the answer to?"

"You're more fun when you fight back. You should do it more often." Priss put the sketches down and backed out of the tent. "Come on, we're going down to that weird cage thing."

"Why can't we just sit still for five minutes?" Davey begged. "Why do we always have to be c-c-c-climbing trees and looking at c-c-c-c-c – argh! – at cages, and g-g-going into people's rooms and - "

"If you stand still too long you put down roots. Come on."

"Let's talk about Isaac," said Priss.

Davey was enjoying the feeling of the sunshine dappling his face as they sat up in the tree's branches once again. He closed his eyes and admired the pattern of the blood vessels on the backs of his eyelids. With his eyes closed like this, he couldn't see the slight swelling of the ground beneath the beech tree. If Isaac had been back here, he had left no flowers to mark his visit. Now he thought about it, surely Isaac's willingness to stay here at all must be proof that both Tom and Kate were innocent. Priss jabbed him hard in the leg with a finger that felt like a bony twig.

"Ow!"

"Then bloody listen. What's up with you now?"

Davey was staring at Priss' fingers. "I'm just checking they're not made of c-c-c-c-cast iron."

"Brilliant. You should be on the telly. Isaac. Discuss."

"I think he's very nice."

"So that's what wilful blindness looks like! Wish I'd got a camera."

"What are you talking about?"

"You do this look," said Priss. "You did it that day Kate told us to stay away from the Dark Side. You did it the other night when Tom was holding court on the ethics of murder. And you do it all the time when you're around Isaac."

"I don't know what you're talking about." He would not look at the ground beneath the beech tree. Whatever was there was private, secret, best left sleeping. He absolutely would not look -

"What are you staring at now? Oh, shit and corruption, what the fuchin' hell's *that?*"

"What's what? Oh my God, is that - "

Priss slapped a hand over Davey's mouth and shook her head warningly. They stared, bug-eyed and breathless, as the panther shouldered its way nonchalantly through the buddleias, and padded silently into the clearing.

Priss put her mouth cautiously against Davey's ear. "Do you

think it knows we're here?" she murmured.

"I don't know. It might be able to s-s-smell us."

The panther was poking around in the undergrowth with a massive velvet paw. Its mouth was half-open. They could hear it sniffing and see its rose-pink tongue.

"How the fuck did it get here?"

"There's stories about big cats on Dartmoor, aren't there? Didn't people keep them as pets?"

The panther had scraped together a pile of twigs and bark fragments. It turned its back towards the pile, and sprayed it vigorously with urine. Priss wrinkled her nose in disgust as the smell reached them and put her sleeve over her face. Davey was afraid she would cough.

"It's not, like, tame, is it?" she whispered through the thin cotton. "I mean, even if it was a pet once, it could eat us?" Davey swallowed hard, and nodded. "What do we do?"

"Wait for it to go?"

"What if it's waiting in the woods?"

The panther padded past the half-closed gate and lay down. It began to lick and nibble at its right front paw, tugging at a fragment lodged between the claws.

"I wonder how high it can jump." Davey whispered to Priss, then wished he hadn't.

"Well, not this high, soft lad."

"You can't possibly know that, stop sounding so smug - "

"Yeah, I can. Nobody builds a cage for a wild animal it can get out of by jumping. This is its *territory*, soft lad. It must have lived here before."

"Before what?"

She shrugged. "Before somebody let it out."

Davey stared down at the powerful muscles beneath the sleek black hide. "They m-m-m-must have been insane."

"Maybe they didn't want it to starve."

"Why would it starve?"

"If you're living in a fucking prison," Priss murmured, "you've got to be sure someone's going to keep feeding you."

Thirty feet below, the panther yawned and stretched. Then it rolled onto its back, writhing from side to side in ecstasy as grit scratched deliciously up and down its spine.

Priss and Davey watched in fascinated terror.

Time passed. For hour after hour, the panther dozed contentedly in the sunlight, occasionally moving to follow the path of the sun. Priss slid her hand into Davey's and held tightly to his fingers. They gazed and gazed, hypnotised.

Davey's legs were cramped. He eased his left leg out from beneath him, then his right. Priss glanced down. The panther appeared to be asleep, and she followed his example. The panther's ears twitched, but it did not wake.

"We should go," Priss whispered. "While it's sleeping."

"What if it wakes up and comes after us?"

"What if we stay here till it gets dark and it comes after us?"

"It might go away again."

"Would you rather walk through those woods knowing where it is? Or would you rather wait till we've got no fucking idea?"

"But - "

"You scared?"

"Of course I'm bloody scared!"

"Yeah, me too. Come on, then." She stood cautiously, her eyes fixed on the panther. "Ready? Three. Two. One. Go!"

Together they raced down the path. A pigeon flew out of the bushes in front of them, its wings clapping, and Davey was mortified to hear himself give a half-choked scream. Priss gasped, "Jesus Christ and all the little angels dressed in fuckin' frilly *nighties,*" and stumbled into him. Even in his terror, he was aware of the soft warmth of her through her clothes. Then they were running again, tearing through brambles and shrubs, sweat cold on their backs, bursting out into slanting sunshine and what felt deceptively like safety as they dashed across the lawn, in through the veranda windows and back into the kitchen.

"Fuch me," said Priss, when she could speak again. "I really thought - " her breath came in deep shudders. "I thought - "

Davey wrestled with the veranda doors. They were warped and reluctant to close. He jammed a chair beneath the handles, wondering if that would do any good. Priss looked very small and fragile. He felt a surge of protectiveness. Maybe he should kneel beside her and put an arm around her shoulders. He could hold her against his chest, maybe even kiss her. He felt the sweat break out on his palms. The taunts of the boys at school – *D-d-d-Davey, never had a g-g-g-girlfriend* – it was time to act, this was ridiculous, he just needed to man up, as they said, and kiss her and get it over with.

"Are we interrupting something?" Kate sounded amused. Davey jumped half a foot, and wished he could stop himself from blushing. Priss' face was radiant with relief.

"Thank fuchin' Christ you're alright," she said.

Kate looked at her blankly. "Why on earth wouldn't we be? We saved you some dinner, did you want some? And is there a reason you're barricading us inside?"

"We, um - " Davey had no idea how to begin.

"Don't shut Tom and Isaac out, though, will you? Oh, there you are. Priss and Davey are sealing off the exits. I almost don't want to ask what's going on. It's bound to be a disappointment."

"We n-n-n-n-need to tell you something," said Davey.

"What's the matter?"

"We, we saw a, a p-p-p - " Davey hit the table in frustration. "Sorry, sorry we saw a p-p-p - "

"It's okay," said Kate, warm and reassuring. "Deep breath."

"Oh, for fuch's sake," said Priss wearily. "He's trying to tell you we saw a panther in the woods."

Davey was appalled by Kate's reaction. The colour drained out of her face, turning it milky white, then grey. She swayed on her feet and put out a helpless hand into space. Tom led her to a chair. She smiled gratefully at him, but her eyes were wild with shock.

"Oh, no," she whispered. "No, no, no, it *can't* be. Isaac, it can't be, can it?"

Isaac came to sit opposite her at the table. After a minute, he took her hand and held it.

"It must be a mistake," she whispered. "It can't be. How long do they live, anyway?" she shivered. "And what is there for a panther to eat?"

"Well, there's us, for a start," said Priss. Tom frowned and shook his head. "What? I'm just *saying*."

Davey remembered the sheep's skull he had found. The animal he had seen in the enclosure was sleek and well-fed, gleaming like polished jet. It could roam for miles across the open moors; it could easily take a sheep, perhaps even a cow. The omnipresent rabbits as a little *amuse-bouche*, perhaps? The occasional unwary walker, dreamy or drunk or both, stumbling across the grass.

"Are you sure that's what it was?" Kate asked. "Oh, Priss, I'm sorry, but - there's no way it could have been a cat, or something?"

Priss snorted. "If I ever meet a cat that size," she said with feeling, "I'll give up cursing and join a fuchin' nunnery."

Kate buried her face in her hands.

Evening melted into night. Rainclouds came scudding in across the moors and drenched the garden in dampness. By unspoken consent, they huddled gratefully in the library. Priss chewed furiously on the end of a pen. As Davey watched her, she bit right through the end and spilled ink out onto her tongue. She spat into her hand and swore, then wiped it on her jeans. Kate grimaced, reached into her sleeve and passed her a tissue. Unexpectedly, Davey felt his heart contract with longing for his mother. He really ought to write, properly this time. Let her know he was alright, tell her he was sorry.

The rain rattled against the window, and he felt the cold deep in his bones. The light that morning had begun to take on that slanted, smoky quality he associated with autumn and bonfires.

What would this house be like in the winter?

Tom, Kate and Isaac were conducting a low, eloquent argument that grew gradually louder. Priss scooched herself along the steps and leant against him.

"I'm freezing," she told him. She picked up his arm and draped it across her shoulders, then snuggled into his armpit. "That's better. Why are men always warmer than women?"

Every inch of Davey's skin tingled. He didn't dare move. "It's going to be really cold here in winter," he said, and swallowed. His voice sounded unnaturally loud. Was it okay to kiss someone with other people in the room? Was it *expected*? What if he did it wrong? Please God don't let him start sweating, she was right under his arm -

"It'll be fuckin' awful," said Priss gloomily. "If we're both still here we should bunk up together."

Davey's palms were damp. He was older than her, she'd expect him to be experienced. *D-d-d-Davey, never had a g-g-g-girlfriend -*

"Hey, no need to panic, soft lad." Priss sounded amused. "I wasn't asking you to shag me. Just keep me warm."

"Um - "

On the other side of the hearth, the argument was growing louder and angrier.

"I'm not letting you," said Kate. She was standing up now, her brown eyes flashing in the firelight. "Do you hear me, Isaac? We've got to think of - well, of everyone."

Isaac was on his feet too, inches away from Kate. His back was to Davey and Priss, but they could see his anger in his shoulders and fists. Davey wondered if Isaac was going to hit Kate, but she didn't seem intimidated.

"This isn't helping," said Tom. He wasn't shouting, but his voice drowned out every other sound in the room, and brought Kate to a stuttering halt. "Isaac, Kate's sorry."

"Don't you dare try and speak for me."

"I know we're all angry," said Tom, although he sounded almost unnaturally calm, "but that's because we're scared. Well, that's reasonable. But we can't start tearing into each other. We can't afford that. Okay? None of us can."

Kate and Isaac were glaring at Tom. He looked back at them, totally unafraid. After a minute, they nodded wearily and sat back down.

"Is he going to make them do a group hug, do you think?" Priss whispered.

"Okay." Tom sighed. "Priss, Davey, come over here, you need to be part of this too. What are we going to do? Are there any guns here, do you know?"

"You're going to *shoot* it?" Davey was appalled.

"We can't leave it hanging around," said Tom.

"But - do you, um, know how to use a gun?"

Isaac cleared his throat, and passed Tom a small slip of paper. It showed a stick-man standing beneath a tree. On the branch above, a panther lay waiting to pounce.

"He's got a point," said Kate. "You can't go yomping off into the woods like Davey Crockett, Tom. You'd be, oh God, you'd be on its territory. It'd know you were there long before you saw it."

They stared at each other in gloomy silence.

"Maybe it's just passing through," said Tom.

Priss looked sceptical. "It was poking around that enclosure like it was right at home." She was watching Kate as she spoke. "You know, like maybe it had lived here before or something."

"You said." Kate stroked Priss' hair. "You must have both been terrified."

"Do you think it might have lived here before?" asked Priss. She wasn't resisting Kate's caress, but she wasn't relaxing into it either.

"I'm not sure that matters, Priss," said Tom. "The point is, what are we going to do?"

We could call someone. The words hovered on the end of

Davey's tongue. Normal people would close the doors, alert the neighbours and phone the police. If they were brave, or possibly stupid, they would creep out to try and get photos, maybe even a video clip. Perhaps they would leave a joint of meat on the lawn to entice the creature closer. Perhaps they might call the press and wait for the junior reporter, eager and cynical, trailing a soundman and camera operator. In no sane, normal universe would the occupants of this house huddle inside and wonder whether they had access to firearms, and if they had a realistic chance of creeping up on a large predator and shooting it dead before it dropped down from a branch and broke their neck with its powerful jaws.

Davey knew how desperately he himself wanted to stay hidden. It simply hadn't occurred to him until now how desperate everyone else was to stay hidden too.

"Have we even got any guns?" asked Priss.

"What?" Kate looked at her blankly.

"Have we got any?"

"No, I don't think so." Even by the kindly firelight, Kate looked tired. Davey could see the deep lines around her eyes, the beginnings of tiny vertical pleats around her mouth. This was how she would look when she was old and papery.

"So can we, like, build a trap or something?"

"And then what?"

"I don't know." Priss was prowling around the floor. "Drop a rock on its head."

"Were you always this violent?" asked Kate, with a faint smile.

"Someone's got to be."

"Could we take it somewhere and release it?" suggested Davey.

Priss snorted. "In what? We haven't got a truck, soft lad. Besides, it probably weighs, like, half a fuckin' ton. *And* it'll be awake. *And* it'll just come straight back. My uncle took a cat twenty miles once, and three days later it was back on his doorstep like nothing ever happened."

"Why did he take it?" asked Tom.

"It was his girlfriend's cat and it hated him. It used to piss in his shoes and jump off the wardrobe. If we catch it, we'll have to kill it."

Davey winced. "I don't think I c-c-c-could. It's so beautiful. How could you hurt something so beautiful?"

"It's a man-eater!"

"You don't know that, it m-m-might not - "

"So why the fuck were you running?"

"It's a hunter, that's what it's meant to do. We're supposed to be civilised."

"You want to take the moral high ground with a big cat?"

"I just don't think it's alright to kill something just because it might want to kill you!"

"You're a waste of carbon," said Priss.

"Look, we can't build a trap," said Tom, cutting across the squabble. "No, really, Priss, we can't. Even if we managed to catch it we've got no idea what we'd do with it afterwards. I know you think you could kill it, but we're not taking the chance. Okay? Okay."

"Sorry," muttered Priss, looking ashamed.

Tom smiled. "That's alright. We're used to you. But thank you."

"So what are we going to do?" asked Kate. She stood up cautiously, as if her bones ached.

"Shall I make a cup of tea?" suggested Davey.

"Oh, that'll fix everything," said Priss. "Okay, I'm *sorry*, I'm just wound up - "

"That sounds lovely," said Kate, and took Davey's hand as he passed her. Her fingers felt very cold. He held her hand tightly for a minute to try and warm it up. When he turned away to go to the kitchen, he found Isaac was watching him.

chapter ten (then)

Davey had always been aware of the dramatic fissure in his mother's life. Photos of her in her early twenties showed a complete stranger. The woman in the photographs had long hair, changed jobs every six months, laughed, smoked, got stoned, drank herself stupid then danced herself sober. His mother wore her hair short and sleek, ate healthily, drank moderately, kept a lovely home, thought before she spoke. Loved her son fiercely. He knew she loved him. It was this knowledge that made everything else so difficult.

Most people presumed Davey's birth had triggered her transformation. "Having Davey was the making of Helen," her parents told their friends, still defiantly proud of their daughter and her love-child even though almost everyone who knew them presumed Davey was James' son. Davey was possibly the only person in the world who knew that it was James who had carefully, patiently, tenderly groomed a struggling single mother into the beautiful wife he had always wanted.

He had a few vague impressions of the three years before James entered their lives (playing with saucepans on a dirty floor; staying with his grandparents; a new bedroom with a strip of peeling wallpaper that cast a frightening shadow), but his first coherent memory was the day they met.

They were in a café, having lunch and waiting for someone to arrive. Helen had explained they were going to meet someone special, but Davey was far more interested in his sausage roll. He was picking the pastry off it to get to the tender pink meat inside. Flakes of pastry littered the floor around him.

"Davey," said Helen, patting his shoulder. "This is James. Mummy's friend. Put that down and say hello, please."

Davey put down the sausage roll and looked at the man. He wore a pink and white striped shirt beneath a dark grey suit. When he hung the jacket on the back of the chair, he revealed red braces, which Davey admired.

"Hi," said the man. "I'm James." He held out a hand. Davey looked, but there was no sweet in it.

"Hello," he said, and went back to peeling his sausage roll.

"Doesn't he know how to introduce himself?" James demanded.

"He's only three," said Helen.

"Time he learned," said James.

Davey didn't like the threat in his voice. He didn't want to learn anything from this man.

"Put that sausage roll down," said James.

Davey stuck his lip out mutinously, and continued to peel it.

"Stop it. You're making a mess. Someone's got to pick that up later."

"Davey," said Helen warningly.

Davey looked at her in surprise. This was how he always ate sausage rolls. What was the problem?

"Do as he says," she said.

Davey looked at the long, half-peeled column of pink meat clutched in his hand. He knew he should let go, but he couldn't make his hand obey. James' hands were coming across the table. The fingers of his left hand engulfed Davey's wrist. The fingers of the right made a flat paddle shape. They went up into the air. Then they came down in a sharp smack on the back of Davey's hand.

"Put it *down*," said James.

Davey stared at James in hurt and disbelief. A grown-up had hit him. Hitting was wrong. His mother said it, his grandmother said it, Mrs Milligan at playgroup said it. Hitting was wrong. As he remembered this, his disbelief dissolved into a slow triumph. Now his mother would tell the man off. He waited expectantly.

"You should have put it down when he told you to," she said, her voice crisp and severe.

Davey felt dizzy.

"And pick up those bits off the floor as well," said James, pressing home his advantage. "Go on. Get down."

Davey glanced at his mother, certain that this time, she would defend him.

"Do as you're told," she said.

And when Davey began to protest, his voice high and panicked, tears spilling over his cheeks, James took him by the arm, lifted him off the chair and dropped him on the floor.

"Do what your mother told you," he said.

Davey glanced wildly around the café. The few grown-ups watching were nodding approvingly, telling James that he was doing the right thing, making the little boy clean up the mess he'd made, teaching him some manners.

Sobbing, Davey picked up shards of pastry and piled them onto his plate.

"Now sit down and eat the rest like a civilised person," said James.

His voice was cold and reasonable, but for a moment they made eye contact, and Davey understood that this man – *James* – was enjoying this, that he was taking a great and horrible pleasure in forcing Davey to do his will. He was too young to know the word *bully*, but when he was older, he would look back on this incident and understand. He'd been hungry when he arrived at the café, but now he felt sick. He noticed that James and his mother were holding hands.

He spent the rest of the meal ingeniously peeling off minute quantities of the sausage-meat and concealing them in the paper napkin, praying his mother would come to her senses and never, ever see this man again.

"I've got something exciting to tell you," his mother said a few weeks later. She took him onto her lap and put her left hand on his knee. She was wearing a new ring, a blue-black stone flanked by two more stones like chunks of glass. Her hair had changed too. It used to be fair and wavy, long enough for him to twirl around his finger at bedtime. Now it was coppery brown and hung in a tidy, polished bell-shape just below her ears. He put his finger on the ring. It felt hard and sharp.

"James and I are getting married," she told him.

James had been his mother's boss. This, like Davey's illegitimacy, was another inconvenient fact that his grandparents continued to take out of the closet long after its relevance had passed away. James himself liked to joke that he'd first seen Helen crawling out from beneath his desk, where she'd frantically been mopping up the coffee she'd just spilled. "I came back from a meeting," he said, "gasping for a coffee, and instead I found this daft wench with a handful of paper towels and my favourite mug in two pieces." A pause. "Fortunately she was a gorgeous daft wench."

James was seventeen years older than Helen, something Davey didn't realise until he was much older. All grown-ups looked roughly the same age to him, and besides, James kept himself in shape, working hard at the gym and choosing clothes designed for young, sharp-dressing men. James was also unable to have children of his own. This was something he'd never officially been told, but had slowly absorbed over years of overheard fragments of conversations.

More than once, people said how fortunate it was that Helen already had a child when she and James met. "He's adopted him as his own," his grandmother told a friend. "And there's not many men would do *that*." The friend made approving noises. "And he's paying for Davey to be privately educated." This said with a strange, pursed-lipped expression, the words escaping around the edges.

"Well," said the friend. "That's a very generous gesture."

"James likes to spend money on the best." Her tone conveyed both admiration and disapproval.

Davey resisted school with all the force in his seven year old soul. How could anyone not come home at night and sleep in their own bed, in their own house, with their own family? But apparently it was not only possible, but desirable, to spend four nights out of seven in a strange building with only other boys and teachers for company.

He begged his mother not to send him away. She insisted it was for the best. He told her he would die without her. She told him not to be ridiculous; he was a big boy and would have a lovely time. He cried and cried, provoking James to exasperation and finally fury.

The blow had seemed to come literally from nowhere, knocking him across the room and against the wall without any visible sign that James had delivered it. Davey, dazed and bleeding from a hard landing against an antique desk, thought for a moment he'd been the victim of an earthquake. He could only reconstruct the event from its aftermath, from his own injuries, and the bruises on James' knuckles. The sight of his stepson's blood on the carpet provoked an even greater rage. Davey was called an ungrateful little shit and banished to his room, before James did something he regretted. His mother came a few minutes later, bringing water and plasters.

"You need to understand what he's doing for you, sweetie," she said.

Davey was transfixed by the sight of his blood, twirling in thin little strands in the water.

"It's one of the best schools in the country. Going there will give you opportunities."

"I d-d-d-don't want opportunities. I want to s-s-s-stay here with you."

"Well, you can't."

"Why not?"

"Because I'm not letting you miss out on this!" Her voice made his head ache. "Because of James we're really well-off, he can do things for you I'd never be able to. My God, Davey, look at everything we've got now. Don't you remember what it was like? I had to borrow against my wages all the time, just to buy your nappies!"

This was an argument he could never win, because he couldn't remember what it was like to live without luxuries, without, sometimes, even the necessities.

"I don't want to go," he repeated stubbornly.

"This is an amazing thing he's doing for you," she said, and stroked his head. "When you're older, you'll thank him."

How could she sit there and mop the blood from his head and still say this man was a force for good in their lives? He knew it was wrong for James to hit him. Why couldn't she see it too?

"He's a good man," Helen said, and kissed Davey on the forehead. "He's not perfect, but he's good. And he's your father."

"S-s-s - " He paused and took the breath his speech therapist was forever reminding him to take. "Stepfather."

"He wants to give you everything he never had. He doesn't want you to struggle the way he did. He's not perfect, but he's doing his best." Her eyes begged him to understand. "Do you see that?"

"But - "

"Just try not to provoke him," she said. "Because you do provoke him, Davey. You act like you don't like him, and that hurts his feelings."

That's because I don't *like him*, Davey thought mutinously. But even at seven, he knew better than to say this aloud.

"And it hurts my feelings too," she said softly. "Because I love you both so much, and I want you to love each other. It's so hard, feeling as if you both want me to take your sides. I want us to be happy *together*. All on the same side."

That pierced him, because she was right. He did want his mother to be on his side.

"So is that settled, then?" she asked him, smiling. "You'll go to school like a good boy? And come home every weekend, and we'll have loads of fun?"

How could it possibly be settled? Had James hitting him somehow been the winning move? Was that really how their lives worked now? He opened his mouth to say *no, I'm not going, I'll never, ever go,* but then he thought again about his mother, stuck in the middle of him and James.

What if she didn't choose him? What if she sent him anyway? Would James carry him, kicking and screaming, in over the threshold?

"Yes," said Davey, in defeat, and buried his face in his arms.

His life fragmented into four discrete territories, all terrible. When he was fifteen he discovered Dante's *Purgatorio* with its seven terraces of torment, and recognised it. There were the days at school, the lack of privacy, the constant tormenting presence of the boys who hated him and who he hated, the claustrophobic knowledge that you could never get away from each other, but would sit on the same table at dinner time and clean your teeth in the same bathroom the next morning. The nights at school, lying miserably awake in a room filled with the sounds and smells of other boys. The nights in his own bed, the passionate relief at being away from school ruined by the knowledge that respite was only temporary, the pressure mounting as the clock ticked inexorably round to 7:15 on Monday morning, the farewell at the doorway, the silent journey to the school gates. Finally, the never-ending tension and occasional explosion of those two dreadful days, the Saturdays and Sundays supposedly dedicated to 'family time'.

"I heard about this new place from Alistair," James said over his paper one Saturday morning when Davey was nine.

"Indoor rock climbing. I'll take Davey next weekend. Just the two of us. Give you some time to yourself. Buy something new, I'll take you for dinner."

She has all week to herself, Davey thought. *Why would she want the weekend alone as well?* He'd said this aloud once, and been slapped viciously around the head and banished to his room for 'disrespecting your mother and not appreciating how hard she works looking after both of us'.

"That sounds nice," said Helen.

Davey looked at her carefully. Did she really think it sounded nice? Was she genuinely pleased at the prospect of getting rid of her husband and son for the afternoon? Did she think they would have a nice time, or even a tolerable one? Or was she just being nice to James for trying, the way she was always kind about the models he made her in pottery? It was impossible to tell.

"Davey?" said James. "What do you think?"

He was always torn between the coward's desire to please, and the boy-child's urge to rebel against the man standing between him and his mother.

"Sounds g-g-g-good," he said, trying to keep his voice neutral.

"You don't sound very keen," said James.

"James," said Helen warningly. Davey felt a quiver of mean pleasure that she was taking his side.

"A bit of enthusiasm would be nice. That's all. When I was your age I'd have loved anything like that. It costs a lot of money, if you're not going to enjoy it then maybe we'll not bother."

"Of course he wants to go. Don't you, Davey?"

The coward knew to say *yes, I'm really looking forward to it*. The rebel wanted to suggest that his mother should take him, and give James some time off to go shopping. Their compromise was a mutinous silence. It lasted only a second, but in that second he knew he was caught.

"Oh, for God's sake," said James wearily.

"He's only nine," Helen began.

"Nine's old enough to appreciate a nice gesture! We always said – haven't we always said? – we always said we will not raise our son to be a bloody spoilt brat."

Helen put a hand on James' arm. It amazed Davey that she was so comfortable touching him. It was like watching someone petting a scorpion.

I'm not your son, he thought.

"Davey, James is right. You are sounding quite ungrateful. He's gone to the trouble of finding a really nice day out for both of you - "

He didn't find it, he didn't! Someone just mentioned it to him!

" - and all you do is look like he's taking you to prison for the day. What's the matter with you?"

"N-n-n - " A deep breath, " - nothing."

"Something's the matter, or you wouldn't look like that. Stop looking so bloody miserable!"

Of course I look miserable, I am miserable! You're yelling at me and you made my mother yell too! How am I supposed to look?

"Sorry," said Davey, burying his nose in his glass of milk.

"I should think so too," James said, and disappeared back behind his paper. Davey watched his mother out of the corner of his eye. Sometimes after a squall she would make eye contact with him and give him a reassuring smile or a wink, telling him that she still loved him and that she was still *on his side*. Not today. He slid off his chair, took his plate to the dishwasher, and started upstairs to his room.

Passing the dining room he heard James again. He was angry, and that meant he was almost certainly talking about Davey. Davey stopped to listen.

"I'm serious, Helen, he was sat right there watching you! Waiting for you to give him a little smile and let him off the hook! He's trying to get around us by going to you behind my back."

"I backed you up, didn't I? I told him he was being rude. What more do you want?"

"I want you to not undermine me. He's got to learn we're a team. He can't get away with splitting us up like that. If we're not consistent, he'll never learn. He's ungrateful, he's getting spoilt. We're trying to give him a nice life and he doesn't appreciate it. It's not on."

"He's a good boy."

"He's not a bad boy, but he's got to learn. He's nine years old, for Christ's sake, what's he going to be like when he's a teenager? We've got to get control of this now or - is he listening outside?"

Davey scrabbled madly for the stairs, but James was too quick for him. He knew now there was no escaping, he was going to be hit. Crying made James angrier, but he couldn't help it. He was only nine years old, and James was strong.

"Right, then," said the climbing instructor, friendly and encouraging. "You're all strapped up. Off you go."

Davey hadn't known what to expect of an indoor climbing centre, but he had certainly not been prepared for the sheer vertical reach of the wall, studded with lumps of moulded plastic. He had no idea where to start. James tutted impatiently, took Davey's right hand and forced it onto a large orange hold above his head.

"There," he commanded. He seized Davey's left hand and jammed it roughly onto another hold. "Now put your feet up, here - " His fingers gouged into the flesh of Davey's calf. He would have bruises later.

"Now pull yourself up," said the climbing instructor. "Come on, you can do it, that's it."

Painfully, Davey inched upwards. There were holds everywhere, cheerful primary colours like nursery school toys. His legs ached and his fingers trembled. James climbed swiftly beside him, his face right by Davey's shoulder.

"Come on," said James. "Keep going. Go for that one there.

No, not that one, you'll never get anywhere, *that* one." Again Davey's hand was seized. He clung to the one remaining handhold in a panic. "Stop being such a wimp, you're not going to fall, now reach up here, like that - "

His arm was stretched painfully high, his fingertips sore and throbbing. He was secure, but stranded, stretched long and tight like a squashed spider. Now James' fingers grabbed at his ankles again, forcing his knee to bend. His kneecap crunched painfully against the wall and he cried out. James slapped his leg irritably.

"Give over complaining, it wasn't that hard. It's your own fault for not concentrating. Foot on here. Here. *Here!*" Another slap. "If I can climb this wall *and* hold you on *and* show you where to put your hands and feet, you can at least listen and do as you're told. Use that leg to push up - "

They climbed higher, higher, higher. Davey's arms were pulling out of their sockets and his legs were elastic bands. James was right beside him, pushing, pulling, grabbing, crushing, jabbing, taunting, criticising. Occasionally the instructor shouted up encouragement. The holds grew sparser. James was forcing him to reach and stretch further than he had ever thought possible. He whimpered in pain.

"Give over," James hissed. "Fuss about bloody nothing. We're nearly at the overhang."

Davey squinted up at the looming out-swelling of brown-painted fibreglass. He remembered looking at it from the floor. It was dangerous to be up here. They were too high. They were too high.

"We'll go up to it and touch that blue hold on the end. Then we'll climb down again. Alright?"

He couldn't move. He was frozen to the spot. He glanced down, saw the rope snaking out behind him, felt his palms turn damp.

"Come on. Don't freeze. Move. Move!"

"I c-c-c-can't," he whimpered. "I'm scared."

"What the hell are you scared of? You're on a safety rope,

you can't fall. Get moving."

"I can't! I can't, I can't, I can't, get me down, I c-c-c-can't d-d-do it, I w-w-want to g-g-g-get d-d-d-d-down."

James peeled Davey's fingers off the hold and pulled his arm up above his head. Davey struggled and sobbed.

"Stop it," James hissed. "You're making an idiot of yourself, and you're embarrassing me. Stop panicking, do what I'm telling you and you'll be fine."

"I c-c-c-c - "

"Grab on there. There. Right? Right. Now this hand. Come on. Let go. Let go!"

Beyond speech, Davey shook his head.

James thrust his face right into Davey's. Davey closed his eyes in terror.

"Look at me. Look at me! Stop that silly performance and look at me!" Davey shook his head stubbornly. "How do you expect me to help if you won't follow a simple instruction?"

"I want mum."

"Well, mum's not bloody here, is she? It's just you and me. So you're going to do what I say for once and stop trying to hide behind her! Now listen. Listen! Give me your hand. Give it to me! And stop that stupid noise, you're safe!"

Davey clenched his fingers even tighter around the grip and shook his head.

"Right," said James, his voice dangerously calm. "If you're going to be such a little brat about it, I'll show you how ridiculous you're being."

And he slid one strong, sinewy arm in the space between the moulded fibreglass and Davey's hunched body, and pushed Davey off the wall.

"I've never been so embarrassed in my life," James said to Davey, threading the car deftly through the late afternoon traffic. "Will you stop that bloody racket? I don't know what you're upset about, I'm the one who should be upset. Telling everyone I pushed you."

"But you *did*," Davey whispered.

"You what?"

"You d-d-d-did push me."

James stared at him. Davey wiped tears from his face and stared back.

"You p-p-p-pushed me off the w-w-wall," he repeated. "With your arm."

To their left was an abandoned pub, windows boarded up, sign faded to a pale greenish blur. James wrenched the wheel sharply left and cut across angry traffic to bring them to a screeching halt in the empty car park.

"Listen to me," he said, his finger inches from Davey's face. "I did *not* push you off that wall."

Davey was baffled. Did James really not remember doing it? Or was he remembering wrong?

"But - "

"I didn't push you," James continued, "because there was no way you could fall. All I did was to demonstrate to you that you were safe. I did it because you were being stupid, and not listening. Do you understand?"

Davey was speechless. A sign above the car declared that these premises were protected by SCAMP security.

"Do you hear me? I didn't push you. I *did not*. I don't want to hear you saying that, ever again, to anybody, and especially not to your mother. Are we clear?"

A dog barked in the distance.

"I said, are we clear?"

"Yes," said Davey.

"And what have you got you say for yourself?"

Davey lowered his head. "I'm s-s-s - "

James waited.

"I'm sorry," Davey managed at last.

"Good. Then let's go home."

James shoved his way back out onto the carriageway. After a few minutes, he turned on the radio and put the volume up loud.

When Davey was fourteen he grew taller than James, and realised that his stepfather was actually shorter than most men and that in a few years, he himself would probably be physically stronger. Davey's greater height seemed to unleash some new fury in James, or perhaps it was merely the ending of restraint over attacking someone smaller and weaker. The beatings became more frequent, more violent; three times in his fifteenth year Davey was unable to return to school on Monday because the bruises were too prominent.

"Why do you keep m-m-making excuses for him?" Davey pleaded with his mother one afternoon. "You w-w-w-wouldn't let him hit you like this. Why do you let him d-d-d-do it to me?"

Helen shook her head helplessly. "He does it for your own good."

"How? How is this for my own good?" Davey held out his arm. His wrist was black and swollen with bruises. "What's he t-t-t-trying to achieve?"

"You make him do it! You know he's got a temper, and you provoke him anyway! Besides, he's got a point. If you're going to amount to anything you need proper qualifications, not some airy-fairy nonsense - "

"I don't *w-w-w-* oh, Christ, I don't *want* to do Economics or Maths! They're b-b-boring and I'm no good at them! I like English Literature and History."

"Maths and Economics are what you need to get a proper degree employers will take notice of. James knows what he's talking about. You need to start listening."

"W-w-why won't you listen to me? I don't want to work in a m-m-m - " deep breath, " - merchant bank. I want to g-g-g-go to university and study English Literature and then - "

"Yes? And then? What comes after that? You don't want to be a journalist, you don't want to work in broadcasting, you certainly wouldn't make a teacher. If you could give us one single, solitary example of what you actually want to be, Davey, maybe we'd listen to you, but as it stands, all you can tell us is what you *don't* want. Well, it's not good enough. I've sent your options form in, and that's that. We've spent a fortune on your education, you're not throwing all that away."

In the solitude of his room, Davey stripped off his sweatshirt and examined the bruises along his ribcage. Would he ever escape? It was wrong for a grown man to hit a kid, he knew that; but what would anyone make of a seventeen year old who let himself be beaten up by a man shorter and older than he was? They'd laugh and tell him to toughen up. There'd been a window of opportunity when he was small and vulnerable, but that window had closed long ago. He was on his own, and he would have to find his own way out.

"Why are you even doing Maths when you're so fucking awful at it?" Simon asked, as they slouched among the trees in the Arboretum. Simon was smoking a cigarette in an elegant black holder.

"Because they made me," said Davey.

Simon laughed. "They can't *make* you," he said.

"Of course they can. They pay my fees."

"Okay, so they can *make* you fill in something on a form, and they can *make* you come here five days a week, and they can *make* you turn up to classes. But they can't actually *make* you learn it, can they?" He blew a smoke-ring over Davey's head. "They can't *make* you write the right answers down on the papers. You straight boys are so unimaginative."

"You were a s-s-s-straight boy yourself till three weeks ago," Davey protested.

"No, I just hadn't told anyone. Just fucking flunk the exam, dimwit. And what the hell can they do about that?"

"Turn over your papers, please."

Davey stared at the paper. A curious exhilaration came over him.

"I just don't understand it," said his mother tearfully. "How could you have failed?"

"I t-t-t-told you I was no good at maths. I really did tell you," he repeated uneasily. "Anyway, an E's technically a p-p-p - "

"Mr Bell said you should get a C at least, a B if you worked hard."

"Mr Bell's a fool," said James. His voice was calm, but his expression was furious. "We're paying a fucking fortune for our son to be taught by a fool."

"James," said Helen.

"I've a good mind to go and sort this out face to face."

"It w-w-won't do any good," said Davey. "It's not the s-s-school, it's the p-p-p-person who m-m-m-marked the p-p-paper who f-f-f-f - "

"Just spit it out, will you!" James yelled.

"I'm s-s-s, I'm s-s-s-s- "

"We'll get you a tutor," said Helen loudly. "You can resit in a year."

"Turn your papers over, please."

Davey stared blankly into space for ten minutes. On the one hand, his future. On the other hand, his mother's face.

He took a deep breath.

It was late, and Andrew was tired, but he had ten more papers to mark. *Seychelles*, he repeated to himself grimly, *the money's going in the Seychelles fund.* Trip of a lifetime. You only get married once. He sighed and picked up another paper.

A quadratic function is defined by

$f(x) = x^2 + kx + 9$

where k is a constant. It is given that the equation $f(x) = 0$ has two distinct real roots. Find the set of values that k can take.

Lower sixth year at school at £7,000 fees a term = £21,000

Repeat Lower Sixth year at school at £7,000 fees a term

= £21,000

School uniform for two years at £2,000 a year = £4,000

Private tutor at £100 an hour, three hours a week for 38 weeks = £11,400

Total my stepfather has wasted on trying to turn me into someone I'm not: £57,400

I'm sorry, but I just can't do this.

He flicked hastily through the rest of the paper, but all the rest of the answers were blank. Well, at least that was an easy one to grade. He scribbled a *U* on the front in red marker and dropped it onto the pile.

chapter eleven (now)

The bathroom was cold. A deep chill radiated off the tiles and soaked into Davey's bones, like the opposite of sunlight. He wrapped the thin towel around his shoulders as he cleaned his teeth. Several times, he turned to check the door was still shut. He was trapped in a huge, isolated house, wearing only a pair of boxer shorts, with four people he knew absolutely nothing about, united only by their fear of the outside world and the need to hide away. On the other side of the door, in the room he called his, was Priss. Reluctantly, he opened the door to the dim bedroom and made his way by touch and memory across the carpet.

"You'll have the enamel off your teeth," said Priss from the darkness.

"Are you, are you in my bed?" Davey asked. His heart was racing.

"Yeah, but don't get any ideas, right? I was cold." The covers slid back. "Come on, get in."

"I, I d-d-d-d-don't think I should - " the hammering of his heart was painful. It was too dark to see if she was still dressed. He wondered what on earth was wrong with him that he was even thinking of turning her down.

"It's okay, I've got clothes on." Priss' fingers clasped his arm. Davey slid beneath the covers, where he lay stiffly, like a corpse. Priss scooted closer and huddled against him.

"That's better. Even the sheets are cold tonight. God, will you fuckin' relax already?" She'd said she was dressed, but he could feel the warm skin of her thigh against his. "You're really bad at being touched, do you know that?"

"No I'm not, I just wasn't expecting to f-f-f to f-f - " He thumped the bed in frustration.

Priss snorted with laughter. "That's just too easy, mate. Chill out, I'm not in the mood anyway." Her hair tickled his face. Shyly, he reached up a hand and smoothed it down. He could make out her profile in the dimness, and hear the click as she chewed furiously on her thumbnail.

"Are you scared?" she asked.

"Yes," he admitted. "Are you?"

"If I tell you something do you swear not to laugh?"

"Okay."

"I think," said Priss, very distinctly, "this house is haunted."

Davey lay rigidly and tried to think of something to say. After a minute, Priss thumped him furiously in the stomach.

"Ow! What was that for?"

"Stop fuckin' humouring me!"

"I'm not, I never said a word - "

"You didn't need to. I can feel you doing it."

"Well, look, you've got to admit - "

"I don't mean like spirits. It's like Kate said. Old houses have bad memories."

"No they don't. It's a building, not a person. Ow!"

"Serves you right. There's only room for one assertive person in this bed." She threw back the covers and flicked on the bedside light. "Get up, I'll show you."

Priss was wearing a skimpy t-shirt and, quite possibly, nothing else. Davey felt a bead of sweat crawl down his spine like an ant.

"No."

"Yes."

"No!"

"Yes! And don't argue with me or I'll fuckin' do you." She got out of bed and he saw the flash of her white cotton knickers.

"But what are we - "

"Look." Priss' face was chalky white and her eyes blazed. "What happened this afternoon, that's got to be the biggest reason on the planet to get out of here, right? So why are we all still here? I'll tell you why, mate. It's because we're all bein' haunted by this place. It's got into our heads, and we won't get away from it, ever, until we find out what happened."

Davey got out of bed. His jeans and t-shirt were still faintly warm. "This is even stupider than your murder theory."

She pressed a pencil-thin torch into his hands. "Here."

Davey padded wearily down the corridor after Priss and wondered what the boys from school would have to say about the long, slender lines of Priss' pale thighs, and the sway of her hips as she walked. Why was she always so naked around him? Was it an invitation? He would love to think so, but he suspected she did it because she knew perfectly well she was in charge, and could look and behave as provocatively as she liked. She opened the door to the Dark Side and held out an impatient hand for the torch.

"We promised not to go in there," he said.

Priss shone the flashlight onto the peeling ruin of the wall. "It's a bad, wicked world, mate."

"But what if - "

"Shush, I'm trying to count." They were picking their way down the corridor now, dust coating the soles of their bare feet. "One. Two. Three. Four. Five. Or is the one on the landing one as well?"

"But why are you - "

Priss paused by a window and peered out. "If I bung you five quid will you shut up? Six. Okay, so now we go through this door - "

"But where - " he tried as they padded delicately across the frayed rectangle of carpet.

"Have you got a death wish?" She flung another window open and hung perilously out for a moment. "Big bush with red flowers. Right, this is it, got to be." She shone the torch onto the wall opposite. "Help me look."

"But what are we - "

"You," said Priss, "are slower on the uptake than my nanna and she's got fuckin' Alzheimer's. There's a door here, thicko, a hidden door. And we're going to find it."

Davey stared at the wall. "No there isn't."

"Yes there is! I said to you ages ago, this house doesn't match up! There's a whole bit of it you can't get to from any other part! It's here, it's got to be, I counted the windows - "

"Are you, are you sure? Or do you just think there might be?"

She took one hand off the wall so she could give him the finger.

"We shouldn't be doing this," he said. "We should go back to bed and - "

"Got it! Give me your hand." She rubbed his fingertips along the paper. "Feel that? That goes all the way up from the floor, and then along the top. And then underneath." She guided his hand across and banged his knuckles against the surface. "Wood. See?"

"Oh," he said wretchedly.

"Right. Let's get it open."

Priss looked young and vulnerable. Her toenails were painted black, and she had a silver ring on each middle toe.

"We shouldn't," he said. "It's private."

"Yeah, good point. 'Cos it's not like we're, I don't know, already fuckin' living here without permission or anything, is it?"

"I just, what if - "

"There'll be a catch you press, I've seen it on films."

"No! What if there's someone in there? Someone bad? You're n-n-n-not opening this Priss, you're just n-n-n-not doing it, I won't let you."

He took the torch out of her hands and switched it off. Then he leaned firmly against the concealed doorway, spreading his arms to stop her reaching past him. Beneath his shoulder, something clicked. The door flung itself open, propelling him into a dark, dusty space on the other side, Priss stumbling after him. Then, just as suddenly as it opened, the door swung shut again, slamming back into position with a deafening bang.

It was absolutely pitch black.

"Shit," said Priss, coughing. "It's blacker than Lucifer's arsehole in here. Get that torch on."

This was the centre of the mystery, the house's secret, rotten heart. Sick and wretched, he flicked the switch. A reedy stream of light poured out. Dust lay on the carpet like felt.

"We should go back."

Priss was already trying door handles. As he watched, she slipped through the nearest door. He followed her, afraid to be left on his own. The bedroom was dirty and neglected, like a room in a deserted hotel. The walls wore an ordered geometric pattern of greens and yellows that Davey didn't like looking at. He moved the torch away and ran its bright finger over a crumpled bed, yellowing sheets bunched halfway down. The green silk eiderdown had coiled itself voluptuously on the floor. A glass of fluff and mould lurked on the bedside table. A cream silk slip, stained and torn, huddled at the end of the bed. The air was musty and cold.

"Like a crime scene in here," said Priss. Davey was surprised to hear a tremor in her voice. "I wonder if the rest of the house would be like this without Kate cleaning it up?" She flicked the light switch. "Bulb must have gone. D'you reckon they put guests here they didn't like? Or did they lock up mad old Auntie Ivy with a bottle of gin and a nice young man for company?"

The bathroom, with a white suite and garish orange tiles, was even colder than the bedroom and smelled of damp. Priss grimaced, and forced the window open. She was openly shivering now, and her fingers were turning blue. Davey looked around for something to wrap her in. A lone towel hung stiff and crumpled from the rail. When he tried to unfold it, black mould fell from its crevices. He shuddered and dropped it on the floor, then went back to the bedroom for the green eiderdown.

"I'm alright," said Priss. Davey wrapped it around her anyway. She was vibrating with cold like a plucked guitar-string. She leaned gratefully against him for a minute before shuffling over in her huge green cocoon to look in the medicine cabinet. A disorderly crowd of plastic containers rattled joyously down into the sink. Priss turned them over in fascination.

"Aspirin. Valium. Lithium. Dexedrine. Hey, look, Excedrin. Like in *The Shining*."

Davey watched as Priss shook out a handful of white tablets. "I don't think you should take that."

"Oh, you think? I just want to see." She poured them back and returned to her rummaging. "Whoever lived in here was proper fucked up - ow!"

"What? What?"

Priss was shaking her hand frantically. A huge spider, its fat body hanging in a hammock of tangled legs, fell to the floor. "That bastard spider *bit* me," said Priss, outraged. "Right, I'll have it for that. Where did it go?"

"Under the bath, I think, but you've got bare feet, you can't stand on a - "

"Look at this!"

The bath was blanketed with spider-silk. Spiders hung like clots from the sticky strands. About half were dead, with crisp-looking bodies and dry, brittle legs. Several others were parcelled up as meals for the stronger survivors.

"That is fuckin' messed up," said Priss, with feeling. She reached for the shower attachment.

"Don't," said Davey, feeling sick.

"Why not? The water's on."

"Just, let's get out of here, okay?"

"They're evil."

"They're only spiders."

"You don't like 'em either."

"I just think we should get out of here."

"Are you worried they're going to run onto your hand or something?"

Davey tugged desperately at the green silk duvet. "Can we please just go?"

Priss sucked the red welt on the side of her hand, and glared into the bath.

"Okay, fine."

They picked their way back into the silent, desolate bedroom. Was he imagining it, or was the torchlight beginning to waver? Priss found a notebook on the bedside table.

"Huh," she said. "Listen to this."

There's a certain kind of cold in this hour of the night
The silence creeps around the curtains and coils around
your knees
The trees are lonely and the moon's getting drunk
So why not join in?
Why not join in?

"What does it mean?" asked Davey.

Priss shrugged. "Here's another one - "

He was nineteen years old and he took his umbrella
Turned it upside down so he could sail it down the stream
At Bristol docks he joined a crew to sail to Argentina
All because he'd seen her face in his dreams

"You reckon this place used to belong to a poet?"

"I don't think poets make that much money."

"No, good point." She dropped the notebook back on the table and turned away.

They returned to the corridor, picking their way gingerly through the dust. Behind another door, the torchlight slithered over a sage-coloured living room with a battered green sofa and two brown chairs that didn't match.

"Like being in a jailhouse," said Priss. "Madwoman in the attic, maybe."

"Maybe it's somewhere to hide," said Davey.

"Why hide back here when you've got a whole house out there - shit!" Priss gave a muffled scream and dropped the torch. Davey heard himself yell with fear. The torchlight had caught the outline of a woman, standing against the wall, not moving.

"Who the hell are you?" Priss screamed, frantically scrabbling for the torch. "There's fuckin' two of us, so don't you fuckin' try anything - " She grabbed the torch, flashed it frantically around.

The woman stared silently back at them with wide grey eyes. She was tall and spare, with broad shoulders and narrow hips. Her thick fair hair hung in an untidy tangle over her shoulders. She was naked.

"It's a painting," said Priss in disgust. "It's bloody realistic, though. Wonder who she is." She padded over to it and ran her fingers over the surface reverently. "This is brilliant, it's like those *trompe l'oeil* things. Come and see."

"In a minute," said Davey.

"Bare tits bother you that much?"

"No! No. I just - " he looked desperately around for inspiration. "I just want to see where the window looks out." He pulled at the thick curtains, dust falling around him like grey rain, and discovered a hidden treasure.

The lamp on the windowsill had a red hessian shade on a pale cream base. Its rosy glow flooded out from the windowsill and transformed the room into a warm bright haven. Gazing at it in perplexity he found himself consumed with a blurry but emotionally-charged memory of standing outside and seeing a red light in a window like a guiding star.

"But it's beautiful in here," he said in wonder.

"It's better with the light on," said Priss grudgingly. She tucked the torch into his front pocket.

"I saw it," he said. "I saw it. The first night I came here.

That's why I - "

"Yeah. Me too."

"Really?" He was surprised by how pleased he was at the synchronicity. "You saw it too? When? How long ago?"

"Never you mind." She was staring at the table. "It's like a beacon. That's what the Ingalls family did, isn't it? Put a lamp in the window to call Pa home. Hey, look, another notebook."

Davey riffled through it. Page after page of hand-drawn staves, with notes and words crossed out, replaced and then replaced again. Little arrows summoned in errant words and musical phrases from the edges of the paper, and banished others to some unknown hinterland. Superscripts directed the reader to mysterious destinations. Some of the pages were so scribbled-over they looked as if they were written in code. The handwriting was familiar. After a moment he remembered the notebook called *Landmark*. He followed her gaze and saw her examining a stack of handwritten sheets.

"Letters," said Priss.

"We shouldn't read them."

"Don't be a pussy." Priss was already unfolding the first one.

"Why would you use that as an insult? That's horrible."

"Good point. Alright then, don't be a knob. Doesn't sound as good though, does it? That just proves sexism's inherent in fuckin' everything. Right, listen to this."

Jack,
Alan told me about Mathilda.
I'm so sorry.
I'm coming home to look after you. It's alright, I'm not expecting anything to happen. I just don't think you should be alone.
Evie
xxxxxxxxxx

"*Love*," muttered Priss, making it sound like a curse. She

unfolded the next letter, and a photograph fell out and landed at her feet. Davey looked at it cautiously.

The girl was all tawny and gold; brown hair, brown eyes, sun-kissed skin. She was pretty in her violet bikini, but her eyes were wide and wary. Priss read the letter out loud.

Jack,

I hope you're having a good summer. I worry about you sometimes. Actually, I worry about you all the time.

I'm staying here in Corfu. It's fun, but I miss you. I miss talking to you. I miss laughing together. I miss meeting up at the end of the day and talking about what we've been doing. I've been trying and trying to understand what happened between us and I think I've just realised something important.

You don't remember, do you? You honestly don't remember.

I know you remember that day in the dining room. You were leaving, and I was crying because I'd just lost my job. They told me that morning. I was being sacked for gross misconduct. You came in and asked me what was wrong, and I said, I've been sacked. And you asked why, and I showed you the letter, and it said, inappropriate relationship with a patient, and you didn't ask any more, you just said how sorry you were and how awful it was. And then you said you'd got plenty of room at your place if I needed somewhere to stay.

But you weren't offering out of guilt, were you? You were offering because you're a nice guy and you didn't like seeing me so upset. You honestly didn't remember the patient was you.

It was that first week you came in. In your first week we checked on you every two hours at least. You were in bits, you were sobbing your heart out. You grabbed onto me and you begged me to stay, you begged me not to leave you. You said you needed me. You said you'd die if I left you. So I stayed.

It was so good, Jack. It should have been horrible and sordid and awkward, but it wasn't. You were so sweet and so gentle. And afterwards, you went to sleep in my arms.

We slept together every night for a week, and then one night I came in to check on you and you were already spark out, so I went away again. But then afterwards we were such good friends I used to look forward every day to seeing you.

And then, those weeks at your place, it was good, wasn't it? We were companions. Not lovers, but my God, you were just out of rehab, we tell everyone to stay celibate for a year. I was willing to wait.

But you don't remember, do you? And now you're living with some girl you only met a few weeks ago, and you wonder why we're all worried.

I know you don't feel the same as I do. But, we were happy weren't we? It was fun. We had a nice time together. We were friends. And you were working, Jack, you were working and it was good, really good.

"Christ," said Priss. "There's pages of this stuff."

It's very quiet here, and I've had lots of time to think. And what I've thinking is this. Everyone says love is supposed to be a wild, crazy, out of control thing, this mad roller coaster ride that takes your breath away and scares you to death. Maybe that's what you have with Mathilda right now, I don't know.

But really, do you need another roller coaster? You said when we met it had all been too much, the life you'd had before. You couldn't hear the music any more. But then it was better and you were clean, and you were just starting to work again. Wouldn't it be nice to live with someone like me, who'll look after you and take care of you and be there for you when you come home?

I know right now you don't agree with me, but I meant what I said. I'll wait for you, Jack.

Always,
Evie
xxxxxxx

"Well, she wasn't completely daft," said Priss approvingly, tapping the letter against her teeth.

"What do you mean?"

"About love. She's right. Fuckin' time-waster it is. So. Evie, Jack, and - " she checked the first letter, "Jesus, *Mathilda*. Bet she had a hard time at school. Wonder who killed who?"

"You've got no proof that anyone killed anyone! Just because they were, you know - "

"Shagging each other?"

"*In love*, I was going to say, well, that doesn't prove anything."

"You think this one didn't end with someone being pissing miserable?"

"I can see what you're talking about," said Davey crossly, "but it's a bit of a leap from that to, to - to one of them actually k-k-k- "

"Kissing their gran. Keying the neighbour's car. Kicking a ball around at the park. Keeping calm and carrying on - look, it helps me think, okay?" She returned to the first letter. "*I heard about Mathilda. Is Mathilda dead?*"

"You're obsessed, it might not be anything like that, it - "

The sudden sound was like a gunshot. Davey jumped, and knocked over a lamp. Priss gave a muffled scream.

"What the fucking hell was - "

The sound came again, a terrible ominous crack that made Davey's hair stand on end. Crack. Crack. Crack. Was it getting closer? They ran back into the corridor. The hidden door swung on its hinges, slamming itself open and shut as if it was trying to break free. Crack. Crack. Crack.

"Why is it doing that?" he said. It reminded him of a hungry mouth opening and closing. "Is it because we left the bathroom window open?"

"Who cares? Just move!" The green duvet slipped from Priss' shoulders and he stumbled over it. Dust coated his hands and body. Crack. Crack. Crack. Priss was shouting at him, telling him to get up and get moving. He stumbled to his feet. Crack. Crack. Crack. The duvet was still tangled around his legs. He shook himself free. Crack. Crack. Crack. The door slammed shut in their faces just as they reached it.

Suddenly, everything was still once more.

"Fuck me," said Priss, breathless in the darkness. "That was awful."

Davey closed his eyes. "Get it open."

"Give me a second."

Davey heard her fumbling with the door handle. "Hurry up," he begged.

"Hang on, I'm trying."

Davey felt his way along the wall and found the door, pushed Priss roughly out of the way. "Just get it open!" He tried to turn the handle. It wouldn't move. He wrestled with it, the cold sweat on his palms making it hard to grip. "Jesus, why won't it open?"

"It's not stuck, is it?"

"It can't be stuck, it can't be stuck, it was fucking open just a second ago, it can't be stuck - " He struggled again with the door handle, then kicked blindly at the panels. "Shit, come on, just open, please, just - fucking - "

"Davey, just chill, okay? Put the torch on, we'll have a look."

A terrible fist had hold of his heart, squeezing it tighter than tight. He put a hand out in the darkness in front of him, and found nothing but blind empty space.

"Put the torch on, soft lad!"

Panic had him by the throat now. This was far worse than the stammer, which merely paralysed his tongue. His hand clutched frantically at something warm and yielding. He couldn't breathe.

"Davey, what the fuck?"

He felt a hand snake inside his pocket, and then there was a beam of light in the darkness and Priss held his hand in hers, her mouth against his ear, murmuring to him.

"It's alright, mate, look, the light's on now, okay? Deep

breath. That's it. And again. Okay. Chill out. Have the torch if you like. Look, it's fine. See? Plenty of room. We're fine. We're fine. Just chill out now. We're fine."

The panic slowly receded, leaving shame in its wake. Priss, on tiptoes, was leaning comfortingly against him. He discovered the warm thing he had grabbed was her right breast.

"Sorry," he managed, dropping his hand. "I didn't mean to - "

"Oh, give over." Priss' voice was surprisingly gentle. "Was it the dark? Or the door being shut?"

He didn't want to think about either of those things.

"Never mind."

"I'm not going to fuckin' laugh at you about it, I know I'm horrible but I have got some standards. But if you're got a problem with stuff like this, you should have said."

"It reminded me of something," he managed at last.

"Like from when you were a kid, you mean?"

He rattled the door again, felt the fear begin to rise. "How can it be stuck? Why the bloody hell did you make me come in here, anyway?"

"Sorry," said Priss.

"Well, so you should be! Because we're stuck! We're shut in here and we can't get out and nobody fucking knows we're in here!"

Davey slumped down against the wall, and put his head in his hands. In the near-darkness, it was easier to ignore the dust.

"I said sorry," said Priss, after a while.

In his head, Davey was concentrating fiercely on the picture of a wide, pebbled beach licked by a slate-grey ocean.

"And that's supposed to make it alright? Why didn't you make me stay outside? Just in case anything happened?"

"Look, I was scared to come in here on my own, okay?" yelled Priss. "I knew this place had to be here, I knew it. And I was scared to come by myself. Happy now?"

"You could have said!"

"What good would it do to know we were both fuckin' terrified?"

"I might not have come with you if I'd known! Don't I get a choice?"

"Yeah, well, too late now, eh?" She sighed. "Sorry."

"I thought that was supposed to be my line."

"I'm nickin' it." She laughed. "Proper little scally."

Davey closed his eyes again and tried to picture the beach, but Priss' gaze was burning through his closed eyelids and melting it away. He murmured under his breath. "Pebbled beach. Grey ocean. Pebbled beach. Grey ocean. Pebbled beach. Grey ocean."

"Are you praying?" asked Priss.

"Visualising."

"Is it working?"

"Not when you keep talking to me." He stood up again and tugged blindly at the door, which remained stubbornly closed. "Jesus Christ, I just, I need to get out! Fuck! Fuck! Fuck!"

"Give it a minute and we'll try again."

"What's going to be different in a minute?"

"I don't know, it just might be! Stop winding yourself up, I don't want to be in here with a fuckin' madman, alright? Sit down and talk to me. Tell me why you're so scared."

Davey laughed hysterically. "Why would I want to do that?"

She was next to him again, her hands on his arm. He was shocked to realise that Priss, who seemed to feel nothing for him but a kind of cheerful scorn, had nonetheless touched him more in the last few weeks than any girl he'd known. He had a vivid mental flash of her striding down the corridor in her t-shirt and knickers; of her expression as she reached to wash away the spiders. The images, erotic and intimidating, burned through his carefully constructed grey pebbled beach. She was probably the most beautiful girl he'd ever met. What would happen if he kissed her? Did she want him to kiss her?

Did he want to? Should he?

"Christ, you're trembling," said Priss, concerned. "Sit down, I'll give you a hug." She draped herself around his back, her firm little breasts pressed against him. He was suddenly immensely tired. Her hands on his forehead were like Alice's sister, brushing away the leaves.

"Don't you fucking go to sleep on me." Priss shook him awake.

"I'm so tired." His eyes were closing all by themselves.

"Stop that. Stop it! Stay with me, Davey, you soft bastard. Are you still awake?"

"Mmm." He was limp and relaxed, the aftermath of fear better than any anaesthetic. Priss was so warm and comforting. The dust was like a blanket he could curl up against. It smelled of must and old, used-up time.

"Don't you bloody dare." Priss hit him very hard on the arm. He whimpered, and put his arm over his head. "Oh my God, Davey, don't you bloody do this to me, stay awake, are you even listening to me, don't you dare leave me on my own in here while you go to sleep, I need you, alright, I can't be in here on my own!"

He could hear the hysteria in her voice, but it seemed far too big a problem for him to deal with. Priss began to wail.

"Kate! Tom! Isaac! Are you there? Come and get us out!"

"They'll never hear us," murmured Davey, feeling the waves close over his head. "They're in the other wing. They might look for us at breakfast time. Might as well get some sleep while we're waiting."

"No, they'll never find us, not in here – they might not even look at all – Davey, stay with me, stay awake, the torch is fuckin' going out."

Davey felt the light strike his eyeballs through his tightly closed eyelids, driving away the comforting lethargy. He sat up. And as if it was the most natural thing in the world, the door had swung open, and Isaac stood in the doorway. Behind him were Tom and Kate.

chapter twelve (then)

Welcome to MSN Messenger!
Online: Elvisgirl, EdwardBulyerLytton

hey elvisgirl online at last J how U doin?
hey ed how RU?
XLnt as always. so how was it 4U 2day?
place is fkn shit-hole Ed
srsly?
YY
yr skool is actual den of sodomy?
LOL no! pedant
i no soz. so wot u mean 'shit-hole'?
BRB.
*" - a non-selective mixed comprehensive school in the
[stranger danger deletion LOL] area of Liverpool. It is
ethnically diverse, with nineteen per cent of its population
coming from a non-white racial background. Thirty-seven per
cent of its pupils are entitled to free school meals. Thirty-nine
per cent of its pupils leave the school with at least five GCSEs
at A - C grade."*
u no all that off top of hed?*impressed*
LOL no. wiki'd it
U no u cant trust wiki rite?
*ha not trusting wiki. using wiki 2 prove point. oh and 9 staff
on long-term sick w stress & supplys keep leaving 'cos we're
a bunch of fuckin' animals*

snds like tuff place L
i'll survive. get GCSEs get out n do 6th form. then world =
fkn oyster. besides 1 or 2 good teachers U no? like eng guy. he
gave us this fkn wild assignment this wk

Heavily made up and with their skirts hitched high, the cream of the Year Eleven girls leaned against the corridor wall and preened at the Year Twelve boys, who watched them from outside the History room.

"You done your assignment?"

"Fuck off."

"Only askin'. Don't have a fuckin' baby, alright?"

"Yeah, well, don't be so fuckin' nosey, alright? Did you do it?"

"Yeah."

"Fuckin' swot."

"Fuck off. Didn't take long."

The girls glanced slyly at Priss.

"Bet Priss did it."

"Priss lurves Mr Jones. Priss has got a crush on him."

"Fuck off, I have not," said Priss, absently.

"Haven't done your assignment?"

"Haven't got a crush on him."

"Ooh. She's denying it! It must be true."

Priss shrugged. "If you say so. Mind you, Katie that means you must fancy Harry Fearn. Which would be a bit of a fuckin' shame, really, since he told his mates he'd rather fuck mud."

Katie reddened. There was a collective *oooh* from the other girls, but Priss had already lost interest. Mr Jones – a professional latecomer who had quit a lucrative sales job to retrain – was making a disorganised passage down the corridor, dropping papers, getting stuck in doors, knocking half-dislodged posters off walls. One of the Year Twelve boys stuck out a foot, but Mr Jones, apparently distracted by a drawing pin on the floor, swerved neatly around, homing triumphantly in on the pin and capturing it in thick fingers.

Everyone swarmed into the classroom.

"Everyone make it here okay?" Mr Jones asked, studying the register. "Who are we missing? Lee-Anne, have we got Lee-Anne? Anyone?"

"She's got her period, sir," said Katie, for laughs.

"Has she really. Thank you for that, Katie, nice to see a true comic genius at work. Anyone with a sensible answer? No? Okay. Anyone else? Mark, have we got Mark?"

The boys stuck their tongues in their lower lips and made spaz noises. Mark Asher was in a wheelchair, and had special permission to go into the classrooms before the teacher got there because if he waited outside, he blocked the whole corridor.

"Locked in the toilet."

"Got lost on the way here."

"Maybe he's taking the stairs?"

"For a bunch of reasonably bright kids, you're all quite horrible sometimes," said Mr Jones severely.

"Mark doesn't mind, sir."

"It's just for a laugh."

"Yes, yes, I'm sure you're all princes among men and Mark is eternally grateful for your kind support and understanding. Alright, here he is." Mark wheeled silently into the classroom. "Any special reason why you're late, Mark? Never mind, you're here now." Mr Jones smiled at the class. "So, I'm sure you all remembered to bring in the piece of writing that made you feel something."

U mentioned him B4. mr jones i mean
so?
so nothing. just sayin. J shows I listen rite?
U rnt gonna ask me if I fancy him RU?
LOL no
good
so do U?
fuck OFF
soz cudnt resist it J tell me more

"Who's going first?" Mr Jones looked around. "Tyler. How about you?"

Tyler stood up and unfolded the magazine he had stuffed in his back pocket.

"Sir, I've brought *Razzle*," he said.

The class erupted with laughter. Priss sighed in disgust, and pulled her hair around her face. Mr Jones rapped loudly on the desk.

"That's enough!" he said. His tone cut the laughter like a guillotine. Everyone looked at him to see what would happen next.

"Okay, Tyler," he said. "Tell us why you chose *Razzle*."

Tyler's face was that of a comedian who's just been handed the setup of his dreams.

"'Cos it made me feel something, sir," he said.

"And what was that?" asked Mr Jones, encouragingly.

"Horny, sir!" said Tyler, grinning like a madman and grabbing his crotch. The class was verging on hysteria, but once again Mr Jones, bizarrely out of character as Mr Tough Guy, rapped on the desk, brought it back under control.

"Horny," he repeated, very loudly.

Everyone stopped laughing.

"That," he said, "is a *great* example of the power of words. Words on a page. A description of events. And just those words – just words on a *page* – twenty-six letters arranged on a piece of paper can evoke our most primitive responses. Just words on a page and they can make us feel like having sex. How is that even possible?"

Priss watched curiously as Mr Jones balanced on the knife-edge he'd found for himself.

"However," he said, "I don't think we'll ask Tyler to give us a reading. Thank you, Tyler, sit down, and I'll have the name of the newsagent who sold you that magazine before you leave. Who's next?"

LOL I wan2B in yr class! mr jones = WIN
mr jones = FUCKWIT. he'll get fired if hes not careful

???

discussing porn wiv 15 yr old kids. FGS. askin 4 trbl. only tks 1 to complain & hes fkn finished

hmm gd point. shame he sounds lk gud guy. still 10/10 4 style YY J

so wot did U pick?

"Priss," said Mr Jones.

"Bet it's, like, fuckin' Shakespeare," Katie whispered to Destiny.

"Romeo and fuckin' Juliet," Destiny whispered back.

Priss held up a battered copy of *The Dark Knight Returns*. Mr Jones raised an eyebrow.

"A graphic novel," he said. "Okay. That wasn't *quite* what I was expecting from you, Priss, but it's definitely an interesting choice."

OMG you picked miller! rock'n'roll!!! go elvisgirl go elvisgirl J J J J J

i blame U & yr influence K a yr ago wud hv picked peyton place

BRB

"**Peyton Place** *is a 1956 novel by Grace Metalious. Peyton Place has become an expression to describe a place whose inhabitants have sordid secrets.*"

that peyton place?

YY

well I spose it did sell 60k copies w/in 10 days of release

thought U sed cldnt trust wiki LOL

damn U got me J so Y wld U pick it?

author made fortune J

that makes it good?

YY it makes it fkn good. her words moved ppl. & made fortune in process. thats wot I wan2 do

hey U will I no it
how do U no? U nvr read my stuff
got faith
tx. doesnt mean much since U hvnt read my stuff but tx J
no prob. how did DK go down?

"Sir, you said to choose something that made us feel something," said Priss, shaking her hair off her face. "I wanted to talk about - " she thumbed through the book. "This page."

"Okay. Why this page in particular?"

Priss took a deep breath. "So this story is, like, set in a time where Bruce Wayne is middle aged. He's been retired for years, but the gangs are taking over Gotham. And he can't watch that happen. So he comes back again, takes over where he left off."

"Okay - "

"And in this part, the Joker's got out of Arkham Asylum and forced Selina Kyle, she used to be Catwoman, to send one of her escorts to kill the president. So all that's, like, pretty standard for a Superhero story, right? But then, he makes her, Selina, dress up in a Wonder Woman costume, and he ties her up and leaves her on the bed."

Connor wolf-whistled.

"Yeah, you would think that, Connor, but that's 'cos you're a div who can't actually read," said Priss, deadpan and devastating. Connor, who had been in the remedial reading programme for as long as anyone could remember, turned pale and slumped down in his seat. Mr Jones looked at her reproachfully. "See, she's middle aged too. And the costume doesn't fit her, it's too small, and her make-up's a mess. So she's never looked worse."

Everyone's eyes were on her; the girls from competitive envy, the boys from low-grade lust, but Priss seemed coolly oblivious to their gaze.

"And then Bruce arrives, and he's still, like, buff and strong and doing the superhero thing, and he finds her – he *sees* her

– looking like that. And she's, like, totally humiliated. 'Cos when she was Catwoman, she was, like, hotter than any of them, right? So she tells him what the Joker's going to do, and then there's this one panel - "

She held the book out to Mr Jones, her slim pale finger with its silver ring and bitten nail resting on the panel.

"This one? Where he's kissing her?"

Priss nodded. Behind her, a spitball war had broken out.

"Yeah. That's the one. That panel. Just that one. It's, like, so totally *not* the way it's normally done in Superhero stories. Like, the men can be ordinary-looking underneath the costume, but the women are always, *always* gorgeous. And the men can get old and maybe a bit fat, and still get laid, but the women either don't age, or they, like, have to retire and disappear. But just this one time, there's a buff, powerful superhero kissing an ordinary middle-aged woman. And I've got no fu - no idea why. Is it 'cos he wants to make her feel better? Is it 'cos he loves her? Is it 'cos he feels sorry for her? Is it, like, a promise? Or is it just 'cos it turned him on to see her all tied up like that?"

The spitball war had now engulfed everyone apart from Priss and Mark Asher, but Mr Jones ignored it.

"You know, Priss, there aren't actually any words on that panel," he pointed out.

"I know, sir. That's why I picked it."

"So how did it make you feel?"

"Frustrated."

Mr Jones blinked. "I'm sorry?"

"Frustrated," she repeated. "Because, as much as I want to be a writer, that panel does something that you couldn't *ever* do with words." She sat down. "That's all." A spitball landed in her hair. She picked it out wearily.

"Thank you." His eyes were warm. "I didn't expect that at all, Priss. I'll give you one thing, you're always - surprising."

She shrugged a little, hiding behind her hair again. Katie made kissing noises.

"Okay, you lot, that's enough," said Mr Jones. "Destiny. You're on."

"Sir, I chose this magazine," said Destiny, holding up a copy of *Closer*.

hey, fkn good analysis. ive trained U well J
corrupted me U mean. I used 2 read real books
oh not this again PLS. graphic novels ARE real books priss
U no that
YY I no. just getting U back 4 asking if I fancied mr jones
LOL J
ha fkn ha. U no how 2 wind me up elvisgirl

u still there?

elvisgirl???

jesus fkn wept ed who the fuck RU
???
u called me by my real name
??? I DK ur real name!
YY you fkn do U CALLED ME PRISS U WANKER SCROLL
BACK UP N READ IT
oh shit
are u stalking me U freak
no priss no
so who the fuck RU n how long hv U known who i am
priss look
no U fkn look U FOUND ME. u sent me frnd request U got
tlkn 2 me U said U wanted 2 get to no me
YY I did cos I do UR amazing
we agreed no real names 4 safety n shit U SAID U DIDNT
WANT 2 DO THE RL THING
let me explain
weve been msging 4 six fkn mths now talking abt all sorts of
stuff hopes dreams wishes books writing drawing every fkn

thing and now UR just some FKN PERVERT WHO WANTS 2 JUMP ME RNT U

priss please please let me explain

OMG RU mr jones? is that why U keep fkn askin abt him n wot I think of him n if I fancy him?

PRISS SHUT UP SHUT UP AND LISTEN IM MARK ASHER

priss? RU there?

priss please please dont do this

mark asher?

YY mark asher! OK? that fkn weirdo twat in the wheelchair. now U no

WHAT? priss talk to me pls

fuck IDK what to say! dont no if I even believe U

Y not? its just my legs that dont work U no. fingers n brain R all thats fkn needed 4 MSN

fuck off didnt mean that

well what then

in RL U never spk U hardly fkn move. online UR funny clever charming rude sarky. if UR rly mark then UR nothing like UR in RL

U never bothered 2 spk to me in RL

yeah well U never bothered 2 spk 2 me U fkn wanker! weve been at skl 2gthr all fkn yr! Y not just talk 2 me? Y the fkn online act?

cos skl is den of sodomy OK? i.e. skl =shithole in case U have 4gotten. fkn animals obsessed w sex no chance 2 just B frnds U no wot hpns if boyz try 2B frnds w grlz? well? do U?

well?

ha. run rings round you logically

oh fkn hell

what? WHAT? come on elvisgirl. talk 2 me

*UR rite wldnt work wld it? BUT STILL FKN PISSED OFF
WITH U, U cld hv said sumthin earlier!*

was scared

??? Ed UR never scared

*online am not scared. online am not crip-boy in wheelchair
ed we R FRIENDS. UR scared 'cos U thk I give a fuck abt
wheelchair?*

every1 has reaction to wheelchair. EVERY1

*yeah well here is my reaction. U ready? NEEDING FKN
WHEELS TO GET AROUND DOES NOT GET U OFF HOOK
FOR FKN WANKER STALKER BHVR. capisce?*

was not fkn stalking U!

YY U fkn were. still not convinced UR even telling truth TBH.

shit Im shaking

shock. go get cup of tea

cant. dad downstairs getting drunk. if I go down he'll hit me

srsly? shit priss. wish I cld help

UR no fkn use UR in wheelchair J

RU laffing at me?

fkn rite

so we R still friends?

DK. still thinking

does it hurt?

LO fkn L ed

mark

*mark. sounds weird. mark asher. UR mark asher. I sit next 2U
in english FFS*

U wr awesome 2day

*U wr silent 2day. Y U never spk up? UR most interesting
person in class*

ed is interesting not me L

*but Ed is U. ED IS U. no still sounds fkn weird. U srs? UR rly
mark asher?*

swear

OK, UR fkn wanker stalker arsehole

???
just following orders J prove it
prove wot?
prove UR ed
now?
next lesson
wot U want me 2 do?
shit
what?
BRB

priss?

U still there?
got 2 go
whats happening
just family stuff. dad is
dad is what?
doesnt matter will sort
priss be safe OK? be safe. pls
sez the psycho fkn stalker who sat next 2 me in English for 6
mths n never said a fkn word J J J CU tomoro

Elvisgirl has signed off

"Class, settle *down!*" Mr Jones shouted, uncharacteristically loud and rapped hard on the desk. "What's the matter with you all today?" He caught Katie's eye. "Has *everyone* got their periods or something?"

An uncomfortable laugh, his usually reliable humour off key this time, everything slightly off balance. There's a strange dynamic in the room. Everyone sensing something different and no-one clear on what or why. Priss was hunched in her seat, chewing furiously on her fingernails, her make-up like a Venetian mask.

"So," he said. "Who's been reading what this week?"

A safe question, a reliable one, reliable answers expected from the usual suspects. Same hands going up: Courtney, Page, Jancey, Tyrone, Jamie. Priss hanging back, as always, waiting for the daft answers to get out of the way first, but he knew she'd have something to say. A new hand, something unexpected -

"Mark," he said, slightly taken aback. Mark's written work was solid, occasionally illustrated with sly doodles of his classmates in the margins, but he never spoke up without prompting.

"Okay. What have you been reading?"

In the background, Tyler stuck his tongue in his lower lip and made the spaz noise. Mr Jones frowned. Tyler made the noise again, slightly louder.

"A novel, sir," said Mark.

"Okay. Which one?"

Tyler made the noise again. Mark flinched, but kept facing forward. Mr Jones got wearily to his feet, but before he could reach Tyler's desk, Priss exploded out of her seat and shot across the room, hair flying, eyes flashing.

Priss had Tyler by his collar. He was a big lad, easily six foot and heavy with it, a slab of muscle, testosterone, fat and stupidity, but he quailed before the look in Priss' eyes.

"If you fuckin' *ever* make that noise again," she hissed. "If you *ever* take the piss out of Mark like that - "

"Yeah?" Tyler sneered, remembering himself.

Mr Jones was striding down between the desks, ready to take over.

Priss smiled sweetly, and put her raspberry-red mouth against Tyler's ear. She whispered something. Tyler's eyes bulged.

"I mean it," she said. "You got it, fat-boy? And don't even *think* about trying to get back at me, I know what you fuckin' did to Jade, don't try that with me or - "

"Priss, stop that right now!" Mr Jones roared. Priss let go of Tyler's collar and he sank back into his seat.

Mr Jones thought quickly. "Both of you out of here now," he said. "Headmaster's office. Go on."

"Why are you sending Priss out?" demanded Katie. "She was sticking up for Mark, Sir, it's not fair."

A chorus of agreement erupted from the girls. Mr Jones waved an ineffectual hand for silence.

"Be quiet! Go on. The pair of you. And you'd better both arrive there. Okay? Now move!"

They were forbidden to hit or even to touch the pupils, but crowding them into movement by invading their personal space was allowed, and Mr Jones used it now. Tyler shrugged and climbed out of his seat. Priss began to retreat down the aisle, but her attention was somewhere else. She was watching Mark.

"What was the book?" Priss demanded, her eyes fixed on him.

"You didn't need to do that!" Mark was pale with anger. "I don't need you to fight my battles for me!"

"Fuck off, you twat, I fuckin' did. What was the *book?*"

"Priscilla, you will *not* use that language in my classroom, you're already in enough trouble - "

"Just tell me what book you read!"

He nearly had them herded through the doorway now, but Priss was still staring at Mark. The classroom was in uproar. Mark had to shout over the noise.

"It was *Peyton Place!*"

"For God's sake!" Mr Jones finally had them outside in the corridor, and closed the door on the mayhem within. "Tyler, off you go. Priss, what's got into you?"

"Sorry, sir." She was looking demurely downwards, but couldn't hide the fact that she was grinning from ear to ear.

"I don't want you to apologise, I want you to explain. What was that all about?"

"Sir, you heard Tyler making that fuckin' mong noise. It's not on."

There was something else, he knew, but he didn't have time to get to the bottom of it now. Christ only knew what they were doing in that classroom without him.

"It's my job to keep discipline in the classroom, Priscilla, not yours, and I won't have you physically attacking other students. Now go to the headmaster."

RU there ed?

cum on I no UR. uve got 'appear offline' on & UR hiding

talk 2 me U wnkr

pls
wot U wan2 talk abt?
why RU hiding?
cos I DONT NEED U TO FIGHT MY BATTLES priss
wot was I spsd 2 do? just sit there n let him get away w it?
YY U were! my fight. not yrs. get it? want yr FRIENDSHIP.
not yr pity
look wasn't fkn abt U OK?
???

realised last nite Ive never hrd U spk. U don't spk cos wen U open yr mth the boys all make fkn noises. thats not rite. U cld be best frnd or worst NME, still not rite. shld hv dun it mths ago. cant sit on arse & listen 2 that shit & still think of self as human being K

ed?
OK thats quite sweet actually
fuck off Ed am not sweet
YY UR. but dont eva fight my war 4me again. dont need it. hv own weapons
Yr wheels R loaded?
LOL am hiding lite under bushel. 1 day will burst out into full brilliance. lk U
am not hiding
YY UR. so do U believe who i am now?

OK yeah. i admit it. UR mark asher
J wot did U say 2 tyler?
sed id tell every1 wot i saw him doing last term
so?
he wuz havin wank in woods
!!! OMG teenage boy has wank!!! call out vice police!!! Y he
care?
was havin it 2 beefcake in mens health
tyler = gay?
must be
huh. feel better about U havin go @ him now I no U got
summat good 2 keep him away
can look after self U no
yeah well so can I. U still showed up 4 me J
so now what?
i got killer idea 4 graphic novel. can draw pics. need writer
U srs?
fkn rite Im srs J so wan2 meet IRL?

"Who is it, Mark - oh, hello, Priscilla." Mrs Asher looked dubiously at the girl in the hallway, a puzzling contradiction and therefore a threat; layers of black clothing, glimpses of pale skin, an abundance of cheap silver jewellery, and the face of Botticelli's Flora.

"Hello, Mrs Asher." An accent far stronger than either hers or her son's, the marker of lower-class roots and a poor education. No, that was unfair. Priss was sweet, nice-mannered, she'd been here eight or nine times now and had only ever been charming. "How's the writing going?"

"Fine, thank you. We've nearly finished the storyboards."

She'd been unable to trace the origins of this friendship, blazing suddenly into life after years of splendid isolation. Priss was too beautiful, that was the trouble, too beautiful, and too female. A nerdy boy with glasses, a geeky, sexless girl, these she could have understood, but not Priss, he was amazing, her son, but to the outside world -

"We're going to my room, okay, mum?" The chair turned, began to roll down the corridor.

"Okay, darling, have fun." *Have fun?* God, she was getting so *middle aged*. Neither Priss nor Mark giggled, which was some small consolation.

"I've done some sketches," said Mark, rummaging in a large black portfolio case. "For the first chapter." His dark eyes were shining, his movements quick and assured. In the school environment he kept still, made no eye contact, left no signs of his passing; but in his room, he sprang into vivid life. When their fingers touched, Priss felt a tingle.

They spread the pictures on the low, wide bed and studied them for a long time, sitting at ninety degrees to each other. Priss was awkwardly tall in the chair Mark's mother had brought in from the dining room. In the background, Jack Laker's *Violet Hour* wove subtle melodic magic out of the air.

"Are those for the scene at the docks?" she asked at last.

"Yeah."

"I like the angles."

"The *angles*?"

"Yeah. The way the shadows all point down to that one spot where they're stood."

"Hey, so they do. That's actually pretty good, isn't it?"

"You didn't do that on purpose?"

He shrugged. "Did you mean that whole section in the city to be a weird riff on Red Riding Hood?"

"No, but - "

"I reckon that's how you know something's really good," said Mark. "When you go back to what you drew or wrote or whatever and spot all this stuff you hadn't even noticed you were putting in, 'cos you were so into it at the time."

"This *is* really fuckin' good, isn't it," said Priss. "I mean, I know we're just kids, but - "

"Forget that *we're just kids* crap," said Mark fiercely. "When we send this in, no-one's going to know. They'll just see our work. We'll submit under fake names and we won't own up until we've got the deal. Okay?"

Priss laughed. "You're so fucking arrogant, you know that? It's not like they'll recognise our names, is it?"

"You've got to think about this stuff."

"If you say so." She yawned, stood up, and stretched, as pretty and unselfconscious as a little cat.

"Am I keeping you up?" asked Mark.

"You are actually," Priss murmured, yawning again. "I was up half the night, I'm about ready to fuckin' drop. I hope you're grateful."

"What kept you up?"

She stared at him blandly.

"Why won't you ever talk to me about your dad?"

"Why won't you ever talk to me about yours?"

"Look, I'm not going to laugh, you know."

"Yeah, you're damn right you won't laugh, 'cos it's not fuckin' funny. And also I'm not telling you, alright?"

"Why not?"

"It's not important."

"If it keeps you awake half the night, it must be. What? Oh God, Priss, I'm really sorry."

"What for?"

"You're crying."

"I am *not* fuckin' crying." She stared at him defiantly. A rivulet of mascara drew patterns on her cheek.

"Hey, it's okay." Mark's voice was carefully gentle. "What are you so embarrassed about? We're friends. Aren't we? Come here." He held out his arms.

"I'm not crying, alright?"

"Alright, you're not crying. Are you going to let me give you a hug now?"

Mark's large, spacious room was suddenly very crowded, and short of oxygen, and the floor seemed a long way down. When she stood up, she stumbled off her platform heels. She made her way around the edge of the bed, and hesitated.

"What?"

"I - "

"I can't exactly stand up and put my arms round you."

She bent awkwardly from the waist, and felt his arms across her back for a brief, electric moment. When she straightened up, there was a smear of mascara on his shoulder.

"That was probably the worst hug in the history of the universe," she said.

"Then come closer."

She moved closer, and bent once more. Her hair fell across his face, and she felt his warm breath against her neck. Her pulse thundered in her ears like a thousand horses galloping.

"That was better," he whispered. His cheeks were flushed.

"Yeah."

"Want to try again?"

She nodded. When she pushed her hair back from her face, he saw her hand tremble.

"Want me to show you something?"

"Like what?"

"Like how to do this properly."

"I don't know what you - "

He put his hands around her slender waist and pulled her towards him until her knees nudged the spaces between Mark's thighs and the side of the chair.

"This," he whispered, "is how to make out with someone in a wheelchair."

He pulled her down onto his lap and they folded into each other, amazed at how well they fitted together, at how right it felt for her to sit astride him, her feet tucked beneath her bottom and her knees crammed into the cramped space between his legs and the walls of the chair. She wriggled into his lap, heard him groan with pleasure, then bent her head so they could kiss, fiercely and deeply, biting each other's lips, tasting each other's mouths and tongues and skin, pressing awkwardly against each other, their hands in each other's hair.

chapter thirteen (now)

Everyone stared at everyone else. The silence stretched tight over several painful seconds.

"What on earth's going on?" Kate demanded at last. Her question was addressed to both of them, but her gaze was fixed on Priss.

"We were - " said Davey, then stopped. "We were, um - "

"Shut up," said Priss coolly. "Thanks for letting us out."

Tom was examining the doorframe. "I had absolutely no idea this was even here," he said to himself. "Kate, did you know about it?"

"Of course not," she said, her eyes not leaving Priss' face. Priss was staring back, her expression a smooth, careful blank. Davey thought that if he got in the way of their gaze he might fizzle up like a fly in a UV trap. Isaac was watching them with a kind of detached fascination, as if they were a particularly interesting documentary.

"Just look at this!" Tom clicked the door closed and ran an admiring hand over the almost seamless join. He opened the door again and peered inside. "I wonder what's - "

"Don't!" said Kate, Priss and Davey simultaneously.

There was another charged silence in which Tom finally seemed to notice the tension between Kate and Priss. Davey could feel Priss' nerves vibrating through the air between them. He didn't dare to move.

"Don't you think you ought to put some clothes on?" said Kate to Priss at last. Her voice was calm, controlled. "The house is cold tonight."

Priss folded her arms defiantly. "I'm fine just as I am. Thanks."

"We can all see your knickers and your t-shirt's tiny," said Kate.

"So?"

"I'm sure it must be uncomfortable for the men to have you wandering around dressed like that."

Priss raised an eyebrow. "Well, *I* don't hear them complaining."

"Well, *perhaps* that's because they're all too polite to say anything."

"I d-d-d - " Davey took a deep breath. "I d-d-d-d, I d-d - " he closed his eyes in desperation. "I d-d-d, oh for God's *sake* - "

"Don't blaspheme," said Tom, then shook his head.

"You see?" said Kate. "Poor Davey can hardly get a word out."

"It's not because of P-P-P- it's not because I can see her n-n-n - " Davey thumped the wall in frustration. Isaac was now watching him instead, his eyes boring into Davey's soul. He wished he could summon the death-stare that James had used for years to keep him in line, the kind of stare that generally preceded a beating.

"Why don't we go down to the kitchen?" said Tom hastily.

Since no-one seemed to have any better ideas, everyone trailed downstairs. As always, the Aga sent out waves of warmth, but the cosy atmosphere that usually prevailed was missing. It was, Davey realised, because of Kate. Her peaceful presence usually spread like a balm over the room. Now, although she was doing nothing to show it, she was boiling over with -

Well, with what? Davey thought to himself in perplexity. *Disgust? But Priss had been wandering around in various states of undress all summer. Anger? But why? It wasn't her house any more than it was theirs. Fear? But that would mean - that would mean -*

He clamped down tightly on the thought. He wasn't going to believe anything about Kate or Tom, or anyone at all in fact, not even Isaac, until he had to. He watched Tom's broad, capable hands pouring boiling water into brown mugs, using one tea bag between two people. Reluctantly, Davey remembered his secret conviction that Tom had spent time in jail.

A mug appeared over his shoulder, and Davey accepted it automatically. Tom's own mug appeared to contain nothing more than hot water. Isaac took a mug and set it politely before him, but didn't drink. Priss and Kate were still watching each other.

"So," said Kate, smiling in a way that might have looked reassuring from a distance. "Would you like to talk to us about what you've been up to, Priss?"

"I don't have a fuckin' clue what you're talking about," said Priss stubbornly.

"Kate," said Tom. "We're not the Gestapo - "

"What were you doing in that annexe?"

"What's it got to do with you?" asked Priss. "This isn't your house. Is it?"

"No, of course it's not my house."

"So why are you so upset about me having a look around?" Priss was leaning forward a little in her seat, her eyes flashing.

"What makes you think I'm upset?" said Kate, very still, very calm. "Of course you can go into any part of the house you want to, although from what just happened to you, that annexe thing doesn't seem very safe. If the door sticks - "

"I was in there too, you know," said Davey miserably. "So if you're going to be m-m-mad with Priss about it, then you ought to be upset with m-m-m- with m-m - "

"Merlin?" suggested Priss wearily. "Meryl Streep? Martin Clunes?"

" - with *me* as well," Davey managed at last, and took a triumphant breath.

"I'm not upset with anyone," said Kate. Her voice was like

cream. "But Priss, since we're all together, I did want to talk to you. I'm worried about you."

"Don't bother your barnet about me, Missus. I'm fine."

"Of course you're welcome to stay here as long as you want, you know that."

Priss looked at Kate wearily. "How do I know the next fuckin' word out of your mouth is going to be *but*?"

"Well, actually, it was." Kate's smile was as glorious as ever, but there was something different this time. *Nothing about this moment feels real*, thought Davey. Kate's gestures were perfectly natural, delivery of every sentence was paced to sound exactly the same as spontaneous speech, but it still felt wrong. His head was swimming. He longed to escape to the cold silence of the library, or – even better – to his room. But he couldn't bring himself to leave Priss here alone. In spite of everything, she was still just a kid really.

"You're still just a kid really," said Kate, and Davey jumped three inches off the bench. "You can't spend your life living like this."

"Why not?" said Priss. "You two are."

"It's different for us," said Tom.

"Don't tell me you fuckin' agree with her?" Priss looked hunted.

"We haven't been talking about you or anything," said Tom gently, "but for what it's worth, I think Kate might have a point. You're only young, you've got your whole life ahead of you."

"You're giving me advice about what to do with my life? *You?* Mr Can't be-in-a-room-if-the-door's-shut?"

"That's nothing to do with - " Tom stopped. "I don't, it's not what you - "

"Anyway," said Priss, triumphant now, "I'm *not* throwing my life away. I'm working. I'm a writer, we can work anywhere, so I might as well work here."

"But you're not working," said Kate, her voice deceptively gentle.

"You what?"

"I read your notebooks, Priss."

"You've been rummaging around in my *stuff*?"

Davey suddenly found he couldn't make eye contact with anyone. When he regained a measure of composure, he found Isaac looking at him shrewdly, and was overcome with a blush so all-encompassing that he felt as if even the palms of his hands were scarlet.

"I'm worried about you," said Kate. "Who's this boy you're writing to? And why are you never actually sending him any of your letters?"

"I don't have a bloody *clue* what you're - "

"I can see you're in love with him," said Kate, her voice so careful, so slow. "But - "

"No she isn't," said Davey, suddenly finding his voice. "That's her writing partner, they're writing a graphic novel together. Priss is doing the words, this bloke's doing the pictures. It's called, it's called - " He found he was embarrassed by the title, even now. "Um, it's called *Crip-boy and Enabler Girl*, they've got a publisher all lined up in New York and - "

"New York," said Kate. "Was that where you were going before you ended up here?"

"I'll be going," said Priss. "Just as soon as the manuscript's finished, I'll be out of your bloody hair. If you were sick of having me around the place, you only had to say."

"It's not that," said Kate. "But that notebook of yours - "

"You mean that manuscript, it's called a *manuscript*, or maybe since it's a graphic novel you could call it a layout - "

"Actually, I'd call it a diary," said Kate. "It's like you're writing a diary about your love life, for some boy who's never going to get to read it. At least, I'm presuming he's never going to read it. What on earth happened between you two? Is that why you ran away?"

"I did not fuchin' run away! I was running *to*, not *away!* I've got a fuchin' *plan*, all rice? I'm goin' to New Yorch, yeah? I know what I'm doin' and I know where I'm goin' and you

rotten lot can all fuch off and stay the *fuch* out of my *fuchin'
stuff -* "

"That's a bit much coming from - " Kate stopped and bit
her lip. There was a bright spot of red colour on each pale
cheekbone.

"What were you going to say?" Priss demanded.

"I wasn't going to say anything."

"Yes, you were. Come on, if we're going to have this fight,
let's get on and have it, shall we? You were about to say it's a
bit rich coming from me. Weren't you?"

Kate stared at Priss, then lowered her gaze.

"Look, it doesn't matter. We need to talk about you. About
what you're going to do."

"Stop trying to change the subject," said Priss.

Davey was surprised to hear the suppressed sob in her
voice.

"What subject would I be trying to change?"

"You know what I'm talking about."

Davey had the uneasy feeling that the balance of power in
the room had somehow shifted.

"Priss," said Kate, "I don't know what I've done to upset
you, but I didn't mean to. All I've done is to try and talk to
you about - "

"You're just not quite sure what I've got, aren't you?"
said Priss. "You know I *might* have found summat I shouldn't
have, but you're not one hundred per cent that I *have* found it.
And you don't want to say anythin' in case you give yourself
away." She laughed. "Jesus Christ, it must really *really* suck
to be you sometimes, you know that?"

"This isn't getting us anywhere," said Kate, with inhuman
patience.

"And why bring up all this stuff tonight?" demanded Priss.
"And while we're at it, what the hell was all that when we got
out of that weird shithole down the corridor? All that stuff
about my clothes?"

"All I did was suggest you put a few more layers on, since

it's cold and there are three adult men here who maybe don't appreciate being able to see quite so much of you on display."

"Are you trying to distract us all from something?" asked Priss. She was leaning across the table now, sure she was onto something. "What is it you don't want us to talk about, Kate? What are you so afraid of?"

Kate's look of bewilderment was so perfect Davey almost believed it. "I don't have the faintest idea what you're talking about, but I'm not trying to avoid any subject at all, we can talk about whatever you - "

"I meant," said Priss, cutting straight across Kate, her voice several notes higher than usual, "the subject of that freaky granny flat thing back there and this whole creepy *house* and - " she looked at Davey with eyes like saucers. "Oh my God, that's where - those flowers weren't for Kate at all, were they? We need to talk about the body that's buried out there in the woods and which one of you bastards put it there!"

Now she's done it, thought Davey despairingly. *Now she's gone and ruined everything. Whatever happens now, we can't ever go back to how we all were. It's not a haven any more, it's just a big empty house with three adults and two kids in it, all frightened of each other, and maybe, just maybe one of them* is *a -*

Kate's laugh of disbelief was the first truly genuine sound Davey had heard her make since they'd been discovered in the annexe.

"What on earth are you talking about?" she said. "Priss, for goodness sake, of *course* there isn't any body in the - whatever made you think there was?"

"Oh, *Priss,*" said Tom, with what sounded suspiciously like a chuckle in his voice. "You daft lass. Is *that* what's been going on? No wonder you were poking around in all the corners. Have you actually been thinking you were living with a - "

"Right," said Priss, with great decision. "If that's going to be your attitude, then we'll just have to fuckin' see, won't we?"

Davey didn't like the determined look on Priss' face, or the way she marched out of the door in the direction of the hall. He was aware there was something ominous about the way she reached for the wellington boots that had rested against the ugly, empty umbrella stand by the front door all summer. But it wasn't until she wrestled the key in the lock, flung open the front door and stormed off into the blackness outside that he finally allowed himself to realise what she was about to do.

"Priss, come back!" he called. His voice annoyed him; it sounded like a lamb bleating hopelessly for its mother. He tried to lower it to a more masculine pitch, and felt ridiculous. "Priss, you can't go out there, it's dangerous - Priss, please!"

He vaguely thought he could hear her yelling something back at him over her shoulder as she disappeared around the corner of the house. It sounded like, "You are such a pussy it's not even *funny!*" And then she was gone.

He stood in the hallway for a moment, undecided what to do. He wanted to go after her, if only because he wanted to be there when she realised how insane she was being. But the memory of the panther out there in the garden – that sleekly-muscled killing machine, covered in black velvet, padding on silent paws through the trees and shrubs – was like a hand on his collar, dragging him back.

"Don't be such a spineless - a spineless *twat*," he said out loud, and took a determined step towards the door.

Except there really was a hand on his collar.

"Do you mean me?" asked Tom. "Or you?" Davey struggled to get free. "No, I'm sorry, Davey lad, but I can't let you go out there too."

"But Priss is g-g-g - "

"Priss is old enough to make her own decisions," said Kate, coming up behind Tom and putting a consoling hand on Davey's arm. "That's no reason for you to get into trouble as well."

"But you were just saying a few minutes ago she's only a kid! Can't you m-m-m - " Davey took a breath, "make up your m-m-m-mind?"

"Davey," said Kate, surprised and reproachful. "That's not very nice, is it? I'm only looking after you."

Davey looked hard at Kate. "Are you?"

"Well, of course I am!"

"You're not just, you know, trying to get rid of Priss because she um, you know, *knows* something about, um - "

"Do you honestly think, that I'd actually *want* Priss to go charging off into the night and get attacked?"

"Killed, you mean, it wouldn't attack her, it would kill her."

"*Killed*, then, by a wild animal? What's the matter with you? What have I done to make you and Priss hate me so much?"

"I don't hate you! I just - "

"Just what?"

He just knew that, however much he wanted it to be true, there was no such thing as Paradise. He just knew there had to be a good reason – or more accurately, a bad one – for two adults to hide themselves away like this, in an empty house in the country. He just knew it wasn't natural for those two adults to welcome in the children of strangers as calmly, as effortlessly as he and Priss had been welcomed; like an act of atonement. He just knew there had been something strange and false about Kate's smoothly-executed persecution of Priss in the kitchen just now. He just knew that Priss had, in fact, been onto something.

He considered telling them all of that, but it seemed far too complicated, and besides, he was tired and unhappy, and he wasn't sure he would be able to get the words out. He glanced at Isaac, who had crept in behind Kate. When Davey caught his eye, he raised an eyebrow. Not for the first time, he wondered if Isaac actually had the power of telepathy. The message arrived in his head as cleanly and simply as a letter dropping onto a doormat.

Come on, then. What are you going to do?

He took a deep breath, and then, just as Priss had done, he bolted for the door.

Tom leapt after him, but for once Davey's youth was on his side, and he easily evaded him. The gravel crunched beneath his shoes as he ran, but he could hardly hear it for the humming in his ears. Would a wild animal come this close to the house? Surely not. It would be in the woods if it was anywhere, maybe lying peacefully on a branch, just waiting for someone to walk beneath a tree and provide an easy meal.

He rounded the corner of the house. Now there was soft grass under his feet, smelling bewitchingly clean and fresh. He wished he could simply enjoy the pleasure of being out in the darkness. Across the lawn, trees loomed like sculptures.

"Priss?" he whispered, then realised that was ridiculous, she would be way ahead of him by now. "Priss?" he called, louder. Would the sound of his voice attract the panther, or frighten it off? He began to make his way through the trees.

The woods looked totally different by night, and they smelled different too, wilder and more earthy, leaf mould tickling in his nostrils, unidentifiable stuff squelching under his feet. He wondered for a wild moment if the entire landscape had somehow been replaced. How was he ever going to find his way? Someone who knew what they were doing would be able to follow the signs of Priss' reckless passage, but someone who knew what they were doing would probably have stopped to grab a torch first. He thought about going back, but the prospect of having to face Isaac's cool, amused stare and admit that yes, he'd got this far, but then turned back because it was dark and scary, seemed somehow even more unbearable than going on.

What was it with Isaac, anyway? It was ridiculous the way he never spoke, probably the most pretentious affectation he'd ever come across in his life. Unless he couldn't speak, of course, there was always that. Or unless he had some sort of social phobia and just didn't dare - but then there was the way he always seemed to be everywhere, watching everyone, and those sly little drawings, and the way he clearly knew Kate from a previous life but wouldn't share anything he knew. And what was the deal with the tent, why was he so unhappy about being in the house? It was like he believed Priss' stupid theory about the house being haunted -

Besides, wasn't Isaac his rival for Priss' affections? He had often seen Isaac looking at Priss appreciatively. Of course, she was unbelievably, scarily beautiful, easily the most physically perfect girl he'd ever seen in his life. And Isaac was an artist. Maybe it was just that. But then, who wouldn't fancy Priss? The important thing was whether Priss fancied him back. Surely he, Davey, was a better prospect than a man Isaac's age.

Feeling cross about Isaac's peculiarities distracted him enough to make his way into the heart of the woods, and then to get himself thoroughly lost and disoriented. Guided by the small amount of moonlight that filtered grudgingly in through the trees, he cast around for a while, whispering Priss' name occasionally in the vain hope that she would hear him, until he fell heavily over a fallen branch.

As he sat swearing quietly under his breath and trying to work out if he had cut his leg or merely bruised it, from somewhere behind him came a terrible, inhuman scream of triumph. It coiled up into the night sky like smoke, chilling him to the bone. As it faded, he found he had leapt to his feet, clutching a half-rotted wooden branch in his hand.

Priss, he thought, *I'm sorry, I'm so sorry, I'm so useless I should have, I wish -*

Was there any chance Priss was still alive?

And who had screamed? Was it Priss, as she died? Or was it the panther, having killed her?

He blundered through the trees in the direction of the sound, aware this was possibly the most insane thing he could be doing, but unable to stop himself. Sweat dripped down his back. He could actually smell it, sour and unpleasant, and realised this was the smell of fear, this was what people talked about when they told him that their scary dogs could smell he was frightened, and that's why they were reacting so badly to him. He wondered if the sound would have carried as far as the house; if the three who remained there, cowering behind the closed doors, would have heard the sound of the panther's successful hunt.

As he pushed through the tough curtain of rhododendron branches, he realised that he had, after all, been on the right track. He was on the far side of the little clearing - he must have actually stumbled past it. There was the little cluster of rowan trees that grew in a tight clump near the doorway to the panther's cage. Up ahead was the huge tree with branches like a Menorah, where he and Priss had sat that lazy afternoon. Which meant that right ahead of him must be the clearing where he had seen Isaac lay flowers.

The ground beneath the tree was disturbed, as if an almighty fight had taken place there. No, it was more than disturbed, it was *dug up*. Something had been digging in the ground. There were leaves and greyish-brown sticks scattered all around.

"Priss," he croaked.

"Right here, you wanker," said her voice, from behind him.

Hardly believing it, he turned around. Her beautiful face was streaked with dirt and her hair was full of leaves, but she was alive.

"Maybe you're not such a pussy after all," she said. "Did anyone else come after me?"

"No, just me, I think, what was that awful noise?"

Priss looked bewildered. "What awful noise?"

"That scream, you must have heard it. It was like - "

"No-one screamed, soft lad." Priss paused. "Well, okay, I might have yelled a bit when I found it."

"Found what?"

Priss' face was white and triumphant. How could she possibly have made that noise? How could that sound have come out of her and she still be alive afterwards? He suddenly noticed she had one hand behind her back.

"Don't freak out, okay?"

Slowly, Priss brought her hand out from behind her.

She was holding a human skull.

chapter fourteen (then)

Like Saul, he could pinpoint the exact moment of his revelation. It was Vespers on the longest day of the year, and the sunlight and the soft singing created a dreamy peace so enveloping it felt like drowning. He closed his eyes and waited for the moment when he would feel the presence of the Divine passing among them.

What came instead was like cold clean air on his face. *But there's nothing here,* he thought. *It's all a lie.*

His name at birth was James Michael Hurst, part of a nice, well-to-do, moderately observant family near Halifax. Church was part of the fabric of the year, like school sports day and the town carnival; not his favourite, but not horrible either, just something you did because everyone else did too.

At fifteen, his feelings changed. Overnight, church became significant, meaningful, desirable. He attended assiduously, and joined the Young Voices bible study group. He was aware of his parents discussing it ("Is it *normal?*" "Oh, come on, love, it's not like he's out drinking and raising Hell, he's only at the church after all." "Yes, I know it's just a bit strange for a fifteen year old, that's all.") and wondered if they'd be more or less reassured if they knew the reason.

There was a girl in the study group called Eleanor. She was slender and dark, subtly beautiful, subtly enchanting. All by themselves, beneath the cover of the study group, she and he staged a quiet teenage rebellion. They borrowed the library books their parents wouldn't approve of – *The Shining, The Thorn Birds, The Amityville Horror* – and exchanged them at the coffee-break. She lent him the albums she loved in secret, *Damned Damned Damned* and *SAHB Stories* and *Lust for Life* and *Violet Hour*, bought with babysitting money and hidden from her parents. Walking home from study group, they found a quiet place behind some bushes in the park where they could lie on the damp, mossy ground. Her breasts were firm beneath his fingers, her nipples tender and rosy. When she murmured with pleasure, he felt that murmur travel through his chest and into his groin. Her hand pressed shyly against him for an instant and he heard himself groan, felt himself press forward into her palm.

October brought sixteenth birthdays and a torn sheet of newsprint.

"He's touring *Violet Hour*," she said. "Look. April next year. The Phoenix in London."

"That's Easter Study week," he said. "We'll be down there. We'll actually be in London."

They looked at each other.

It was only because their public personas were so faultless that they got away with it, but get away with it they did. They crept out via the hotel fire exit, navigated the tube, found their way to the Phoenix (the easiest part - follow the crowds and the screams). They shared a flask of Ribena laced with a nip of everything from her father's drinks cabinet and lost themselves in the pure beauty of the music.

Afterwards, Eleanor insisted on trying to get backstage. Somehow they did that too, slipping past harassed doormen who had far too many people to cope with and not enough support.

The noise was incredible, a continuous inarticulate wailing he could hardly believe was coming from people. Angry, sweaty roadies carried amps and speakers off the stage and out of the doors. A man in a duck egg blue suit with no tie and his shirt open at the neck beckoned girls out of the crowd with an imperious finger. They were crushed and pushed and jostled. Eleanor was beside him, then suddenly she wasn't. Had she been summoned to join that line of girls?

"Jesus fucking Christ." A man's voice behind him.

He'd never heard the words *Jesus* and *fucking* spoken together before, and he was surprised by his own outrage. When he turned around, the man behind him looked familiar.

"Sorry," the man said.

"It's okay."

"Just out of interest, which was worse? *Fucking*, or *Jesus*?"

"Um, both - "

"Sorry," the man repeated. He shook his head dazedly. "It's just, I'd never really - does this look as utterly fucking awful to you as it does to me?"

"Erm, I'm just looking for my girlfriend, she's in there somewhere, oh, she's there." The man in blue was beckoning Eleanor through the crowd, pointing towards the end of the growing queue of girls.

"Your girlfriend." The man followed Tom's gaze. "That's your girlfriend?"

"Yes, and I think I'd better go and get her - "

"Jesus God, how old are you both? Fourteen? Fifteen?"

"Sixteen! We're sixteen, we're old enough to be here - "

"Shit." The man's face was unhealthily pale and the pupils of his eyes were huge. "I'm so sorry."

"It's alright, I'm not a kid, I've heard people curse before."

"I wish cursing in front of a schoolboy was all I had to be sorry for. I never realised, I mean, I thought maybe they just sort of, oh, shit, if I'd known - "

The man in the blue suit was pacing out the line of girls, studying, examining. Behind them was a door stapled with a sheet of paper that said *Dressing Room*.

"Right," said the man with great decision. "That's it. Game over. Time to cash up." His smile was unexpectedly sweet. "And when you grow up, mate, you can tell everyone you were the very last person to speak to Jack Laker alive. Just try and be a better man than I was, okay?"

He had no idea how to respond, but it was too late anyway. Jack was disappearing through the crowds, head down, shoulders hunched, unmemorable, like a man who had willed himself to become invisible.

"I love you," he breathed in her ear, as they lay wrapped in each other's arms, their clothes scattered on the hotel room floor.

"I love you too," she whispered back.

"I'm sorry," he said a month later. She cried, which felt bad. But he couldn't ignore the command laid on him. Seven words, spoken by a man lost and frantic, a man who was carried unconscious from a sordid hotel room six hours later. A man who might well be dead now. *Be a better man than I was.* A strange way to hear the call, but then what way wouldn't be?

"What did I do wrong?" she asked. "Was it because I wouldn't - "

"No! No."

"What, then?"

"I think I have to be a priest," he said. It was the first time he'd spoken the words out loud.

His family were baffled, briefly angry, then proud and resigned. He obtained the recommendations he needed. Seminary was hard work but satisfying. He waited patiently to discover God's plan. Almost on a whim, he made a retreat to an Abbey in Hertfordshire.

At the age of thirty-one, he became Brother Andrew.

Then, on 21st June more than two decades later, Brother Andrew quietly and painlessly died. The man who raised his head in the church and thought: *But there's no-one listening. There really is no-one listening,* was someone entirely new.

He did the things they all did when their faith was weak, and he did them many times over. It was like trying to make himself believe in Father Christmas. The door in his head had opened and he'd walked into a new place. There was no going back. The year rolled on; the garden disappeared back beneath the ground, the swallows flew south, the frosts and the robins came. The Abbey was cold, and the light grey. His faith did not return.

In the spring, he thought. He loved the slow triumphant swell of returning life as the year turned towards Easter, the terrible mystery of the Passion and the glory of the Resurrection. This year, he looked at the crucifix above his bed and thought, *You poor bastard. You poor, poor, lonely bastard, dying up there alone and in agony for what you thought was true.* Easter Sunday came and they sang the hymns of Resurrection, and he thought: *This is a lie.*

The pressure of pretending was becoming unbearable, but to his angry bafflement, no-one seemed to notice. In the enforced intimacy of their daily lives, how could these other men not see that he was in Hell?

And yet, he was desperate to contain the impurity within him. His greatest terror was that he would share his doubt (he called it *doubt*, although it felt exactly like *superior knowledge*) with the others, and they'd see he was right. What if he did that? What would happen then? What if he single-handedly brought down the community?

Time crawled on, hour after hour, day after day. This must be how a bad marriage must feel, twin demons of Guilt and Loathing tearing at your insides every minute. He fantasised about going to the Abbot. *I've lost my faith. I need to leave. Let me go to Rome so I can make my plea for laicisation.* He never got further than the door of his cell. How could he look into the face of a man he had worshipped alongside for so many years and admit it was all a lie?

A rainy October Sunday; the end of harvest, the smell of bonfires in the air. If he was free to choose, he would have spent the day in the garden, letting the rain soak into him while he put things to bed for the winter, but of course he was not free. He made the rounds of the Abbey before Vespers, making sure everything was secure. He had to smile at the irony of a man locking the door to his own prison.

As he squatted to shoot the bolt on the door to the outside world, someone knocked on the other side of it.

"Yes," he said cautiously.

"I, um - "

It was a man's voice, strained and exhausted.

Like all religious institutions, they attracted their share of the wanderers, the lost and the mentally ill. There were clear policies for this, balancing compassion and charity with personal protection.

Fuck that, he thought, relishing the strong Anglo-Saxon sound reverberating in his head like a sword dropped on stone. He unbolted the door.

The man on the doorstep was thin, tired, and soaking wet. He wore a t-shirt, jeans and flip-flops and had a canvas bag and a guitar slung over his shoulder. They gazed at each other in perplexed silence.

"Hi," said the man on the doorstep at last. "I'm really sorry, I don't know the right way to, um, address you." He held out a hand and then dropped it. "Christ, is it even okay to shake your hand? Sorry, I didn't mean to start out by blaspheming. I'm not usually this uncouth, it's just been kind of a bad night and - "

"Do you need help?"

"I was wondering if I could spend the night in the church," said the man on the doorstep.

"You mean you want to make a retreat? There's a procedure - "

"Actually I was just looking for shelter for tonight. I don't know if that's allowed?"

Despite the clothes, the man didn't look homeless. There

was a certain bone-deep grubbiness that came after a while, a stain that nothing but the confidence of a roof over your head seemed to scrub off.

You're supposed to be back in your cell. You're supposed to be asleep. This isn't your job. You're supposed to pass this along.

"Why not?" he said, and held the door open.

The presence of the forbidden visitor was like a klaxon screaming. Any minute now they'd come boiling out of their cells and bombard him with questions. And then what? Time to own up? Maybe they'd throw him out. Or maybe they'd just turn on him and kill him. That might be a relief – his own shame washed out by the tidal wave of someone else's crimes – but no-one came to investigate. No-one heard the creak of the Abbey door. He closed it carefully behind them, and guided the pale and shivering visitor into the nearest pew.

"Sorry," the strange man muttered. "It's just been a - "

"Don't apologise."

"Thanks so much for letting me in. You don't have to stay, I'm sure you've got better things to do."

Even without Seminary training, he would have recognised the desperate plea for someone to talk to.

"No, I don't," he said. "I'll get some food and keep you company for a bit. Can I ask your name?"

The man's smile stirred a sense of memory within him.

"I'm Jack."

When he returned – still amazed at the ease with which he had smuggled a stranger into a closed monastic community – Jack was gazing up at the exquisitely painted ceiling. When he turned around, his face was awed.

"How did they do that?" he asked.

"It's egg tempera and gold leaf."

"But how did they *do* it? I mean, they were just normal blokes, right? They didn't pick you to be a monk because you were good at art, did they? So how did they make something so beautiful?"

"Are you an artist?"

"No, I don't paint."

"But you're a musician," he said. It was a statement, not a question. He already knew who he was talking to.

"Well, yeah. I am."

What did it mean that this man had come back into his life, now, at this moment? Did it mean anything at all? Or was it just an enigmatic coincidence?

"Are you working at the moment?"

Jack's shoulders slumped in what could have been defeat, or relief. He reached for the canvas bag by his feet. Without speaking, he unpacked six bottles of vodka and a cornucopia of pill bottles brimming with vivid, gleaming capsules.

"My major occupations right now," he said, "are Not Drinking, and Not Taking Pills. Not exactly productive, but, you know. And today, today - "

He saw Jack's shoulders heave. "It's alright," he said softly.

"I just don't know how much longer I can do this," Jack managed, and buried his head in his hands.

He waited patiently for Jack to speak again.

"There was a girl I loved," Jack said at last.

"What was her name?"

"Mathilda."

The syllables hung in the air.

"And what happened?" he prompted at last, since Jack seemed to have run out of words.

"It was my fault," said Jack. "I fucked it up. But she was the one, you know?"

"How long has it been?"

"She was the one," Jack repeated, not appearing to hear the question. "Until I met her, I never thought that was real, but she was. I met her one night in my garden, and that was it, I was gone."

There was grey in Jack's hair, and the lines on his face

were not all from exhaustion and cold. *We've both grown old,* he thought.

"It's still all for her, you know? Every song I wrote, every tour I put together, all for her, trying to be the man she'd have wanted. I've written whole albums for her, for what we had, for the life we should have lived, if I hadn't - " He took a deep breath. "My entire career since then has been like a massive exercise in necromancy."

So she died.

"You know that feeling, when there's something you love so much, you just have to make it yours? All yours and nobody else's? Whatever the cost?" He shook his head. "I'm sorry, I'm sure *you* don't. I'm sure you're a much better man than I am."

I tried to be. "I'm just as flawed as anyone else," he said out loud.

"I seriously doubt that. Not many people would take in a total stranger and let him ramble on like this."

"How long is it since you and she - ?"

"More than twenty years."

"So why's she haunting you now?"

"It was at a gig," Jack said. "There was a girl in the front row."

He waited patiently, knowing each confession had its own rhythm. He was good at this. They all were.

"She was wearing a green dress," Jack said. "A sea of denim, and this one girl in green. They say it's unlucky, don't they?"

"Do they?"

"See, I do know how unbelievably fucking lucky I am. I really do. I get sackfuls of fan mail. I was rich before I was thirty. But what's the point? What's it for?"

"So you brought your problems to God?" *Who isn't listening because he isn't even there.*

"Not really," Jack admitted. "I actually don't believe. I'm so sorry. But I couldn't face Rehab and my sponsor relapsed three months ago and my manager would only tell me to get laid, and I thought a man of God might just be the only other person who'd take me in. I'm the biggest fucking hypocrite in the world, and I'm taking complete advantage of your good nature. You can throw me out if you want to."

He hesitated. "Actually," he said slowly, "I don't believe either. Not any more. I lost my faith. And now I don't know what to do."

The blood throbbed through the chambers of his heart. Silence pressed heavily against his eardrums.

"I just realised I don't know your name," said Jack, sounding dazed. "I'm really sorry. I want to help but I don't know what to call you."

"I don't know what to tell you. They called me Andrew, but he's gone now. I suppose I need a new name."

"And how long have you, um, known?"

"A year. Longer. Long enough to be sure."

"Have you said anything?"

"What is there to say?"

"That's a hell of a thing to live with. What are you going to do?"

"I have no idea," admitted the man who used to be Brother Andrew.

"You could leave, though, right?"

"I'm not a prisoner. But I made a promise. It's like getting married. Is it fair to bail out just because you're unhappy?"

"Haven't you already broken it, though?"

"It's not just that," he admitted. "I haven't been out in the world for decades, literally decades. I have no money, no family, no friends. Where would I go? What would I do when I got there? I'm sorry. I'm supposed to be helping you."

"No," Jack protested. "I just wish there was something - I could offer you a drink?"

Their laughter sounded thin and light in the vastness of the vaulted air.

"You know," said Jack, "I have this house in the West

Country. I haven't been there in years. I just walked out the front door and left it. Never went there again."

"Why?" He suspected he already knew the answer.

"It's where - where we lived. We had one summer together. I don't think I'll ever go back there. But you could."

"Sorry, what?"

"If you need somewhere to go. Christ knows what state it's in by now, but the power's still on, and the water, and it's totally safe, or at least - no, it should definitely be safe by now." The oddness of the phrase was striking, but Jack was still speaking. "If you want to, you're welcome. Stay as long as you like. No-one'll bother you."

"I couldn't possibly - "

"You get the train from Paddington," said Jack. "Change at Truro. Then you get the ferry - "

"I really can't," he said. The prospect of freedom made his head swim. "But thank you. You're very kind."

"I've got a lot to make up for," said Jack.

Later he leaned against a pillar and watched Jack sleeping with his head on the empty rucksack. An unpleasant thought burrowed at the back of his mind.

Of course there was no way to tell by looking. It was at once the oldest and most amateur of crimes, and it left no mark on those who committed it. And it was more difficult to be objective because he actually liked Jack. He didn't want to believe it could possibly be true.

He awoke a few hours later in a panic, it was nearly four o'clock, time for Vigils, and found he was alone. There was no sign of Jack, or the rucksack, or the guitar, or the vodka, or the pills. The blanket had been wrapped awkwardly around him, and when he stood, a piece of coloured cardboard, plumped around a roll of ten-pound notes, fell from its folds.

He was holding the inlay card from a cassette. On the front, a painting of a house, seen from a distance and in darkness, a single rosy lamp glowing in a high window. The dimensions of the cassette didn't suit it; the image felt hemmed in from the sides, as if it longed to breathe. The words *Jack Laker* and *Landmark* were crammed around the edges like an afterthought. He turned the card over and found the note.

I meant it. The house is yours if you want it. Here's a picture of it someone did for me once. It looked better on the vinyl. Thanks for keeping me sane and sober.
Jack
PS You look like this guy I knew years ago called Tom.

And below, a scribbled list of directions that leaped out at him in confusing bursts:
Paddington - change at - ferry to - up the street - key's underneath the -
And one more strange command:
Be careful in the woods.

chapter fifteen (now)

There was no question about it. No possible way it could be anything other than what it looked like. Davey had seen them before, of course, in cases in museums, shielded behind glass and silence. He had read little white cards explaining how information gathered from skulls could give important information about diet and nutritional status, the mystifying secrets that could be gleaned from this simple shard of bone.

But he had never until now considered that each skull had once been part of an actual human being. This wasn't some interesting relic somebody had carelessly broken one afternoon and then thrown away, like clay pots and worn-out scraps of fabric. This was the skull of a person who had once lived and breathed just as he did; and had then died, and been buried beneath a tree in someone's garden.

There were black spots dancing in front of his vision. He felt Priss grab him hastily.

"If you pass out, mate," she told him, "there's no way I can catch you even with two hands. Why don't you sit down or something?"

His knees folded beneath him and then he was sitting on the ground, which suddenly felt dirty and polluted. He glimpsed the thick crust of dirt on Priss' fingers, saw the glint of blood, black in the moonlight, where she had cut herself as she scrabbled furiously in the soil. How much of the muck on her hands was actually rotted human flesh? How could such a beautiful sanctuary contain such ugliness? His stomach lurched and he heard himself whimper. Priss slapped him hard on the arm.

"Give over," she ordered, and put the skull carefully on the ground before them. "I didn't want to find this, but I did, so there's no going back. We need to think, okay? We need to decide what we're going to do."

"What do you mean?" Davey asked faintly. "We just found a b-b-b-b - "

"Bacardi Breezer, bison, Bert Bacharach, Bavarian sausage, banyan tree, *no!* Sorry, I just can't help myself when I get nervous. A body, okay? I get it. We found a dead body."

"Was it - "

"Did it smell, you mean? No, it's just bones. Well, I'm saying that." Priss sniffed cautiously at her fingers. Davey struggled not to vomit. "No. Definitely just bones. So who do you think it is?"

"I don't know."

"Well, of course you don't fuckin' *know!*" Her fury took him by surprise; he had been too busy with his own terror and disgust to realise that she, too, was shivering with cold and tension. "But you could at least, you know, *speculate* a bit, right? We've got to decide what to do. We're out here in the cold with a dead body. There's three grown adults – well, okay, two grown adults and Isaac – back in the house. So we need a strategy. And that means we need a theory. So - " She poked thoughtfully at the skull with her foot. " - who do we think this is?"

Davey tried to focus on the skull in front of him. The expression 'Beauty is only skin-deep' had never seemed more apt. It was a hideous, ugly thing, blind empty eye sockets and yellowed teeth. He looked away again.

"It's got to be something to do with that fuckin' annexe," said Priss. "And those letters, and those two women, what were they called? Daphne and Miranda, or something?"

"Evie and Mathilda," said Davey, relieved to have something to contribute. "Where did you get Daphne from?"

"Probably the purple bikini," said Priss.

"Um - "

"Scooby Doo, you culturally-derelict twat. Maybe that Jack guy, maybe he killed one of them."

Davey tried to remember what he had read in the letter. In books and films, people always seemed to have perfect recall of any piece of information they were given. The plot frequently depended on it. He had often wondered what would happen in reality: policemen arriving, perplexed, at the wrong address because they'd heard *street* instead of *avenue*, codes forgotten or mistyped leading to endless Doomsday devices going off.

"Wasn't there something in there about one of them leaving him?" he asked. "And the other one was coming back from her holiday to c-c-comfort him - "

"Ha! To make her move on him, more like." Priss sniffed. "She must have really liked him to come all the way back from Greece just to hold his hand and listen to him sob into his beer about how special his girlfriend was." She began picking dirt from beneath her fingernails. "Maybe she killed him in a fit of jealous rage when he told her he wasn't interested."

"That's a bit extreme, isn't it?" It was easier to talk about possible motives than it was to actually look at the skull.

"Murder is extreme?" Priss laughed. "Hold the fuckin' press."

"Well yes I *know*, but would you kill someone just because they wouldn't s-s-sleep with you?"

"I might kill them if I thought they'd only done it out of loneliness." Priss grinned. "Or if they were a really crap shag."

"Don't make jokes like that," said Davey. "It's horrible."

Priss laughed scornfully. "How can you sit here with an actual murder victim in front of us and tell me off for bad-taste jokes? You'd want to get your priorities sorted. Maybe he'd already killed her, the other one I mean. And Daphne - "

"Evie - "

"And then maybe *Evie* helped him bury her out here."

"Only he was filled with remorse, and left," said Davey.

"Remorse." Priss savoured the word thoughtfully. "D'you think you could feel something as poetic as *remorse* for killing someone? It ought to be a bit more visceral than that. Besides, running away doesn't sound much like *remorse* to me. More like terror." She sighed. "Do you think running away is an inherent act of cowardice?" Davey swallowed uncomfortably. "No, don't answer that, since we've both done it." She looked at the skull gloomily. "For Christ's sake. What are we going to *do?*"

"I don't know," said Davey miserably.

"Yeah, I know you don't. You're no fucking use at all." Priss leaned against him affectionately. "You're quite warm, though."

This, he thought, was his cue to put his arm around her. That was the first move. Once you had your arm around her, you were halfway home. Then you could turn her face up towards yours and kiss her -

His arm hung uselessly from his shoulder like a huge slab of dead meat. *Just move,* he thought to it furiously, but he couldn't get the right neurons to fire up. *Just get on and move, she must think you're absolutely retarded.*

"Can you hear something?" asked Priss.

And now that he stopped to listen, he could. A slow rustling, a cracking of twigs, something shouldering its way towards them. He suddenly remembered the panther.

"Shit and corruption," breathed Priss. "What do we do?"

He was too terrified to think of an answer.

And then they saw a glimpse of torchlight, and Tom whispered, "Priss? Davey? Is that you?" and Tom and Isaac, pale and breathless, appeared through the trees.

Afterwards, Davey's memory of the return to the house was a slow, surreal nightmare. Branches clawed and clutched at them as they passed; shadows crouched everywhere, ready to spring. The wind rustled threatening branches on the edges of their vision. Priss stood in a rabbit hole, twisted her ankle and had to hobble the rest of the way clutching onto Davey for support, white-faced and speechless with pain. Isaac silently offered to take her other arm, but Priss looked at him in disbelief until he turned away again. And throughout it all, Tom marched silently behind them, staying a few paces back, as if either he or they were infectious, carrying his grim burden.

The house finally loomed up across the lawn. They could see Kate's silhouette against the light that streamed out from the French windows in the kitchen; she was pacing up and down, her arms wrapped tightly around her.

"What are we going to tell her?" Davey asked.

"Fuck, my ankle hurts," Priss muttered, biting her lip.

Tom said nothing, but merely gestured them all onwards. Kate saw them and threw the doors open wide. Isaac hesitated, then followed Priss and Davey over the threshold.

"Thank God you're alright," she said. "Thank *God*, I thought, oh my God, I thought when I heard that scream, Tom, what on earth, oh, *no* - "

"Is there somewhere I can put it?" said Tom. "I'm sorry, I know this is a terrible thing to ask, but is there a basket or something, something you won't want to use again - "

Kate groped blindly behind her and found a plate. She looked at it, then laughed hysterically. "Bring me the head of John the Baptist," she said, laughing and laughing. "Oh my God, this isn't funny, why can't I stop laughing? There must be something better, something more appropriate, somebody slap me, please, I think I'm going into hysterics here."

Isaac took the plate from Kate's hand and replaced it with a gardener's basket from beside the doors. Tom gratefully placed the skull in it, then immediately went to the sink and began to wash his hands, scrubbing hard at them with the stiff wire brush Kate used to clean potatoes. Kate pressed both her hands over her mouth to smother the awful, mirthless laughter and finally managed to force herself into silence.

"It must be an old one," she said at last, swallowing hard. "Bones last for centuries, don't they? It must be old, medieval maybe, or Tudor, there have been people living here for thousands of years - "

"It's not thousands of years old," said Priss wearily.

"We don't know that," said Davey.

"Yes, we do."

"How do we know?" he asked. "It might have been there for centuries, it really might have."

"A body buried in a shallow grave decomposes in just a few years," said Priss. "The bones last about another fifty. If it had been there for centuries I wouldn't have found even dust, never mind bare bones."

"How would you even know that?" asked Davey weakly.

"Because I'm the fucked-up product of the digital information age," said Priss. "I know all sorts of awful shit. You wouldn't believe some of the stuff I've got in my head." She limped painfully to a chair and lowered herself into it.

"What happened to your ankle?" Kate knelt at her feet. "Priss, this looks like a sprain. Sit still and I'll get some cold wet cloths."

"Leave it," said Priss. "It's fine, *ow* it'll be fine if you stop doing that, anyway - "

"It's already swelling. If I don't wrap it, tomorrow morning you'll look like the Elephant Man. I know it'll hurt, but it'll only take a few minutes."

"Stop it!" Priss screamed.

Kate looked at her in astonishment. "Stop what?"

"Stop being so *nice!* Stop looking after all of us like you're all of our mothers fuckin' rolled into one, alright?"

"Priss, I know it hurts, but there's no excuse for - "

"I just turned up on your doorstep," Priss said. "I was going to kip in the shed for the night and then maybe break in the next day and nick anything worth selling, did you know that? And instead, you just came down the garden path and invited me in for lunch!"

Kate stood up and went over to the sink. Hunting in the cupboard, she found a clean cloth and began to fill a basin with cold water.

"You looked hungry," she said over her shoulder.

"I was! I was starving, I hadn't eaten in, like, eighteen hours! And you were like a dream come fuckin' true, alright, like something out of a fairy tale. Taking me in, making me feel at home. You can stay as long as you want, nobody minds. You and Tom, the pair of you, you never asked me where I'd come from, what I'd done, I mean, come on, right? A big deserted house, and two people who just *happen* to be living here, and just *happen* to be really happy with a couple of teenage randoms moving in with them. It doesn't take a fuckin' genius to figure that one out, does it? One of you killed him, or maybe you both did it together, or why else wouldn't you call the police when that beast turned up in the woods?"

"We didn't call the police because of *you*," said Tom, raising his voice so he could shout Priss down. "Because of you and Davey. You're obviously both on the run from something. If you must know, Priss, we thought maybe that was why you were hiding. Because the police were after you."

"Just me? Just because I'm from Liverpool and common as a Burberry pushchair in Starbucks? Not Posh Boy over there?"

"Well, aren't you on the run from the police?" said Kate, very gently. She had taken an ice-cube tray from the freezer compartment of the fridge and was dropping the cubes into the bowl of water one by one, slow and careful.

"Why the fuck would you think I was on the run from the police?"

"We found a car key in your room. And before you say anything, you're too young to drive at all. Let alone a top of the range Audi. We didn't call the police because we were trying to work out what to do."

There was a silence. Davey took a breath to say something, but Isaac grabbed his wrist and squeezed it sharply. When

226

Davey turned to him in surprised reproach, Isaac frowned and shook his head. Then he tapped his finger against Davey's wrist, where his watch should have been. *Later.*

"I don't believe you," said Priss at last. "I want to. Fuch me, but I want to, but I can't. One of you knows *something* about that body, I know it. Why else would you be so nice to Davey and me if you're not making up for something?"

"Priss," said Tom gently. "Did it never occur to you that maybe we just like you and we want to help?"

"The world doesn't work like that."

"Not always," Tom agreed, "but sometimes. Sometimes we see a fellow human being drowning, and we reach out a hand to pull them out of the water."

"Is that something the prison chaplain told you?" said Priss. "Don't even pretend you weren't inside, you bastard, because I know, I *know* - "

"Okay," said Tom.

"No," said Kate. "No, you don't have to, *you don't have to* - "

"I was behind walls for more than three decades," said Tom steadily, "but not the way you think. I was a monk, Priss. I was a monk, and then one day I lost my faith and I wasn't a monk any more, and I didn't know what I was going to do. Then ten months ago, a stranger gave me a way out. He came to me for help, but he ended up helping me. He's a musician called Jack Laker and he owns this house, and he said I could come and stay here if I wanted to. Maybe he made that offer to Kate too, I don't know, I've never asked." He glanced at Kate, but she was still busy with the cloth, cutting it into strips with kitchen scissors and then meticulously submerging each strip in the bowl of icy water. "I don't know where Jack is right now, but it's definitely not his body buried out there in the woods, Priss, I promise you."

Priss was staring at him as if the universe had just tilted on its axis. "Jack Laker? Are you serious?"

"Do you think I'd make this up?"

"Do you know who he is?"

"Yes, he's a musician! He gave me money and directions to get here, he wrote them on the inlay card of one of his albums, look - "

Tom fumbled in the pocket of his jeans and unfolded a worn oblong of cardboard. Davey felt his spine crawl with recognition. He glanced at Priss. Her face was perfectly expressionless; the look he suspected she hid behind when something happened that had moved her too profoundly to be shared with the world.

"And this is really his house," she said.

"Yes, he told me - "

"He told the whole bloody world," she said. "Every nerdy arty kid for the last thirty years has had a copy of that album cover on their wall. I can't believe I didn't - " she shivered. "Fuch me, I really thought - "

Kate smiled. "That I'd done him in? Or that Tom had? Well, I hope you aren't too disappointed. Now, are you going to let me bandage that ankle or not?"

Her right ankle was twice the size of her left, and she winced and swore when Kate touched it. The silence as Kate bandaged it lay over them all like snow.

"I do *want* to believe you, you know," Priss whispered as Kate lowered her ankle gently to the floor. "I don't actually *want* to think you're a murderer."

"Well, that's something, I suppose." Kate reached up and took a leaf out of Priss' hair. She flinched away, but then let her do it. Her eyes were filled with tears. "Now I think we should all go to bed, and talk about this in the morning, don't you?"

Priss wiped her eyes with the back of her hand, leaving a streak of dirt across her cheekbone.

"We can't just walk away from this, you know. You can't fix everything with fresh bread and bandages. Some poor bastard died, and whoever it is, they deserve a hearing."

"I swear to you, Priss, I'm not trying to walk away from

anything. But we're all tired and cold and we're not going to get anything done tonight."

"We could call the police tonight."

"Is that really what you want? With you still on the premises?"

Priss looked at Kate in despair. "Why are you doing this?" she asked. "Really? Just tell me. Are you taking care of me because you're some sort of fuchin' saint on earth? Or are you doing it so I'll feel guilty and not dob you in to the coppers after all? Which is the real you?"

"I'm just myself," said Kate. "I'm me. I'm not a saint, but I'm not a murderer either. I know you want there to be a simple explanation, but this is real life. Sometimes life is just a whole lot of stuff that happens, just one thing after another, and then suddenly you're at the end of it all thinking, *so, what the hell was that all about?*" She held out an arm. "Come on. I'll help you up to bed."

Priss opened her mouth to protest, then closed it again. Davey watched silently as Priss, Tom and Kate left the kitchen. He listened to them climbing the stairs, Priss' progress heavy and reluctant, followed by Kate's light, even footsteps and then Tom's slower, firmer tread.

He made sure the door to the kitchen was shut, and then he turned to Isaac, who was sitting silently at the table, just waiting for the time to pass until he and Davey were alone. *Like a condemned prisoner,* Davey thought, although he had no idea how a condemned man would behave in real life.

"It was you, wasn't it," he said sadly to Isaac, and sat down opposite him at the table.

Isaac, naturally, didn't say anything. He just looked questioningly at Davey and waited for him to continue.

"I saw you that afternoon," he said. "That afternoon when you put flowers under the tree. On her grave, I suppose. You killed her, didn't you? That's why you went to visit the grave. To say sorry."

Silence.

"You and Kate know each other from - from before," he said. "Of course, you don't ever speak, so we've never had to hear you get her name wrong, but she's not called Kate at all, is she? She's really called Evie, isn't she? That girl who was in love with Jack. We found some letters and a photograph of her up in the annexe. I don't know why Priss didn't recognise her, I noticed it at once. Her hair is shorter now, but it's still the same colour. That's where you two know each other from."

Isaac's face was in shadow; Davey had no way of telling what he thought about all of this. He ploughed desperately on.

"The body was that woman called Mathilda," he said. "That's what happened to her, isn't it? The girl Jack was in love with. Maybe you made it look like an accident, but you killed her. Jack helped you hide the body, before Evie got back from Greece. That's why he left afterwards and never came back. And poor Kate, Evie I mean, she's been waiting here all this time waiting for him to come back one day, except he never *is* coming back, is he, because he knows what's out there and he can't bear to be near the house where you k-k-k-killed his g-g-g-girlfriend!"

He paused dramatically, convinced that at last, in this final extremis, Isaac would finally speak, but Isaac remained stubbornly silent.

"You're not even going to deny it, are you? Oh my God, I'm right, aren't I?" Davey felt a vast, hollow triumph open up inside his chest. "I'm right! You did kill her! Jesus God, you killed her, and it's not just that, is it? It's not just that poor lady out there in the woods, it's Jack and Evie too. You're the reason they never got together, because he left before she got here, and she's been here ever since. The only thing I can't work out is why you ever came back here."

Silence.

"No, hang on," said Davey, breathless. "That's why you've been sort of hanging around me and Priss, and giving us all these little hints. You sort of w-w-w-w-wanted us to find it, and sort of didn't. Because you know what you did, don't you? You know how terrible it was."

Silence.

"Or is it because you l-l-l-like Priss? I've seen you looking at her. Well, she's n-n-n-n-not interested in you, okay? It's absolutely dis-dis-dis-disgusting the way you fawn over her. She's young enough to be your daughter, you know, it's vile for you to even be thinking of her like that. And it's not just because I l-l-l-like her, I do like her, of course I d-d-do, but I'm not stupid enough to think that means she has to like me in return - " he stopped, grabbed the light that hung low over the table, and angled it towards the other side of the table. "Are you, are you laughing at me?"

Isaac put up one hand to shield his eyes from the brightness. The corners of his eyes were creased with mirth and, despite his best efforts, his mouth turned irresistibly up at the corners.

"How can you possibly be laughing? What part of this is funny? What's the matter with you?" Isaac's shoulders were shaking. Davey felt a cold spasm of terror clutch as his stomach. *This is real,* he realised. *I'm in a deserted country house with a murderer, and now he knows I know.* "Look, I'm sorry, maybe I shouldn't have said anything, we can talk about this. No, don't, stop it, *stop it - "*

Isaac was making his way around the table towards Davey, still laughing. Davey retreated. Isaac was going to attack him; Isaac, possibly, was going to kill him, and then melt away into the velvet night outside. He knew he should defend himself, it was ridiculous for someone his size to be such a coward, but the mechanics of hitting anyone, even in self-defence, even when in fear of his life, simply eluded him, all he could do was back away. He retreated across the kitchen, holding his hands uselessly out in front of him. Isaac was still coming towards him, still laughing. Davey felt the edge of the worktop against his back and realised he had run out of kitchen. *Why didn't I go towards the door instead?*

Isaac was right in front of him now. He effortlessly seized Davey's hands in his own and forced Davey's arms down by his sides.

"Don't - " said Davey, pointlessly, and closed his eyes.

And then, instead of the blow he'd been expecting, he felt Isaac's mouth settle over his, and his entire body fell into a sweet and utter stillness. Isaac's tongue slipped between his teeth. He could still feel the quiver of laughter in Isaac's chest. He felt his knees buckling treacherously beneath him, and was grateful for the support of the worktop.

"Don't," he said weakly, when he could breathe again. Isaac moved obligingly back, leaving a courteous distance between them. He could hear his own pulse thumping in his ears. Isaac waited to see what Davey would do next.

There was an invisible hand in the small of his back, pushing him forward. Someone else had taken over his body, Priss was right, this was a ghost story after all, he was being haunted, possessed, taken over. Someone else was making him reach out and take Isaac's hand in his, caress those crisp dark curls shot through with grey. This wasn't what he wanted, it was Priss he wanted, in fact he thought he might even be in love with her. This was someone else's wishes and desires. Someone else put his arms around Isaac's waist.

No, he thought in amazement. *It's me. Of course it's me. This is me. I'm doing all of this. This is who I am.*

Isaac led the way to Davey's bedroom and closing the door behind them, he gently pulled Davey – shivering with desire – onto the bed and closed the curtains around them. The world around them was shut out and they were enveloped in a dark and private space where there was no sight, only an abundance of touch and sound and scent and taste. When Davey laid his hand flat against Isaac's chest, he felt again the quiver of his silent laughter.

chapter sixteen (then)

Naked and content, Priss lay on Mark's bed with her eyes half-shut, basking in the sunshine. Mark lay beside her and watched her greedily. Priss was studying the cover of the CD that played in the background. The proportions were right, but the image – a house with a rosy light burning in a high window – looked as if it had been designed for a larger space, like the vinyl covers Mark had framed on his wall.

"If we got caught," she asked at last, "what d'you reckon we'd be in the most trouble for? Bunking off, or having sex?"

Mark considered this for a while. "Having sex, probably."

"Why? If you bunk off enough they get the law on your parents. You'd think that's the thing that'd annoy them more, right?"

"We're underage," Mark pointed out.

"Only just. What's going to happen in the next - " she counted on her fingers " - the next seven weeks that means we're magically allowed to shag?"

"I wonder how much we're allowed to do *before* then?" asked Mark, getting interested. "How far can we go before we're officially breaking the law?"

Priss rolled over and rested her chin on his chest.

"I don't know. I always just assumed it was, you know, the actual deed. It's all meant to stop you knocking me up, isn't it?"

"So if I get you off and you get me off, but I don't put it in you, then we're in the clear?"

Priss laughed. "I suppose so."

"Yeah, well, that's not what they said in PSD. It's all supposed to be about emotional maturity and stuff."

"*And stuff?*" Priss looked scornful. "Are you, like, totally going Valley Boy on me?"

"We need to be sure we're ready for the emotional side of physical intimacy. Mrs Alsop said it so it must be true, right?"

"So basically they're, like, the orgasm police?"

"I wonder which is worse," said Mark thoughtfully. "Getting each other off but not doing it properly, or doing it but neither of us comes?"

"Depends what you mean by worse, I suppose."

"How about if we do it and one of us comes but not the other?"

Priss' smile was luminous. "Now that's a fuckin' crime, alright."

Davey sat in his bedroom holding the unopened envelope. He had never in his life felt such a profound peace. He had finally broken free. James could rant and storm all he wanted. This was it. This was freedom. The front door opened. He went downstairs to meet them.

But James stood alone in the hallway.

The man who had been Brother Andrew looked in the small shaving mirror he kept among his few, sparse possessions in the cell that had become his prison.

"Hello," he whispered to his reflection. "I'm Tom. Tom. I'm Tom. My name's Tom. Fine, thank you. I'd like to buy a railway ticket - "

No. He wouldn't need to give his name. All they'd be interested in was his money. And he shouldn't call it a *railway ticket*, he'd be buying it at a railway station. What other kind of ticket would it be? He thumbed through the money again. The notes looked different to how he remembered them. Of course, the bank notes must have been through several design changes since he'd last handled cash. Jack had given him six hundred and fifty pounds, an appalling amount of money. Would the train ticket cost that much? He had no idea.

"Tom," he murmured again, trying the name on for size. He wasn't sure if it was the name he would have chosen for himself, but then, how many people did get to choose their own name? Why should a failed monk be any different?

Priss rolled reluctantly off the bed, and stretched. "We should do some work, mate. We've not touched that last chapter for days. What? *What?*"

"You are so unbelievably sexy," said Mark huskily.

She grinned, and reached for a t-shirt. "You're not so bad yourself."

Mark glanced down at his thin, pale legs. "Don't take the piss."

"I'm not." Priss reached for the huge black art folder at the end of the bed. "Sexy's not the same as physically perfect, is it? It's about what's inside."

"The outside helps." Mark reached out an urgent hand and stroked her thigh. "Especially when - fuck, Priss, you're just lush."

"Fuck off and stop objectifying me."

"I'm not objectifying you, I'm giving you a compliment."

"No you're not. How would you like it if I only fancied you 'cos of that fuchin' contraption?" She gestured at the wheelchair that stood beside the bed.

He grinned. "And you're really hot when you're angry."

"Fucking give over, would you?"

"Look, I just really fancy you, alright? I see you naked and it turns me on! Massively! So shoot me for being a boy. I can't help it."

Priss looked remorseful. "I want to get this first draft finished, is all."

"Yeah, well, we can do that later, can't we? My mum's coming back in an hour." He hitched himself up to a sitting position and kissed Priss' navel.

"The quicker it's finished, the quicker we can get it sent off to a publishers and the quicker I can - "

"What?"

"Nothing."

Reluctantly, he stopped kissing her breasts. "You alright?"

"Fucking known for it. I'm just looking forward to not living with my dad."

"I don't get why finishing the book means you can - "

"New York, remember?"

"Oh yeah." He pulled Priss down onto the bed beside him. "What's the deal with your dad, anyway?"

"Nothing I can't handle."

"He's not, you know, like, hitting you, is he? Or um - "

"Look, he's not hitting me and he's not fiddling with me and it's none of your business anyway."

"I wish I could keep you safe, that's all."

"You?" Priss laughed. "You're no use to anyone. You're corrupting me sexually, you're interfering with my education for your own selfish pleasure, and every time I try and get some real work done you start distracting me." She pushed him onto his back, and climbed briskly on top of him. "It's a good thing you've got a big knob or I'd be running for the hills."

"I've sent your mother to get her hair done," James told Davey.

Davey felt the first stirrings of unease.

"Let's have a look, then." James held out his hand for the envelope. "You haven't even opened it. That confident, are you?"

Davey watched James' broad thumb slide beneath the flap of the envelope and remove the thin slip of paper.

There was an ominous pause.

"You did this on purpose," said James, his eyes fixed on the slip of paper. "You conniving little shit. You deliberately failed your exam."

"I - I - "

"*Don't* try and pretend you didn't. You're not stupid unless you want to be. This is worse than last time!"

Davey suddenly saw no point in pretending. "Yes," he said, and shrugged. "I did."

Going over the wall. The image implied something dramatic, exciting, requiring ropes and grappling irons, or at the very least torn-up bed sheets and a perilous descent from a window. But of course, none of that was really necessary. No-one was imprisoned here. Everyone had chosen the life they now lived. The wall existed only in his mind.

Nevertheless, it took another six weeks of agonising waiting – six weeks of nerving himself – six weeks of obsessing so painfully about the envelope stuffed full of banknotes that he was more convinced than ever that the love of money was, indeed, the root of all evil, before he was finally able to run. The moment arrived unexpectedly, one afternoon during the time set aside for private prayer and meditation. He was sitting on the edge of his bed, staring blindly at the crucifix on the wall, feeling the familiar misery folded around him like a blanket.

"So stop it," he said out loud. "Stop being miserable. Come on. Time to go."

And suddenly, astoundingly, it was possible. He was over the wall. Now all he had to do was to walk away.

He reached beneath his bed and found the envelope, taped carefully to the underside of the bed frame. He was afraid that if he looked back he would lose his nerve, so he simply walked out of his cell, leaving the door open behind him. His footsteps echoed in the stone corridor, but he knew no-one would disturb him.

On the doorstep, he hesitated. He wanted to go and say farewell to the garden, perhaps even to visit the bees and let them know what has happening but he recognised the impulse for what it was, the last spasm of procrastination, holding him back. The bees would be fine without him. The whole place would be fine without him. The men he was leaving would continue to make their prayers to the silent, empty places in the universe, a way of life that had made sense to him once, but no longer.

What would be the meaning of his life now?

He thought of the man he had seen in the dank, sweaty vestibule at the back of the Phoenix, of that same man stumbling in over the doorstep of a church. What if the purpose of his life was, after all, to help someone else?

Whatever you did, he vowed recklessly, *whatever you did, Jack, I'll keep your secret. You gave me my freedom. Now I'll give you yours. I'll guard your house for you. If I can stop it happening, they'll never find out what you did.*

It lacked the weight of the vows he had made as a young man, but what good had come of them? This was a burden he knew he could carry; the right payment for the freedom and the second chance he'd been granted. He walked down the dusty private road towards the smooth black tarmac that unwound like a ribbon, leading him out into the world.

It wasn't until the third car slowed, swerved and stopped, until the third window rolled down, until the third face looked out and asked if they could offer him a lift, they didn't normally pick up walkers but they figured they'd be safe with him, right? - that he realised he was still wearing his monk's habit.

The corridor outside the changing rooms was the usual chaotic riot. Miss Langland blew a sharp blast on her whistle, and the shrieks and curses and laughter mumbled to a reluctant silence, punctuated with an occasional giggle.

"Stop messing around and get changed," she ordered them briskly. "What's the matter with you? Sixteen years old, most of you are now, and you still haven't got the nous to get into your kits without me telling you? You're pathetic, the lot of you. Priss, where do you think you're going?"

"Taking Mark to the toilet, miss."

"He can take himself." Could he? They'd done their best with inclusion, but so far they'd been unable to organise a sports-friendly wheelchair. Instead, she and Mark had established a wordless *detente* where she turned a blind eye to him quietly wheeling himself down the corridor towards the library. Miss Langland still felt the occasional pang of guilt about this, but since neither Mark nor his mother had made any waves about it, the staffroom consensus had been that they could let things slide, on a sort of don't-ask-don't-tell basis.

"It's the building work, miss," said Priss. "He needs help to get the wheelchair past."

Miss Langland looked searchingly at Priss. Her face had that perfectly smooth and expressionless look that set alarm bells ringing.

"So can I go, miss?" asked Priss, meek and demure, eyes downcast.

Oh, for God's sake, thought Miss Langland wearily. *What the hell could she be getting up to with Mark Asher?*

"You come straight back here once you've taken him," she said.

"I'll need to wait till he's finished, miss. So he can get back."

"What? Oh, I suppose you will. Alright, then. But straight after that."

"Yes, miss."

"I'll check."

"Yes, miss."

She watched Priss all the way down the corridor. Everything about Priss' body language told Miss Langland the girl had just put one over on her. But, she thought again, what could she possibly be getting up to with Mark? After all, he was in a wheelchair, wasn't he?

As always, the blow seemed like the action of some unseen

spirit, rather than the fist of the man who stood before him in the hallway. Davey's ears rang. He shook his head to clear them.

"I did it on purpose," he repeated, tasting blood in his mouth. "I did it on purpose. I did it on p-p-p-p - " deep breath, " - I did it to make you listen! I'm not going to do Economics at university, I'm not g-going to come and work in your bloody bank, I'm n-n-n-n - "

He was flattened by a hailstorm of blows and kicks, a furious attack accompanied by an unearthly growling that was coming, it had to be, from his stepfather, but how could a human being make such a terrifying noise? It was like being savaged by a wild animal. He closed his eyes and tried to endure; to disappear; to hide in some secret part of his mind while his body underwent its inevitable, terrible punishment.

After refusing nineteen offers of a lift more or less on a reflex, he gave in and accepted the twentieth; an articulated lorry with a trailer so vast he couldn't begin to imagine what it contained. The logo on the side was a black West Highland terrier with a basket in its mouth, and the word *NETTO*. Some sort of pet food? He climbed into the cabin, taking a childish pleasure in his vastly increased height. The lorry driver seemed delighted with his capture of a genuine man of the cloth, and talked sporadically and at length about his life on the road, its trials and its unexpected benefits and finishing each disjointed anecdote with an apology for any offence caused.

In the nearby town, Tom slithered out at a traffic light, waved goodbye to the driver, and found a row of shops. The names were a mystery, conveying nothing beyond a general intention to sell him things, but he peered in through windows until he found what he was looking for - a charity shop, with racks of clothing laid out, in an approximation of attractiveness on ugly tubular display racks and mismatched hangers.

It was like walking into every church jumble sale from his childhood. He inhaled the scent of old clothes and books and felt dizzy. Who knew this was how freedom would smell? The three volunteers – two women in their fifties, who he'd expected, and a man in his twenties, who he hadn't – fell respectfully silent as he came in. He could feel their gaze moving over him like fingers. Hastily, he picked out trousers, a shirt, a pair of shoes. Took them to the counter.

"That's twelve twenty-five," said the woman, then hesitated. "Although since you're um - "

"No, I insist," said Tom, appalled. "Really." He thumbed through his envelope of cash, found a twenty pound note, handed it over.

"Well, if you're sure."

He glanced at the name on the plastic bag she was offering him. What on earth was Scope?

"Of course I'm sure," he said firmly. "Thank you very much."

"D'you know, I never knew - " the young man was looking at Tom's robes in fascination. "Doesn't it get really hot with real clothes on underneath?"

Did this man actually imagine he was wearing an entire other layer of clothing beneath his habit? Tom laughed. It felt good. It had been years since he'd last felt like it.

"Actually," he said, "it does. Thank you both, I'll maybe see you again soon."

Outside the shop, he inspected the handful of change: a note, five coins. The only one he recognised was the fifty pence piece. The others might as well have been from another country. Now he needed to change, but where? Were there still public toilets? What would happen if he went into a pub and tried to use the facilities? And what time did the pubs even open?

He was aware that he'd changed, deeply and utterly, from the man who had walked into the monastery decades ago. Nonetheless, he'd somehow imagined the world on the other side of the wall had remained mothballed. Staring at the mysterious assemblage of coins in his hand, he realised that he was a stranger, lost in a strange land. The thought was unquestionably thrilling.

He could go anywhere. He could do anything. And no-one, no-one would know.

He had to stop himself from skipping down the pavement.

When Davey opened his eyes again, he was lying on the hall floor. James stood over him, panting and flexing his fingers, perspiration turning him back into the malign giant who had haunted Davey's dreams since he was three years old.

"What have you got to say for yourself?" James demanded.

The word *sorry* fluttered automatically up to Davey's lips. For the first time in his life, he swallowed it.

"Did you ever think," he said instead, forcing the words out between swollen lips, "that maybe there's a bloody good reason Nature fixed it so you'd never get to be a real father?"

After that, James beat him until he lost consciousness.

"We'll have to be quiet," Priss whispered as Mark drew her onto his lap. His mouth was flushed and rosy. His hands fumbled for her breasts.

"You mean you'll have to be quiet," he whispered back. "You're the screamer, not me."

"Fuck off, I am not, ohhh - "

"Jesus, Priss, you feel so *good*."

Struggling for silence, they moved together in constrained ecstasy. On the other side of the wall of the disabled toilet, they could hear the headmaster Mr Yates tearing a clinically efficient strip off Dean Reynolds, who had apparently been caught selling speed at break time. Mouths pressed tightly together, they reached orgasm to the news that the police had been called and would be arriving in Mr Yates' office shortly.

Everything, everything felt different. The babies rode in prams like miniature space capsules and entered every shop ahead of their mothers, who wore tops like vests that showed smooth gold arms and shoulders and white linen trousers that showed the line of their underwear, and sunglasses perched on top of their heads. He didn't mean to stare – he didn't want to be conspicuous – but he couldn't help himself. The last time he'd taken any notice, mothers wore flowery frocks, babies waited outside, and people stopped to peer in and pat them on the heads like dogs.

About half the people he saw were busy with phones, either pressing them to their ear and chattering away to thin air, or weaving their way through the throngs of people while simultaneously tapping frantically away at the keys. Their progress was smooth and effortless; they never walked into each other, or collided with anything. How had they acquired this new skill? Could he do it too? Would he have to, in order to live in this world?

In the middle of a square, a huge oval corrugated capsule bore the label PUBLIC TOILET. Its shape reminded him of a French *pissoir*, but he couldn't see how you got in or out. There were buttons and lights, and something about time limits after which the door would automatically open, and Tom walked away from it in amused despair. How could even this most basic of human functions have become so mysteriously complicated?

He could ask for directions, he supposed, but who could he ask? Who should he pick? They all noticed him, the habit saw to that, but once they'd processed the simple fact of his presence *(Whoa look a monk / that's kind of cool actually / didn't realise they still existed / oh well)*, they swerved away, avoiding contact. His habit apparently projected a personal force field that kept everyone at a distance of three feet, in all directions.

A road sign caught his eye – white parallel lines crossed with a zigzag, reversed out of a red oblong – and he seized triumphantly on this icon of familiarity and set off in the direction it pointed in.

Now Davey was lying on the floor of his bedroom. He could not conceive of the strength it must have taken for James to have dragged him, six inches taller and a dead weight, up the stairs. He tried to stand up, but black dizziness pinned him to the floor.

"Not so fucking cocky now, are you?" said James, from some unknown space on the edges of his vision. "I'm meeting your mother for lunch. I'll be telling her exactly what you've done, so don't get any ideas about spinning her some nonsense when you see her."

"Are you g-g-g - " He clenched his fist. He wanted to ask, *Are you going to tell her what you've done? Are you going to tell her you beat me to a pulp?* But the words wouldn't come. James had beaten all the strength out of him. Defeated, Davey lay quietly and tried to focus his eyes.

"And after that," said James, "we're going to talk about what you'll be doing this summer. You're going to pass those fucking exams if it's the last thing you do, I can tell you that much. No more allowance. No going out. Private tutor every day. And I'm clearing out all this shit - " he saw James wave a contemptuous arm in the direction of the bookcase, stacked untidily high with dog-eared paperbacks and notebooks. "No distractions. We're taking your CDs as well. You can stay in this room until your tutor reckons you're ready to sit those exams and actually pass them. And if you fail them again, you'll stay in here some more, and study harder, until you *do* pass. Okay?"

Davey closed his eyes. The carpet felt itchy and unyielding against his cheek. He could feel the blood beginning to dry and crust against his skin. James bent down beside him, grabbed a handful of hair so he could lift Davey's head. Davey whimpered.

"I said, okay? Look at me when I'm speaking to you."

"No," said Davey.

"Excuse me?"

"No," Davey repeated. "No, it's not okay. It'll n-n-n - " he kicked his foot against the carpet in frustration. "It'll never be okay. You'll have to k-k-k-keep me locked up in here until I d-d-d-die, because I'm n-n-n-n-never going to - "

"Give over," said James. His voice was quiet, but his eyes were burning with triumph. "Look, we've been fighting this battle since you were a kid, haven't we? I've been trying for years and years to turn you into something worthwhile. Someone your mother can actually be proud of."

James' face was inches from his own. He wanted to look away, but he couldn't.

"And in all the time you've known me," said James, his voice sounding almost gentle, "have you ever won? Hmmm? Even once?"

"Shall I come round later?" asked Priss, picking her blouse up off the floor of the toilet.

Mark hesitated. "I might be out later."

Priss shrugged. "Okay. Tomorrow, then?"

"Um, yeah, maybe. I'll call you, alright?"

He changed in the station toilets, stuffing his habit in the unpleasant space between U-bend and the tiled wall. Then he went to look at the destinations board. Paddington didn't feature on any board he could see, but Kings Cross must be close enough. The ticket clerk looked at his envelope of cash with deep suspicion, but sold him the ticket anyway.

"This can only be used on the specified train," the clerk told him. "If you get on the wrong train you'll have to pay a penalty fare. Platform Three, over the bridge."

"Thank you," said Tom. The clerk handed him two oblongs of green and orange card, which he presumed must be his tickets. He stowed them carefully in his left pocket, re-folded the envelope and shoved it in his right and set off to look for Platform Three. The force field was still in place. People moved out of his way as he approached, careful not to catch his eye. Was it so clear that he was an outsider?

As he left the ticket office, he saw a tired, middle-aged man, wearing fusty-looking clothes and worn shoes and an expression of amused bewilderment, approaching the plate-glass door. The man had no coat and no luggage. Even to Tom's eyes, he looked poor and lost and isolated, possibly even homeless, but he seemed strangely cheerful about it. He stopped politely to let him pass through first.

It was only when the other man halted too that he realised he was looking at his own reflection.

"Your problem," said James, "is you're weak. You're weak and pathetic and useless. But I'm going to make you into a man if it kills us both. I won't raise a spineless little bastard."

The worst thing wasn't the pain, or the dizziness, or the blood, or even the fear. It was the bone-deep knowledge that James was right. James was stronger. James was stronger, because his mother would choose James over him.

"Okay."

He hoped James would let go of his hair now and leave him in peace, but instead he felt the painful pull on his scalp become more intense.

"I didn't hear you."

"Okay," repeated Davey. His voice was a slow croak.

James smiled. The look in his eyes could probably have passed for affection. "That's right, pal. And it's for your own good, you know. In ten years' time you'll thank me for this."

Welcome to MSN Messenger
Online: Elvisgirl, EdwardBulwerLytton

U there m8?

come on U dozy twat i can see UR online

mark U no its priss rite? talk 2 me
hey priss how RU?

at last it speaks J wassup? wot U doin?
not much just chillin U no
tht U wr out 2nite?
WTF RU checking or summat? changed mind OK?
fucking hell m8 only asked
soz
should think so 2 U twat J can still come over if U like
no its cool im busy
ok whats wrong
nothing
YY there is am not thick talk 2 me
nothing wrong its cool honest just not in mood 2nite
this isnt fkn booty call you twat weve got work 2 do
I said not 2nite ok?

priss? U there? sorry L
never mind fkn sorry whats wrong w U?
just in funny mood tonite
like last week u mean? and 2day B4 PE? starting to thk U only
want me 4 sex m8

you utter bastard
?? didnt say a fkn word!!!
YY i no U fkn didnt cos theres nthg 2 say is there? FFS all
that BS abt partnership n stuff UR just like all other men only
wanted 2 get into me
look Priss its not like that OK
YY it is EXACTLY lk that fk me all that fkn shit about NY was
just to get me to shag you wasnt it
id lv 2 meet U hun but shld warn U tho am not lk utha guys J
???

U utter twat UR seeing some1 else
??? no im not
YY UR. FFS RU sum sort of msn fkwit or smthng? UR msg
sm1 else RITE NOW &U just xpost w me go bk n chk history

U fkn loser. again

?? WTF Priss is just sum guy not another girl honest so Ive got 2 wndws open so fkn shoot me

fuck off mark am not fkn thick not that fkn thick anyway just fkn thick enuff to shag U when UR bored n horny rite

look Priss im sorry shldnt hv dun this pm at skl i no it wasnt fair on U but U came on rl strong and

dont even thk abt pulling that shite U >o<

lk ok UR rite sorry this isnt how I mnt 2 tell U its just run its course U no? was gr8 rly gr8 but

NY was nvr fkn real 4U was it? was real 4 me not 4 U

lk I mnt it at the time all rite

no U didnt U just knew wot I wanted 2 hear n said it FFS how stupid am i NY FGS I wld hv dun it 2 wld hv gone w U wld rly hv dun it thats how much U got under my fkn skin

oh come on don't get all hvy on me priss pls it does my hed in

IT DOES YOUR HEAD IN?

shit soz didnt mean it like that i dont mean 2B horrible i just look im sorry ok? can we talk about this?

priss?

dont B so childish priss UR still signed on now UR msn loser rite? J

Elvisgirl has signed off

The Underground was like something out of a Bosch painting; long echoing tunnels, vertiginous escalators, people pushing impatiently past him, knowing where they were going, and what they would do when they got there. He hung around and watched in fascination as an endless stream of people walked confidently up to the machines in the wall, manipulated the information they found there, received their tickets. The sense of adventure was still on him, he could still feel the schoolboy fizz of excitement in his belly; but he was also a middle-aged man who had seen more strange people in the last six hours than he had seen in the previous thirty years, and his feet were tired.

At the foot of a white-tiled pillar, a woman sat quietly, her hands in her lap, her head bowed, radiating the word *despair*. The crowds brushed past her as if she did not exist.

Why was she sitting there? She must be homeless.

My God, he thought in sudden horror. *So am I.*

But no there was one crucial difference. He had money and a destination, and she had neither.

He put his hand to his right pocket, and realised the envelope was gone.

Davey wanted to stay asleep, but his body wouldn't let him. He could feel oblivion retreating like an ebbing tide, leaving him to face the pain. When he opened his eyes, the light hurt them. He whimpered, then cringed. How could such a pathetic sound come out of him? No wonder James hated him.

What had happened? James must have beaten him again, that much was clear, but why? What had he done this time? And where was his mother? It was hard to stay focused. The thought frightened him. Had James done something really serious to him this time?

He thought he could hear music.

"Okay, so who's missing?" Mr Jones ran a finger down the register. "Alisha?" He looked around. "Alisha, come and sit back down in your own seat, please."

"I've changed seats," said Alisha, looking demure. In the seat beside her, Shaun snickered. One hand rested ostentatiously on the desk. The other was out of sight. They were sitting very close to each other. A few strands of Alisha's hair, silky and meticulously straightened, trailed across Shaun's shoulder.

"No, you haven't," said Mr Jones. "Move back."

"Fucking fascist," Alisha muttered, quietly enough so that

he could ignore it. She stood up, pulling her skirt down. Shaun brought his hand back out onto the desk. Mr Jones grimaced, and prayed he wouldn't have to watch Shaun sniffing his fingers for the rest of the lesson.

"Katie?"

"She's off sick, sir."

"Okay. Priss? Has anyone seen Priss?"

"She's not here, sir."

"No sh- No, I can see that," he said. "Anyone got anything more than *she's not here?*"

There was no question about it; his right-hand pocket was empty. Had he dropped it? Or had one of the myriad strangers he had brushed against stolen it from him? He clutched blindly at his left-hand pocket, and heaved a sigh of relief. He still had the tickets, at least. The tickets, and a handful of change, enough to buy, enough for - he stopped in perplexity. How much could he buy with this strange handful of metal shapes, this crumpled sliver of paper?

He leaned against a cool, tiled wall and examined each coin in careful detail, knowing how strange he must look, not caring. The note was worth five pounds. The thick round coins with the milled edges were worth one pound each. When had pound notes disappeared? He shook his head in bafflement. The fifty pence was unchanged, familiar. Its miniature double was a twenty-pence piece; a sensible innovation, he thought, and found himself nodding approvingly. Did they still make ten-pence pieces? If so, he didn't have one. Instead he had this miserable dot of nickel, so small he was tempted to try and pick it up with a moistened finger, that was, apparently, worth five pence. What had happened to one-pence pieces, he wondered? Did they still exist? Had they shrunk down so small that he'd be unable to find them?

Someone jostled his elbow, sending his precious hoard flying. He scrabbled madly to collect it up again. His adventure was turning sour on him.

No, he thought stubbornly. He was still out, on the other side of the wall, and free. He'd make out somehow. Nothing worth having was easy.

What *was* that music? Davey sat up, flinching at the pain in his head and his ribs and his stomach and his back and his left leg, then warily climbed to his feet. Blackness crept around the edges of his vision, then receded again. He limped over to the window. The sunshine streamed heartlessly in, oblivious to the shooting pain it set off in Davey's head.

Outside in the street, two men knelt on the pavement. They were perhaps a few years older than him, one fair, one redheaded, dressed in the coolly shabby kind of clothes that Davey automatically associated with art students. They were sketching something on the pavement in chalk. He had seen people do this before; usually the result was a strange, ghostly copy of an Old Master, immaculately rendered but with all the colours a little too pale, a little too thin. The man with red hair was adjusting a set of portable iPod speakers.

"What do you fancy?" he asked. His companion shrugged agreeably.

"You pick."

"Something from the master, I think." A flick of the wheel and a complex, haunting tune spiralled up from the speakers, climbing the heavy air and insinuating itself in through the bottom of Davey's sash window.

Davey closed his eyes. He had learned long ago that, when the pain from one injury became too unbearable, he could distract himself by focusing on another instead; it was as if his brain could only process a certain amount of pain at one time, and which pain he processed was within his gift to choose. Crammed awkwardly into the window frame, he began making a slow tour of his injuries. *Head. Ribs. Stomach - ow,* ow, *bad one, don't go back there. Back. Leg. Head. Ribs. Sto - no, Back. Leg. Head. Ribs. Back. Leg. Head. Ribs. Back.*

As night fell, the words *novelty* and *adventure* began to dissolve, to be replaced with a darker and more frightening vocabulary. *Alone. Homeless. Vulnerable. Hungry. Tired.* He fought them as well as he could, but they stalked his footsteps as he hopelessly roamed the crowded streets. Did nobody sleep in London? Were these the same people he'd seen earlier, or was there some sort of shift system? Eventually he was too exhausted to continue, and squatted hopelessly in a doorway. When a woman around his age touched his elbow, he stared at her in dumb terror.

"It's alright," she said, very gently. "I'm Jane, I'm an outreach worker. I know most of the faces around here. You're new, aren't you?"

Priss knew exactly why the driver had stopped – even with her hair plastered to her skull and her huge baggy anorak on, she knew how she looked – but that was okay. It was getting late and it was pissing with rain, he had a nice car and he was going in the right direction. He held the door open, making elaborate efforts not to invade her personal space and put the heater on to try and dry her out.

Priss' new driver turned out to be called Neil, which was pretty much the name she would have given him if she had to pick. He was about thirty-five, maybe a bit older. He was sort of ugly, boringly dressed, a bit skinny, the should-have-gone-to-Specsavers type. He told her he worked in IT, and was on his way to a conference on the security implications of cloud computing. She could imagine him playing World Of Warcraft in his spare time. He was formal and polite, asking conventional questions about where she was going, why she was going there, what she did.

She began with two truths, one lie. She was headed for London, she was going there to meet a friend, and she didn't do anything, she was still at school. When she told him her age, she felt the car twitch and slow as he involuntarily took his foot off the accelerator and clutched the steering wheel a little tighter.

"Erm - " he was stammering a little. "I um, I hope you don't think I'm, I mean - "

You mean you hope I don't think you're a disgusting old pervert for wanting to get my knickers off, Priss thought cynically. She smiled, and looked at him shyly from underneath her eyelashes.

"I know hitching is really dangerous," she said, breathless and girlish. "But I've really got to get to London. My mate – Aleesha, she's called – her boyfriend's been hitting her and I've got to get her back home."

After that, she knew it would be easy. As the road grew dark, she yawned a couple of times – easy to conjure, the warmth and comfort of the car making her sleepy – and he hesitantly asked her where she was planning to stay the night. She loitered nearby as he checked in at the desk, and heard him ask in a voice that was noticeably louder than it needed to be if he could change from a double to a twin. *A real knight in shining armour,* she thought to herself, which was a damn shame given what she was about to do to him.

Inside the room, Neil elaborately nominated one of the beds as *hers*, then disappeared into the bathroom for ten minutes. When he came out he had changed into ironed jeans and a black shirt. He had a taxi-sharing friend in the lobby to meet and a pre-conference dinner to go to, he said as he took forty pounds in cash and two credit cards out of his wallet, but of course she must order room service for herself. She quite enjoyed the way he fussed around her, as if she was a brand new rescue kitten he'd just adopted, who might leave at any moment.

She took a long, hot shower and finally felt warm for the first time in three days. Then she ordered herself two burgers with fries and two large cokes and spent a contented forty-five minutes devouring every last morsel.

Then she went to the drawer where he'd left his car keys and wallet, took out the remaining cash – there was a decent amount, nearly two hundred pounds – grabbed her rucksack, ran down the back staircase and out to the car park, and stole his car.

Before they'd let him in the shelter, Tom had to promise he wasn't carrying any drugs or alcohol and agree that if he did turn out to have lied about this, they would be entitled to evict him. If he hadn't been so exhausted, he would have found that pretty funny – where did they imagine he was hiding it? – but he supposed it must just be standard procedure. Jane gave him a plate of eggs and bacon and a mug of tea.

"Want to share your story?" she asked him. "You don't have to if you don't want to. But some clients find it helps." She hesitated. "Or is there anyone you'd like us to call?"

"Do you meet a lot of people with someone to call?" he asked, curious.

"Oh, yes. More than you'd think. Especially the new ones. Like you."

He opened his mouth to ask how she was so certain he was new to the streets. Then he remembered the night Jack had turned up at the door of the monastery, and his instinctive opinion: *too clean to be homeless.* For now, he was still visible, still capable of attracting help, still looking as if help was possible. How long did he have before the street closed over his head?

"I've done what you're doing, you know," he said suddenly. "Taking people in, I mean. Helping them. It's really strange to see it from the other side."

"We all spend a night sleeping rough as part of our training."

"It's not the same, though, is it?"

"No," she said. "It's not the same."

He drained the mug of tea, surprised by how thirsty he was. He wondered what he would do for water, where homeless people went to drink. You could survive without food for weeks, but lack of water would kill you in days.

"You never answered my question," said Jane, gentle but persistent. "If there's someone you'd like me to call, let me know and I'll see what I can do."

"No. Yes. No. There's a man I know, Jack. But I don't have a number, I've only got an address."

"Is it family?"

"A friend." He bit his lip. "Well, sort of. I mean, we don't know each other all that well, but, no, I can't, it's not fair to ask him. I need to make my own way - "

"It's up to you," said Jane. "But in my experience, it's best to make the call. Whatever you've done – even if you're running from the law – you'd be better off in the long run. It's not too late to go back. Are you alright?"

Out of nowhere, Tom found himself in the grip of a fragment of memory. He was standing in a crowd in an over-filled hall, Eleanor wedged closely alongside him. The room smelled of hair gel, sweat, and fanatical devotion. The audience had been screaming earlier, but now they were rapt and silent, almost afraid to breathe in case they missed a word of the song. The performance was acoustic, just the singer and his guitar; the backing group had melted away into the shadows. And the words:

It's too late to go back
But there's still something to do
It's hard but it's simple
The only way out is through

Had he been unconscious again? Or had he just been asleep? He grabbed onto the windowsill and pulled himself painfully upwards. The morning sun lit up the dust hanging in the expensive city air. It couldn't even be ten o'clock yet. His watch – an ugly Patek Philippe James had bought him for his eighteenth birthday – had stopped working. The face was cracked. It must have happened when James threw him to the floor. James had broken it, but it would be Davey's fault. It always was.

The men outside had left, perhaps because so few passers-by had stopped to admire their work. Davey wondered briefly why they had chosen this quiet and expensive residential street to work on, where the most likely reaction would be demands that they wash it all off again.

They had drawn a picture of a large country house, standing on high ground. The walls were a soft rosy colour, either because it was painted that way or because of the warm, sleepy light of the setting sun. A single light burned in one small window. Across the top right-hand corner of the picture, written in flat white lettering, was the word *LANDMARK*.

The car was easy to drive. Far easier than the decaying heap of junk belonging to her father, which pulled hard to the left and had a tendency to stall at traffic lights. It was tempting to put her foot down and scream down the outside lane as fast as she could go, but she needed to stay inconspicuous. She cruised down the M6, keeping an eye out for the police. It had been three hours. Neil's dinner was probably finished, he might already be back in the hotel room, discovering she'd cleaned him out and stolen his car.

As she approached the junction, she realised that going to London, at least in this car, was possibly the worst plan she could come up with. She'd told Neil she was headed there. If they were going to look for her anywhere, they'd be sat on a bridge over the M40, waiting for the black Audi A4 to cruise smoothly by beneath it. She flicked on her indicator and turned onto the M5.

The M5 was quieter, the traffic moving faster. She drove and drove and drove, foot pressed hard against the floor, fighting to stay awake, stopping at a quiet garage to use the Ladies (disgusting) and nick several cans of Red Bull (easy, the attendant was doing a Sudoku puzzle). The fuel gauge crept inexorably downwards; the tank had been full when she stole it, but even a car this size would run out of petrol eventually. The motorway came to an end and forked into two A roads. Because it was the easiest choice, she picked the left-hand fork.

Now she was driving over empty moorland, nothing for miles but grass and the occasional pony. She was getting tired. She rummaged in her rucksack for another can of Red Bull, gulped it down, and carried on.

Was it safer to find a lay-by and sleep in the car? Or should she head for a big town and sleep in a doorway? She could even afford a crappy hotel room if she wanted, but she'd rather save the money for now. She drummed her fingers on the steering wheel. Five hours since she'd stolen the car, it must have been reported by now. Best to ditch it. Large town it was.

As she parked up in a scruffy-looking side street, a police car nosed its way down the road towards her. The jolt of adrenalin made her jump and curse. She slung her rucksack over her shoulder and began to walk away. The police car continued its leisurely progress. A trickle of sweat ran down her spine. Had she shut the door properly? Fuck, was the interior light still on? She didn't dare look back to see.

The sound of the car slowed; the engine was idling. They'd stopped. Two coppers in the car. One to inspect the vehicle. One to run a check and see if it was reported dodgy or missing.

As soon as she reached the corner, Priss began to run. Downhill was easier, so she ran that way. Her Doc Martens thumped the pavement as she ran down and down, through traffic, over junctions, past shop windows, faintly registering the change in smell from petrol fumes and rubbish bags and frying-oil to diesel fumes and salt and rotting seaweed, getting damper, getting cooler, and then suddenly she was on a busy quay and people in going-out clothes were climbing onto a pleasure-boat, clutching plastic beer glasses and laughing in the kind of accent that made Priss want to scream and thump them very hard. She fumbled breathlessly in her rucksack, found the cash she'd stolen from Neil, hurried aboard and collapsed onto a seat, chewing her nails until the boat pulled away from the quayside, before finally allowing herself to relax.

As she tried not to listen to the stories being told around her – stories about other superior boat trips, taken in Lausanne, Sydney, British Colombia and the heroic amounts of alcohol they'd all consumed – she saw a huge house, rose-coloured and beautiful, in the middle of what looked like empty moorland.

When Jane came back, she had an extraordinary expression on her face.

"I managed to find a number," she said. "Eventually. It took me quite a while. You didn't tell me your friend was a famous musician. And I never knew *he* lived in the West Country. I'll be honest, when I realised whose house you were talking about I nearly didn't make the call."

"I, um - "

"He wasn't there," said Jane. "But a lady called Kate answered the phone. She said it would be fine, of course Jack would want you to stay with him. She said she'd organise a train ticket for you and she'd come and meet you at the station." She smiled faintly. "Whoever you are, Tom, you're a lucky man, do you know that?"

Davey moved feverishly about his room, bundling things into a bag. What should he pack? What would he need? It was difficult to concentrate through the taunting voice in his head; the sound of James' voice, saying the words Davey knew he would say if he was here: *Where the hell do you think you're going to go? You idiot. You're a failure, Davey. Running away is just the kind of thing I'd expect from a spineless little toe-rag like you.*

"Shut up, shut *up*," he wailed to himself. He stopped by the drinks cabinet, took out a bottle of Stoli vodka, and swallowed several hot, oily mouthfuls.

Don't even know what to pack, do you? You've never been

anywhere on your own, have you? When I was your age I was already living on my own, fending for myself. You'd never last five minutes without me and your mother to look after you. Look at you, failed your A-levels for the second time, can't drive, you're completely bloody unemployable.

And where the hell are you going to go, anyway?

He had no idea, but he knew he couldn't stay here any longer. He had to run. He went back up to his room, stared wildly around. What else, what else, what else?

As he slung his bag over his shoulder, he heard the key in the front door.

chapter sixteen (always)

The canopy over Davey's bed was the same faded red damask as the curtains. Last night the curtains had been tightly closed, but now they were folded tidily against the bedposts, the extravagant loops of old gold rope back in place. He'd gone to sleep with his head resting on Isaac's shoulder, but he had woken alone.

"I'm gay," Davey said to himself, trying out the sound of the words. As personal announcements went, it felt about as significant as *I'm left-handed.*

"I'm gay," he said, more loudly, trying for drama. Surely it should sound more apocalyptic than this? He pictured James, glowering like a basilisk. Had James sensed this about him, all those years ago? Was this why he'd tried so hard to mould Davey into someone else?

"I'm gay," Davey told this imaginary James. But he couldn't imagine what would happen next. Sighing, he pushed back the sheets.

A tiny scrap of paper lay on the empty pillow. It was a corner torn from one of Priss' notebooks, he recognised the smooth, yellowy paper, the elegant, closely-spaced grey lines. Written in meticulous handwriting, condensed into the smallest possible space, was a brief message:

You're lovely
- I

Davey stowed the note carefully in his back pocket, and went downstairs. The horrific discoveries of last night felt distant and unreal, separated from now by an ocean of time; time in which he'd discovered he was entirely different to how he'd always imagined himself, someone greedy and needy and demanding and impetuous, someone who begged without shame and cried out in bliss, someone who did things he'd never dared to dream about. He laughed to himself as he went down to the kitchen.

"Morning," said Priss. She looked white and tired, and as she went to the coffee pot, she limped painfully on her bandaged ankle. "You're up early. For once."

"I'm gay," Davey told her.

Priss poured coffee into her mug in a luxurious brown stream. "D'you want some? I've made about a gallon."

"I said - I'm gay."

"Duh." Priss reached for another mug.

"What do you mean, *duh*?" Davey demanded. "Are you even listening to me? I only just found out myself! How can you possibly have known?"

"Because it's fucking obvious," said Priss, yawning. "It's, like, the third thing anyone notices about you. Tall; dark hair; gay; nice shoes. Probably not a murderer."

Davey took the mug she was offering him and sat down.

"Did you honestly not know?" asked Priss.

"No."

"Christ." Priss grinned to herself behind her mug.

"So where is everyone?" asked Davey crossly.

"Why? D'you want to tell them as well?"

"No! I mean, well, I suppose I - I'm not expecting them to be interested or anything, but actually, I - I think we ought to talk about, you know, the, um - "

"I heard them talking in Kate's room last night," said Priss. "While you and Isaac were fucking each other's brains out." Davey blushed. "They're not sure what to do. Tom thinks Jack might have done it, he feels dead guilty about dobbing him in. I caught him looking at the phone this morning like it was going to bite him."

"Stop being such a wanker."

Jack cradled the phone between his ear and his neck, and reached for the pen that lay, tantalisingly out of reach, on the smooth teak surface of the console table. The phone slipped away from him and rattled against the table leg. He picked it up guiltily.

" - better not have thrown it at the wall," said Alan. "Are you still there?"

"Of course I am. Sorry, I dropped the receiver." He reached for the pen again. It was no closer than before.

"I'm not your mate," said Alan menacingly. "I'm your manager. Or I would be, if you'd let me, you know, fucking *manage* you and your career? Ten dates. That's all I'm asking for. Ten dates. It's nothing! UK only, and we'll get a private helicopter to take you back to the country pile afterwards. They'll be the hottest tickets in the whole fucking town - "

Jack suppressed a yawn. They'd stayed up late last night, drinking and talking out on the veranda, wrapped in blankets as the night became chillier. They were celebrating Isaac's first draft of the *Landmark* album cover, although Isaac had been oddly reluctant to show it to him. Instead he had rolled it up into a long tube and walked the five miles to the village post office to send it to Alan. Jack had only known what it was because Mathilda mentioned it at lunchtime. He'd tried not to be jealous that Isaac had confided in her. After all, Mathilda wasn't responsible for what Isaac told her, was she? It was only Mathilda's response that mattered.

He suddenly discovered a large, loopy knot in the cable. If he untangled it, the phone might stretch far enough for him to reach the pen.

"Jesus Christ," said Alan. "I can actually hear the sound of you not listening to me."

"I'm listening," protested Jack.

"No you're not. You're waiting for me to get bored and start talking about something else instead. That's how well I bloody know you, Jack. I can actually sense when you're not listening to a bloody word I'm saying."

"Sorry! Sorry, I'm listening now."

"Forget it, pal. Now I *am* bored. For fuck's sake. That's how well *you* know *me*, right?" There was a click then a long, slow sigh as Alan drew deeply on a fresh cigarette. "How's the new album coming?"

Jack winced. "Slow. Painful."

Alan laughed. "You always say that."

Did he? Maybe he did. Maybe it was always this terrible. He seemed to spend hours just staring at the page, trying to fit together the words with the music in his head, getting nowhere. It was so much easier to lay down the pen and dream about Mathilda instead.

The cable was free, surely now the phone would reach. He stretched out, grabbed the pen, enjoyed the small thrill of victory. Now he just needed some paper.

"Going back to this tour," said Alan, fortified by nicotine.

"Let's not," suggested Jack. "I hate it when we fight." He found a folded piece of paper in his pocket and took it out. It was covered over in writing so dense it looked like it was written in another language. Was this actually his work? He peered at it in appalled fascination.

"I've got a proposal for you."

"I'm not marrying you."

"Fuck off. Don't you ever call me a fucking poofter, okay?"

"Jesus. It was just a joke."

"Yeah, well, some jokes aren't funny. Not that I've got anything against poofters, I'm sure their mothers love them. Would you do the tour if I got you a babysitter?"

"Sorry, mate, did you say a *babysitter*?"

"Yeah. Someone to look after you. Keep you on the straight and narrow. Make sure you don't end up taking anything you shouldn't." He chuckled. "Tucking you up in bed at night.

What do you think?"

"I think you've actually lost your mind."

"Hey, there's no shame in it, you know. Plenty of the greats have had minders. Leaves you free to concentrate on what's important, right?"

What was important, was Mathilda. She'd been restless over the last few days. She'd been on the phone for hours to her agent, a man called Irving Something, American by birth and from the sounds of it, aiming to get back home and take Mathilda with him. It was pathetic to eavesdrop but impossible not to. Everything she did mattered to him. If she wanted to go – to London, to Hollywood, to the moon – he had to know, so he could plan around it. What was Alan saying? It sounded like something about the Borgias -

"Sorry," said Jack. "I could have sworn you said something about Lucrezia Borgia."

"I did. I was checking to see if you were still listening. So what do you think?"

"About being babysat by Lucrezia Borgia?"

"About being babysat by Evie." Jack spluttered. "Alright, alright, no need to fucking choke. Why not? You know her, she knows you. She'd take good care of you. She's willing to do it - "

"If you ever mention this halfwit idea to me ever, *ever* again," said Jack, "I'll fire you. Swear to God."

"No you won't. No other bastard would sign you, the way you behave. Look, I'm not pushing for this tour because I'm some sort of sadist. You do know that, right? You do actually remember I'm on your side? All I'm trying to do is get a bit of exposure for your music, which, mind-bogglingly fucking brilliant as it is, is not going to sell itself."

Jack could hear the sound of Mathilda's laughter, that low, dirty laugh that thrilled down his spine. He was bored of sitting in the hallway. Was he so difficult to work with? Was his behaviour so outrageous? Other musicians drove limousines into swimming pools. "I'll think about it," he said.

"Liar."

"Fuck off, Alan, I will. Okay?"

"Twenty notes says you'll hang up and forget every word I said until next time."

"If I pay you the twenty quid will you promise not to phone again until tomorrow?"

"It's a deal." Alan hung up without saying goodbye.

He put the phone carefully back into its cradle.

"So is this it, then?" asked Davey, following Priss as she painfully climbed the stairs to her room. "The end of the summer?"

Priss shrugged. "What do you think? You saw them last night. They'll talk a lot, but they'll give it up and call the coppers in the end. They're probably just waiting for us to get out of Dodge before they do it. So what about you? You going home to get beaten up by your dad again?"

"Stepdad. And how did you know he - "

"Didn't take a genius to figure that one out," said Priss. She sighed. "For God's sake, I just wish - I just wanted to know. You know?" She shook her head. "And you've got to admit, it would be pretty fucking cool to be able to say you'd lived with a murderer."

"You know," said Davey, "I um, I mean, you actually - "

"You want to come in?" Priss held open the door to her room. "Special invitation."

"Oh. Thank you. Um, I wanted to tell you - "

Priss was staring at her bed. "What the fuch's that doing there?"

Davey looked, but couldn't see anything unusual. The smooth sunburst-orange of the bedspread was immaculately smooth; Priss' heavy black notebook lay on her pillow.

"I never make my bed until just before I get into it," said Priss. "And I never leave my notebook out like that, it looks poncey." She picked up the book and leafed through it. "That bastard Isaac, he's been using my notebook to *draw* in. I'll kill him when I see him. No, hang on a minute. Shit. Okay, maybe I won't - "

Davey peered over her shoulder. The smooth yellowy pages of her notebook were filled with black and white sketches, laid out in panels, like a graphic novel. Crowds of people swarmed up the driveway and through the door of a beautiful house – the house, Davey realised, they now stood in – while, in stark contrast, a man sat alone in the branches of the huge candelabra tree in the garden, carefully nailing up a round paper lantern.

Mathilda was pacing out the thick carpet of the chill-out room, muttering to herself under her breath, occasionally referring to the copy of *Lysistrata* in her hand. He perched on the arm of a magenta couch, unsure if she knew he was there or not. Part of her talent was to create the illusion of being alone before an audience. He was struck again by how self-contained she was, and how little she needed him to be happy. Her beauty and her separateness were a sharp pain in his chest.

At last, she put down the book and came to him. "Isaac's gone."

"Good," said Jack, before he could stop himself. "Shit, I didn't mean - "

"Didn't you?"

"I just meant it's nice to have the place to ourselves again."

"Because we were falling over each other all the time?" She was smiling, but he could sense the argument threatening to come to the surface.

"Yeah. He was such a pain, always chattering away when I was trying to work - "

"You were jealous, weren't you?"

As always, her directness wrong-footed him. "No."

"Yes, you were. It burns you up that he's seen me naked, doesn't it? You were lying when you said it was fine."

He wondered if she was looking for an excuse to argue. "No, it didn't - oh, alright, yes it did. Okay? Is that what you wanted to hear? Why did you model for him if you knew I didn't like it?"

"Because I didn't care."

He was unsure if he'd heard her right. "I'm sorry, what?"

"This," she said, enunciating with great care, "is my body. Not yours. Mine. You don't own it. I do."

"I know that! But I love you. I *love* you. It's only natural to be jealous - "

"Jealousy is for cavemen. What happened to trust?"

"I do trust you, I just - "

"No, you don't. For God's sake, Jack, is your definition of *love* lying awake at night wondering if the woman next to you spent the afternoon fucking somebody else?"

"Well, have you? Have you been fucking him?" Jack was vaguely aware how destructive this question was, but was too angry to stop himself. The words had hovered on the end of his tongue for weeks now. He couldn't keep them caged any longer.

"Well, what if I have? What then, Jack?"

"Then - then - "

"Then I wouldn't be all yours after all? What makes you think you get all of me anyway? Did you think I was a virgin?"

"I never really - it's none of my business, is it? I mean, obviously we're all entitled to our past."

"And what about your past? Your past that keeps turning up on the doormat every morning?"

"If you mean Evie, we were only ever just - "

"Jack, if the next word out of your mouth is going to be *friends*, you're the biggest fucking hypocrite I've ever met in my life."

"What are you talking about?"

"You could at least own up to what you've done. You've already lost one woman her career. You're not doing the same to me."

"I have absolutely no idea what you're talking about."

From between the pages of *Lysistrata*, she took out an

envelope. A letter from Evie, already opened.

"You opened my post?"

She dropped it beside him onto the magenta velvet. "Get the plank out your own eye first. You bastard."

Together, Priss and Davey leafed through the pages. A girl with long hair climbed the tree and sat next to the man. Another girl, naked, her eyes huge and black, trod a perilous path down through the woods to the enclosure where a black shape prowled impatiently behind the bars.

"This is fucking brilliant," said Priss.

"Why aren't there any words?" Davey asked.

"That's the writer's job." Priss turned over more pages. "Look, she's jumped into the cage. Hey, is that who I think it is?"

In the corner of the page, a man with dark curly hair watched in horror as the girl plunged into the panther's lair.

"That's Isaac," he said incredulously.

You'll find it hardest when you're stressed. Knowing it didn't make the craving easier to ignore. The medicine cabinet in the annexe called to him. The only way to stay ahead of it was to walk and walk, pacing out rooms and corridors through luxurious decadence to crumbling ruin and back to decadence again, as he tried to put together what he'd just read in Evie's letter.

He forced himself to examine the few shards of memory he'd held on to. The journey from the hospital, sweating with fear, trying to hold it together in an office somewhere, lying through his teeth to the shrink, *no, nothing, nothing since I was admitted, not a thing, I swear,* knowing the shrink wasn't fooled. Being searched, his suitcase and then himself, the blaze of panic when they found his stash. Understanding murmurs, worse than accusations. Hallucinations, things slouching in corners, voices whispering and giggling, creatures on his bedclothes and on his skin. The haze of pills clearing, leaving a dreadful clarity filled with everything he'd been running from. No sleep. He'd lost eleven days he worked out afterwards, and was glad to have done so.

And somewhere in all of that, he'd apparently -

Was it even possible? Was Evie telling the truth? He didn't believe her. He'd barely been able to walk when he arrived, never mind have sex. And surely, surely he'd have some vague recollection? But there was simply nothing there. Nothing but an eleven-day gap in his brain.

He could see Mathilda coming out onto the lawn from the woods.

Which would sound worse? To tell Mathilda that yes, she was right, he'd ended Evie's career and then abandoned her without remorse or hesitation? Or to confess he'd fucked up his brain so profoundly that he simply had no recollection of the events Evie described? Would it make things better or worse to go and talk to her?

She caught sight of him, beckoned him impatiently outside.

"This must be the story of what happened here," said Davey.

"I bet you were ten minutes late for your own birth." Priss flicked impatiently through the pages. "That's Evie, look, she looks just like her photos. That girl from the tree, that's probably Mathilda - and that guy must be Jack Laker." She shook her head in disbelief. "Jack *Laker*. We're living in Jack Laker's house. No, that still sounds ridiculous. I mean, I don't even *like* Jack Laker. Christ, if he's killed someone every fan in the Western world'll be sobbing into their Cheerios."

"You really didn't know, did you," said Mathilda as soon as he got close enough. "I thought maybe you were faking it so you didn't have to talk about it. But you really, really didn't know."

"I still don't know," he said. "I can't remember a thing. Not a thing."

"I don't believe you."

"That's how bad it was."

"That's how bad what was?"

He was in court, under oath. No escape. No excuses. His chest was tight. "I was out of contract with Island," he said at last. He scrabbled in his pocket for something to destroy, found a biro, pulled out the ink-tube. "I was going to sign with Gumshoe, but then they went up in smoke. And I really thought that was it. Fifteen minutes over. Then Alan turned up at a gig one night with a contract in his pocket. Next thing I know, *Violet Hour* was double platinum and I had four top ten singles off it. I still don't know why."

"I know you don't."

"So there I was, a freak superstar with forty dates booked in these massive venues. And it's like a deal with the Devil, you know? I don't know why I was surprised. It's not even a secret, not really. You know when you start it's going to be screams whenever they see you and mad people hanging around the stage door afterwards, and hotel rooms, and a messed-up sleep schedule, and everyone treating you like some kind of holy idiot, and never having time to work, and forgetting to call your mother, and absolutely no personal space, and sycophantic interviews, and girls in the dressing room, and junk food, and drugs. You know what it's going to be like, but somehow you think you'll be different. No, I mean, *I* thought *I* was going to be different."

"You don't have to tell me this."

"Yes. Yes, I do. See, the thing is I'm a writer, not a jukebox. Once the album's finished, I just want to put it out there and get onto the next thing. But the fans aren't there for *new*. They want *familiar*. So every night, the same show, over and over, note-perfect, and they'd be ecstatic, then every morning I'd be in the hotel room with my ears ringing, trying to hear the music, the *new* music. But I was too tired. So Alan got me these Dexedrine tablets."

"And then you couldn't sleep."

"And then I couldn't sleep. So he got me some Valium.

That made me sleep alright, Christ - the first time I took one I thought I was going to die. But then there was always the speed to wake me up. And that's how it started."

"So could you write then?"

"No, that's the fucking stupid thing. It *never* worked. But once I'd started, I couldn't stop it. See, *I* wanted to write, but nobody else cared if I did or not. They just needed me to perform. They were getting me everything they could think of to keep me going, and trying to cheer me up by - " the pen snapped in half. "Oh, fuck, I still can't believe I - "

"The girls in the dressing room?"

"Yeah. I mean, you always get groupies, but suddenly there were so many more of them. There was this one gig. The Phoenix. I met a kid back stage. Just a kid. And his kid girlfriend. Alan was picking girls out of the crowd. I saw him pick her. A fucking schoolgirl! And Christ, if you think what I did with Evie was - " he shook his head. "That was the worst night. The very worst one."

"Did you? With her, I mean? The schoolgirl?"

"No. I took every goddamn pill I had. And then a pint of Jack Daniels on top. They found me in my hotel room, passed out in a pool of piss and vomit."

"She looks like him," said Priss, studying Isaac's drawing of the girl in the cage. "If he grew his hair, he'd be the spit of her. I bet she's his sister." She turned the page and disclosed a double-page spread showing a row of beds with Evie, in a nurse's uniform, moving between them. One of the patients was Jack, lank-haired and skeletal. In another bed, Evie bent low over the girl with the dark eyes.

"And did you really say all that to Evie?" Mathilda asked. "Did you tell her you'd die without her? That you needed her? That you couldn't survive without her?"

"I might have done. Addicts'll say anything when they're desperate." He paused. "I mean, *we'll* say anything when *we're* desperate. But I honestly can't remember."

"Not even a flicker?"

"Not even a flicker. Look, I should have told you all this before, I know I should. I'm sorry. I should have warned you how bad it can be, living with an addict. I mean I damaged my brain, didn't I? It'll never work quite right again. I can't drink or take drugs, or risk going anywhere near anything that might make me want to drink or take drugs. It could happen again, at any time, from now until the day I die. All that fucking grandstanding about that stash I keep up in the annexe, that story about the landmine - that's bullshit. The truth is I'm too weak to get rid of it."

She was looking across the lawn into the woods.

"Look," said Priss, "they're having a massive row. Jack and Evie and Mathilda. D'you reckon he asked them for a threesome?" She paged on through the manuscript. "And what's Isaac doing in all these pictures? Did he, like, live with them or something?" She turned over the pages. "Oh, no! No fucking way!"

"What? What?"

"He did the artwork," said Priss, sounding outraged. "Fuching Isaac fucking painted the fuching cover artwork for the fucking *Landmark* album. Isaac! I've known guys who'd walk over their mother's entrails to meet the guy who painted that cover. Damn it, I wanted to meet a murderer."

"You know," said Davey, "you still might have - "

"Give over, posh boy. I want to see what happens next."

"I'm sorry," Jack repeated. "I wish I was a different man, a better man. And I really wish I was the kind of man who wouldn't get jealous just because a young, good-looking, talented guy who you clearly get on with got to see you naked." He waited, but she kept silent. "You know, you *could* tell me you think he's repulsive and it drives you nuts the way he never speaks."

"Isaac's queer," said Mathilda.

"He's *what?*" Jack was astounded. "Are you sure? How do you know?"

"Does that bother you?"

"No, I suppose not, but - " he shook his head, feeling the events of the last two months rearrange themselves into a surprising new pattern. "I had no idea, are you sure?"

"I'm sorry too," said Mathilda. "I was jealous, you see. I didn't like reading all those things Evie said you said to her. And I wanted to see how the painting would turn out." She took his hand gently. "But I should have known you wouldn't have walked away from her like that if you'd known. I don't think you've ever been knowingly cruel to anyone in your life, have you?"

Hand in hand, they stood on the lawn and felt time flowing past them. The argument felt to Jack like a lock in a canal; a necessary pause in a dark and frightening place, to allow their closeness to move to a new level.

"I need to go and feed him," he said at last, reluctantly breaking the peace.

"Why have you got that panther? You've never really explained."

"I told you, I won him in a poker game."

"Yes, but how?"

"It was when I was looking for a house. I met this old guy in a big falling-apart place in Devon. He said he'd only sell to the right person. Apparently that wasn't me, but we got talking and then we got drinking, and we started playing. He bet me anything I wanted out of his animal collection. I was most sorry for the panther, so that's the one I took."

"That makes sense, actually," said Mathilda. "It's one of the nicest things about you, you know."

"What is?"

"How kind you are."

He kissed her hand. "I won't be long."

Twenty minutes later he was running madly through the

woods, blazing with a rage so pure and incandescent it felt like a series of electric shocks.

"This would be much easier to understand with the words," said Davey.

"Easy's boring," said Priss. "So, Jack and Mathilda are living together, Mathilda's modelling for Isaac. Whoa." Sprawling across a double-page, Isaac had drawn first the panther, and then Mathilda, both of them sleeping in a barred cell in the shape of a heart.

"Prisoners of love," said Davey.

"He must have used half my pens on this one, the robbin' little bastard," said Priss gloomily. She turned the page.

"What the fuck have you done!" Jack yelled. He slammed the veranda doors shut. "What the bloody hell have you *done?*"

Mathilda looked at him blankly.

"I don't know. What have I done?"

"The cage door! You let him out! You went into the woods this afternoon and you bloody well let him out! Why would you even do that? I know you don't approve of me keeping him, but Jesus Christ, Mathilda, why would you *do* that? He'll get killed out there, there are roads - "

"He's miles from any roads," said Mathilda, reaching for her glass of wine.

Another white-hot stab of rage. "So you admit it? It was you?"

Her face was smooth and blank as she took a considered mouthful from her glass. "I didn't say that."

"Well, you might as well, because *of course* it was bloody well you!" His hand went to the chain around his neck. "Who the fuck else was going to get the key off me?"

"How do you know you didn't forget to lock up?"

"Because I check. Always. That's what you have to do when you're keeping a - "

"Prisoner?"

"He is *not* a prisoner!"

"Of course he is. It's disgusting to keep anything caged like that. Now he's free. He can do what he's meant to do."

"Which is what, exactly? Maul sheep? Get shot? Starve to death? Die of loneliness?"

"He can live!" Mathilda's sudden fury, as white-hot as his own, took him by surprise. "He can get out there and live his life! And yes, sometimes that includes getting hurt, and being hungry, and wishing you were somewhere safe and warm, and being lonely but that's what makes the good times worthwhile! Life is painful sometimes! That doesn't mean you should shut yourself away and hide from it!"

"He was happy where he was!"

"Then why," said Mathilda, "did he walk out the door as soon as he got the chance?"

"He was safe."

"*Safe.*" Her scorn was so huge and visceral that he thought she might actually spit. "That's a worthwhile goal? *Safe?* What's the point when you give up everything else to achieve it? You want to wrap everything and everyone up in cotton wool, don't you?"

"If you'd seen the state he was in when I found him - "

"Not everyone," said Mathilda, "needs to hide from the past. Some of us can actually get better while living in the real world."

Jack looked at her in total silence.

"Shit," said Mathilda. "I'm sorry. That was unforgivably rude and cruel."

"If it's what you think, you should say it."

"Is that really what you think? Or are you just saying that to paper over the cracks?"

He felt a cold clutch of dread in his heart. "What do you mean, *cracks*?"

"I'm sorry I said that, I am. But I'm not as nice as you are, and sometimes I can't help being rude. You're trying to shut yourself in here and keep everything that matters to you in here with you. You're like a little kid building a fort under blankets. Well, I'm not going to live in your fort with you, Jack. I can't. It's time to call it a day."

"He's not shy about drawing himself, is he?" said Priss.

Isaac was removing a key from a drawer in the kitchen. He was shirtless, his hair tousled. Davey felt a tingle of desire. Now Isaac was wrestling with a huge, heavy padlock. The cage door stood ajar as Isaac lay in the grass above and watched, the panther walked out. It sniffed the air, then padded off between the trees. A high-angle view of two people glimpsed, arguing, through the veranda doors of the kitchen. Mathilda walking down the drive, not looking back. Jack hunched over a notepad. An envelope dropped in a post box. Jack, his guitar over his shoulder, putting a key under the porch doormat.

He followed her out of the kitchen and up the stairs. She opened the door to the annexe and rummaged through drawers for the few clothes she had brought with her.

This can't be happening, he thought. *This is just another row, like the one we had this afternoon.*

"You're not serious," he said.

"Of course I'm serious. I should be in London anyway. I've wasted the whole summer here."

"But you'll come back."

"I don't think so."

"You can't mean that. You *can't*. I love you, you love me. That can't disappear because of one stupid argument - "

"I do love you," she said. "Are you listening, Jack? *I do love you.* And I know you love me. And it's been a wonderful summer. But it's not going to work."

"I'll come to London," he said. "I'll sell this place if that's what it takes."

"Will you warn the buyers that there might be a wild beast loose in the woods?"

He bit back the spasm of fury. "I'm serious. If you need to

be in Hollywood I'll come with you there too. Whatever you want, I swear, wherever you want, I'll marry you tomorrow if you'll have me - "

"No, no, no," said Mathilda.

"Why not?"

"Because you've got your own career, and it's a good one." Jack started to protest, but she held up a commanding hand. "I can't ask you to traipse around after me all over the world. I'm just starting out, I might never get anywhere. We might as well face it, Jack, two artists together are a recipe for disaster."

"Don't decide now," he begged. "Don't write us off. Give it a few months and see how you feel then. I'll wait for ever, Mathilda, I swear - "

"Don't you dare," she told him. "Don't waste your life waiting for me, okay? Find someone who's unselfish enough to put you first."

"This can't be how it ends."

"I'm afraid it is." She kissed him gently on the cheek. "Isaac left that painting of me in the living room. I'll understand if you don't want it, but don't burn it or anything, okay? He'll be very famous one day, I think."

"Please don't do this."

"I have to."

"How can I get in touch with you?"

"Why would you want to?"

"Because - "

"It's like ripping off a plaster," she said. "This way hurts like hell. But doing it slowly only prolongs the agony."

He thought he heard a tremor in her voice. "If you ever want to come back," he told her, "the door will always be open. *Always*, do you hear me? I'll leave the key under the mat for you - "

"Will you do one thing for me?" she asked.

"Anything, you know that."

"Don't try and catch that panther. Leave his cage door open too. The world's more interesting with a wild beast roaming around in it."

"Are you fucking nuts?"

"That's better. I'd rather have you furious than broken-hearted."

"How dare you try and manipulate me? I'll feel however the hell I want to feel - "

"I know," she said, and walked out of the room.

"So whose body is in the woods?" demanded Priss. "And who did it? Someone killed somebody, we know that much."

"About that," said Davey. "I wanted to tell you - "

"There's Evie again," said Priss, pointing. A woman with soft dark hair walked down the drive towards the door. "Remember that letter we found? She did come back after all."

Jack had heard it was usual not to remember the times of deepest grief; that the days passed in a blur. Instead, he lived each day with a dreadful clarity that trapped each moment in amber.

He slept in a different bed every night, hoping this might vary the content of his dreams, which were all wish-fulfilment fantasies so banal and predictable he got angry with himself even while he was still asleep. Mathilda appeared around every corner he had ever known in every house he had ever lived in, emerged from cars he had owned and cars his mother had owned and the buses and trams of his childhood, speaking the words he longed to hear. *I'm so sorry, I made a mistake, I'll never leave you, I swear, never again, oh God, I've missed you.* He awoke thinking of how she'd have laughed if he'd been able to tell her.

He spent hours in the library, that sanctuary they had all three instinctively gravitated to, writing ferociously, savagely, desperately. Oddly, he found the music flowed easily now. It didn't stop his pain, but it gave it shape and dimension, turned it into a structure he could step back from and look at and think to himself, *Yes. That's what happened. This is how you describe love, and brokenness. That's what it is.* He had the feeling sometimes that someone else was in the house with him – bringing small food items like loaves of bread and bottles of milk, taking pens and the occasional item of clothing in return – but it was a big house, and he had often had that feeling before.

At least once a day, he went to look at the portrait Isaac had left in the annexe. It was painted on the back of one of the old plywood doors he'd had torn out and replaced; if he looked closely he could see the places where Isaac had carefully adjusted the perspective to take account of the dents and scrapes in the wood. It was a beautiful, haunting painting.

Every evening he swallowed the fear in his throat and went down to the cage to see if the panther had come back. There was no obvious sign. Perhaps it had already died. Occasionally he found minute scraps of rabbit flesh and fur, but foxes could just as easily have left these. Besides, surely such a huge creature couldn't just live off rabbits?

After four weeks, six days and thirteen hours, the letter arrived, airmail, the address typed.

It was from Evie. As he read it, he felt the stirrings of life again. He had glimpsed a prospect even more terrible than staying here forever on his own.

In Priss' notebook, Evie picked her way through the rhododendrons. The panther lay on a branch and watched her.

"How does he know?" Priss muttered. "Look at that, that's fucking unnatural, no-one should be that good with a biro. Or is he making it up?"

"He saw it," said Davey, turning the page. "Look. He was in that tree. That candelabra tree."

Isaac had drawn himself in back view only. He was very small, as if he was reluctant, even now, to confess to his part in Evie's terrible death. Davey didn't like touching the paper where her blood soaked into the earth.

Had Isaac cried out to try and warn her?

Jack took Evie's letter upstairs to the annexe, trying hard not to notice the disorder in the deserted bedroom, the half-opened drawer, the bedspread that lay on the floor after that last time they had made love. He put it carefully with the others, although he could not have said why he was keeping them; he had no intention of seeing Evie ever again. Perhaps, he thought, it was because he had finally come to understand the pain of unrequited love.

He kissed Mathilda's portrait.

"I mean it," he said to her. "If you ever need to come back. Ever."

Alan was out, so he left the message with his secretary: *You win. Fifty dates, wherever you want, worldwide if you can get them. No babysitter.*

In the kitchen, he wrote the final draft of the letter, taking his time, concentrating hard, determined to get every word right. With his guitar over his shoulder, he took the long walk down to the village to post it.

On the train, he took out his notebook. To his surprise, the notebook was almost full. To his even greater surprise, he liked what he read.

He made a few amendments, a word here and there, a chord, a flourish; but the structure felt right, the melodies were good, it was falling into place. Scraps of music drifted through his head. He scribbled frantically in the margins. People watched, and smiled, but he was oblivious to their attention.

"I really thought Kate was Evie," Davey admitted.

"You dozy twat," said Priss, staring at the next page. "You utterly dozy twat."

"Why?" said Davey hotly. "She's got the same coloured hair, it's not that stupid an idea."

"Not you," said Priss. "Well, not just you, anyway. I can't believe I didn't recognise her."

The left-hand side of the woman's face was a copy of the exquisite painting they had found in the annexe, of the woman who now had a name, Mathilda. The right-hand side was a photograph of the same woman, torn from a copy of a newspaper, older and with her hair dyed red and worn in a long bob, exposing the lines of her cheek and neck, subtly re-presenting her features into an eerie re-coloured resemblance of the woman who had welcomed them both into the house. And the third part was a headline, torn from a gossip magazine:

KATE: HEARTBREAK AS MARRIAGE COLLAPSES
Tragic Kate Mathieson has abandoned her five-year marriage to toy boy Anders Johns after rumours of infidelity, close friends have reported.
The timeless Hollywood star – who turned 51 last year and whose real name is Mathilda – left their home in exclusive Oriel Springs after a

"Oh my God," said Davey in wonderment. It was like suddenly seeing the other side of an optical illusion. Now he saw it, the previous condition of not-seeing was unimaginable. Kate's bold, arresting features had stared out at him from cinema posters and DVD covers for films good and bad, art-house and commercial, Hollywood blockbusters and clever British classics and Shakespearian remakes. He had seen her in *Hamlet* once, a starry remake with Kate in the title role, and a woman rumoured to have been her lover playing opposite her as Ophelia.

"But she's got brown eyes," he said.

"So? She had green eyes in *Starburst* and blue eyes in *Sons et Lumieres* and cat eyes in *Practical Cats*. She's an actress. Looking like other people's what she does for a living."

"I suppose," said Davey dubiously.

"Christ," said Priss. "I'm losing the plot here - so the panther did it. And Isaac buried the body." She shook her head. "Do you think we saw the same actual one?"

"How can we have done? This was decades ago. Maybe it was its descendant."

"Or its ghost."

"Sorry?"

"If I can't be in a murder mystery I'll settle for a ghost story. What's this?"

"You know, you actually - "

"No!" Priss screamed, clutching a long cardboard wallet. "See what he's given me."

With some difficulty, Davey pried the wallet from her hand.

"I'm going to New York," said Priss, dazedly. "I'm going to *New York*. Isaac paid my plane fare."

"Have you got anything to sell when you get there?" asked Davey.

Priss waved the notebook. "I'll sell *this*. I'll write the script for it, it'll be fantastic - "

"It's got real people in it."

"So? I'll get someone to redraw them a bit, no-one'll know. Let's see the ending."

Davey was looking out of the window. He had never been in Priss' room before. She had a fantastic view, straight down the long expanse of gravel drive to the entrance, guarded by the two stone pineapples. They were too far away to see, but he remembered them with a vivid clarity, and the way the stone wall had felt against his cheek as he made his drunken circuit of the outer wall the first night he arrived.

He thought he could see someone in the distance, walking slowly down the driveway.

Jack was in New York when the packet from Alan caught up with him. In an age of electronic communications, the notion of sending a physical object thousands of miles to communicate one's wishes and desires seemed like a charming whimsy from a forgotten time. He let it lie on the bureau for weeks, knowing it would be Alan's semi-regular selection of Jack's most obscene, amusing or baffling fan mail. He finally got around to opening it one boring, sticky afternoon when the outside world felt like an armpit and his room like an air-conditioned cell.

He was always amazed by the inventive banality of the human race. If a teenage boy could make a copy of the *Landmark* cover from clippings of his own pubic hair, what would that same boy be able to achieve if he really put his mind to it? At least Alan had taken the time to put it in a plastic wallet first. The blank envelope was the last thing he found. Alan had scribbled a note in the corner:

Classic of the genre, this one. Apparently it's for you. Apparently. Hand-delivered to the office. I had a look, it's not a letter bomb. Fuck me, mate, but your fans are strange little boys and girls.

He opened it, expecting another pubic-hair picture.

Inside was a blank sheet of paper.

Ten minutes later he plunged into the angry, sticky New York heat, and frantically flagged down a taxi to take him to the airport.

The figure walking down the drive was coming into focus; a thin man with grey hair and a lived-in face, travel-worn and unsuitably dressed, a guitar slung over his shoulder.

"I need to tell you something," said Davey desperately.

"I might have to rethink the ending, though," said Priss. "It needs more violence, this story. A proper murderer would have gone down a treat. "

"There is a murderer in this story," said Davey. "Well, there might be, anyway. I'm not really sure but, um - "

"Maybe a bit more about the hospital. That might do it."

"Priss, sorry, but we haven't got much time."

"Or some extra back story. Or compress the timescale a bit, get them back together in ten years, not thirty."

"Will you please just shut the fuck up and listen?"

"What are you on about, soft lad?"

"I'm trying to tell you. The day I - the day I left. You wanted to live with a murderer. Well um, I - I might be. Sorry I didn't tell you before. But I might be."

"Are you having me on? You killed someone? *You* did?"

"I don't know. It was the day I ran away. My stepfather, he b-b-b he b-b-b-b - " he took a deep breath. "He beat me up. For failing my A-levels on purpose. He came back just as I was leaving. I - I shoved him down the stairs. I'm not sure, but I think I might have killed him." Priss' expression was impossible to read. "When I remember it, I can sort of picture it both ways. I can see him with his neck sort of b-b-b-b-broken and floppy, and I can see him just lying there, out of it but basically alright. And I d-d-d-don't know which is the real version." He shrugged. "I suppose I'll have to go home and find out now."

"You," said Priss, "are a garden of hidden wonders, mate. Why did you keep that quiet for so long? Actually, scratch that. Why are you telling me now?"

"Because it's nearly over. We'll have to leave soon."

"Why? Look, just let me finish the rest of this and we can talk about it, I just need to see how it ends - "

"It's ending right now," said Davey. "This is it. This is how it ends. But how did he know?" Priss was thumbing frantically through the last few pages. "Oh, will you please put that book down and come and look?"

"Will *you* come and fuchin' look?"

"But I am looking," said Davey, in a daze. "How did Isaac know – he must be a witch or something – how on earth did he *know*?"

And Priss and Davey looked up from the last page of the notebook to see the same scene repeated in front of them; the man stopping in front of the door, hesitant even though he stood at the door of his own property; and Kate, her arms held wide, flying out of the door and into his arms, both of them sobbing out loud, gasping, clinging to each other as if, after years adrift on the wide ocean of time, they had finally sighted land.

Mathilda,

Here's what I won't do in this letter. I won't beg you to come back. I won't try to prove you were wrong to leave. I won't threaten to do anything stupid. And I won't try and pretend that, just because I love you and always will, you're obliged to feel anything for me at all.

Here's what I will do in this letter. I'll acknowledge I was wrong. I'll be honest about how I feel. I'll tell you my plans. And I'll tell you how you can find me.

I understand why you left me. I do. You're right. I'm possessive and selfish, and I want you to myself. I wish I could say I could change that, but I probably can't. I can't imagine a future where I'll love you less, or when I'll want less of you to belong to me.

But because of that, I'll always, *always* wait, if you ever decide you're ready to leave the life you're living and come home to me. I say this with no expectations. I know it may never happen. But my heart's yours until the day it stops beating.

I know how much you hate people who mope. If there's one thing you've taught me, it's that life is for living, not dreaming. So this morning, I called Alan and told him I'd do the tour. And when I've done it, I'll write another album, and maybe I'll tour that one as well, if the fans will pay to come and see me. I can't say I'm looking forward to it. In fact I'm scared as hell. But I want to live a life that's worthy of yours. I want to live a life you can admire.

I know you all the way through, my love. So I know you're